THE LAST THING SHE DID

KATE MITCHELL

Print ISBN 978-1-913419-76-9

For Hazel and Gianfranco, in the year that you two become three.

ROISIN

2019

1

Nobody says he's dying; they don't need to. With his yellow skin and his hair all spiky where he's been pushing his fingers through it, and his elbows like little bumps in twiggy arms, Roisin is reminded of that advert for cheesy strings. Except the cheesy strings on TV run about and her daddy just lies there. He's string-thin though. He probably weighs less than Aodhan, who's only ten. No, they don't need to tell her. She knows.

Nanny's voice comes from the doorway. 'No talking now, just sit nicely and let him see you. I'll be getting him some dinner, so.' The latch drops with a slight click and Roisin listens to Nanny's slippers flapping into the kitchen, and then there's silence.

She sits on the stool and reaches across the bed to hold his hand. Paper-thin skin moves under her fingers and she thinks it's about to peel off. She drops his hand. He opens his eyes. He's lost most of the colour to the yellow of his sickness.

He says, 'Help me up.'

She pushes an arm under his shoulders. A sharp bone pokes into her wrist. She can't remember when he last ate anything except those slops Nanny gives him. Nanny will be in the kitchen now, mashing some of the veg they'll be having later. Maybe Roisin should cook him a pizza, or a chocolate cake; he's always liked her baking. His head drops back, over her arm, his mouth opens, and she smells mouldy oranges. His tongue has disappeared. Maybe he's swallowed it.

'Jesusmary.' Roisin pulls her arm away and his head falls back on the pillow. She freezes. Seconds pass. Should she call Nanny? Then his tongue flicks out and along his lips. That's okay then. She lets out a long breath, but her hand is shaking.

Hearing a motor, she walks to the window, lifts the curtain, and watches Father McDonnell pulling into the yard in his fancy black car with its tinted windows, getting out carefully, tucking his scarf tighter into the collar of his overcoat and stepping on tiptoe to avoid the mud, coming towards the house. A shaft of sunlight reaches under her hand, and she follows it across the room. It touches her daddy's whiskers with a silvery glitter and she realises how much the illness has aged him.

His lips are glued together in a 'mmm' sound. He licks them again. She sits back on the stool, reaches his glass on the night table, dips her finger in and dabs some water onto his lips. He licks it off, and she does it again, and again.

He's trying to say something. She leans over him to put her ear close to his mouth. Now she can smell the skin on his neck. It doesn't have the sour smell that's coming out of his mouth. His neck smells of soap and woodsmoke. That's because Nanny dries his pyjamas over the fire, but when Roisin thinks about it, that was always his smell. It reminds her of being little, and him coming in from working in the fields; she'd snuggle into that smell and he'd read her a bedtime story while Nanny got the meal ready. Her daddy has always been a cuddler, making a fuss of her, stopping everything to talk to her. Even when he was working. She'd go into the fields to find him, and soon as he saw her, he'd stop whatever he was doing and open his arms wide and she'd run up to him, jump onto him, her arms around his neck and her legs around his middle. He'd grab her legs and she would drop backwards and stick her arms out as he turned around, faster and faster, and as they twirled, she'd be screaming, and he'd be laughing with the fun of it.

She whispers into his neck, 'I miss you.' His hand rests on her arm, with a slight squeeze.

He says, 'Rosie.'

She lifts her head, steps back. Rosie? Her name is Roisin. Nanny went mad, that time she got her school friends to call her Rosie: *it's a proper Irish name, is Roisin; we'll have no English nonsense, so.*

He lifts his head off the pillow, and breathes in a long, shaking, thin kind of breath. Roisin thinks it's the death rattle. She knows about that. He told her, when Buttercup was dying, and he sat with the cow's head in his lap, and there was this desperate sucking in of air, and it rattled out again, and then she was gone.

But it's clear as anything when he says, 'Your – name – is – Rosie.'

He falls back on the pillow, saying something about the end. She knows it's the end. Her throat feels scratchy and she swallows hard to stop herself crying again. Not now, when every second counts if he's trying to talk to her.

She sniffs, swallows. 'Sure, I know, Daddy.'

'No, Rosie, listen. Find your mammy... End...'

Her mammy? Does he mean his mammy – Nanny? She starts to get up, to call Nanny, but stops when he says:

'I'm sorry, Roisin... Rosie, so sorry. Find your mammy... in England. Tell her I'm sorry.'

'Don't you be taking any notice of his ramblings, so.' Nanny appears at the other side of the bed, pulling the sheet up to his chin. Its starchy whiteness contrasts with his yellow skin. 'Get yourself off and let the priest have a minute with your daddy.' She waves an arm at Roisin. 'Off you go, now.'

In the doorway, Father McDonnell brushes past her. As he shuts the door in her face, she looks across to the bed and sees her daddy's eyes boring into her.

2

In the church, Aodhan hangs onto Roisin's hand, wiping his nose with his other arm, leaving a shiny snail trail of snot along his sleeve. Wrapping an arm around his shoulders, she pulls him close, as much for herself as for him. Nanny turns her head, shakes it; she disapproves of making a cissy of the boy. On the other side of Nanny, Aunt Anne Marie is stony-faced. Roisin knows what she's thinking: her vagabond brother has got his comeuppance at last. Anne Marie doesn't mind speaking ill of the dead. Roisin overheard Mrs Sullivan talking to her as she arrived at the church:

'Will ye be moving into the farm now, Anne Marie?'

'It makes sense, so it does.'

Nanny has other plans. Roisin went with her yesterday, to meet Father McDonnell to discuss the funeral arrangements, and he asked what she'd do now. Nanny said she was going to sell up, move to one of those new bungalows in the town.

As they left, she tapped Roisin on the arm. 'There will always be a room for you, wherever I live. Mind now, you must promise not to say a word to Anne Marie about the plan. She'll say I'm demented and get the courts to put me in a home.'

Now, Nanny hooks her hand through Roisin's arm as they follow the coffin out. Anne Marie beckons Aodhan away from Roisin and Nanny to walk between herself and Niall, behind them. Roisin feels Anne Marie's eyes burning into her back all the way to the open grave. As the coffin is lowered, she wants to jump after it, bang on the lid and shout to her daddy, 'What did you mean?'

Back at the house, Roisin goes into the kitchen to help Nanny and finds her and Anne Marie standing either side of the table. Aodhan is looking from one to the other, like watching a tennis match.

Anne Marie piles sandwiches and little plates onto a tray, while saying, 'It makes sense, Ma, for us to move in. Sure, you can't manage the place by yourself, and Roisin's going to be off to university within the year.'

Roisin hands Aodhan a plate of cakes. 'Not to eat. Come and help, pass them around.' She picks up a plate of sandwiches and he follows her into the parlour, which is crammed full of neighbours and friends. While she hands out the sandwiches, Aodhan walks behind, copying her with his cakes. She knows Anne Marie will never get over it, when Nanny tells her she's not getting the farm. Niall will have to carry on with his job in the city, doing insurance or sales or some such.

When she slips back into the kitchen to swap her empty plate for a full one, Anne Marie is hissing, 'Niall slipped out of line just the once with that woman in Kilkenny, and you're still punishing him, not trusting him with the farm. And the Prodigal Son, meanwhile, who lived a dirty life over in England, and the liver cancer was the proof of it...'

Roisin has heard it all before. Anne Marie always thought

Nanny was too soft on Daddy, shouldn't have taken him back. But he promised Nanny he was off the drugs, that he'd work hard and make it up to her, and he did. Anne Marie has always been angry with him, not just because he was what she calls a junkie, but she seemed to be equally angry that he sorted his life out. She overheard Anne Marie once, calling Roisin '*his bastard daughter*'. When she told Daddy, he said Anne Marie was jealous that she and Niall waited so long to have Aodhan, and then they had to do it with the IVF which made them bitter because it put them into debt, while he had Roisin all that time.

As she turns to go back into the parlour, Roisin catches Nanny's eye and winks. Nanny's lips twitch, so maybe it cheers her up. Mrs Sullivan sticks her head around the door, calling for Nanny to come and sit down, but Roisin knows she won't; she'll be keeping herself too busy to think about it.

There's just the clearing away to do. Roisin gathers up all the glasses and takes them into the kitchen, where Nanny and Anne Marie are washing up. The air between them is electric. Aodhan sits at the table, trying to work out a puzzle which involves unlocking a bottle of beer from a wooden box that has chains all around it. He gave it to Roisin's daddy last Christmas, and try as they might, neither of them could manage it. Roisin did it. It put her a few steps up in Aodhan's opinion. She didn't let on that she'd downloaded the solution from the internet. Let them think she was that clever. She'd put it back together again, and he's been trying ever since. The tears are running down his little face, so he can't really see to do it anyway.

Roisin ruffles his hair. 'He'll be watching, laughing his head off at you.'

Aodhan's eyes fix on the damp patch on the ceiling as if it could be her daddy's face, but at least he's smiling now.

Mrs Sullivan brings in a heap of plates from the parlour, puts it down on the press, and goes over to Nanny. 'That's the last, Bridget, so I'll be off.' Patting Nanny's hand, she says to Roisin, 'Be a good girl, now, take care of your grandmother.' Why is everybody saying that to her, today? What makes them think she's not going to be good?

Nanny's wiping the same saucer, round and around, her cloth making circles in the suds, while she stares out into the yard. Roisin follows her eyeline and thinks for a split second that he might appear, kicking the pile of leaves in the gateway, lifting his arm to wave to them as he comes in from the fields. That's what Anne Marie doesn't get, that they were a proper family: Roisin, Daddy, Nanny. He had changed back to the lad his mammy brought up: kind, hardworking. Nanny forgave him and probably loved him all the more for coming back to her.

He never made a secret of the years he spent in England. He said to her once, 'I've done terrible things, Roisin. I've been badder than you could ever imagine.' But the cancer came out of the blue. The doctor said that's how it happens with the hepatitis, it lays there, in your system, for years, decades sometimes, then it's up and attacking your liver and before you know it, it's too late.

Every glass, bowl, plate, cup and saucer has been washed and put away. Roisin has pushed the carpet sweeper around the parlour, cleaned the spots off the carpet where folk walked the mud in from the yard, and flicked a duster over all the surfaces. Nanny has taken herself upstairs with a cup of warm milk. Roisin is alone for the first time today, probably the first time since her daddy passed. From the darkening parlour, she looks out at the moon sitting on top of the line of trees at the far field, a jagged quarter of it still missing, like a bright but broken Christmas bauble. She remembers Daddy explaining about the waxing gibbous moon. And then she hears his voice, and the words she's been refusing to listen to, for the past five days: *Your name is Rosie. Find your mammy. England. Tell her I'm sorry...*

His room is along a short, flagged passage behind the kitchen. Perhaps intended as a scullery or a cookhouse two centuries ago, it had long since lost its original purpose and was in use as a storeroom when Roisin was growing. It was decided he would move in here so that Roisin could have a room of her own and there could still be a guest room for when Nanny's friend from England came to stay. The room reminded her of one of the monastery cells she'd visited with the school, with its plain white walls and stone floor: the only splashes of colour had been imported by herself and Nanny, with their rag rugs and the bedspread they had made together from knitted squares.

Nanny has been in and cleared and swept and scrubbed, and the bedding is folded. There is nothing personal to be seen; even his paperback book has gone. Roisin turns to the chest of drawers where his best jumpers are folded and piled on top, ready to go to St Vincent de Paul, while his working clothes are in another pile. She opens the little left-hand drawer. Nanny has started to roll his socks into pairs and put them in a carrier bag, then she must have faltered, for the half-full bag has been left in the drawer. Roisin can understand why. The very opening of the drawer has released that smell of woodsmoke and it catches in the back of her throat. Tears drip off her chin onto the sock she is holding, its heel darned on top of darning. She wipes her face with the sock and stuffs it into her pocket. Taking a deep breath, she sets about finishing the job, packing the socks and underwear into the bag, until the drawer is empty. The lining paper is creased and when she lifts it out, she sees it has been lined with old newspaper underneath. She is about to scrunch it up when she sees the headline.

She drops two logs on the dwindling fire, switches on the table lamp and curls into the corner of the settee, cuddling a cushion for comfort, and reads the newspaper article again. Throwing the cushion onto the floor and pulling her laptop towards her, she presses a key and it kicks into life. She brings up the browser, her fingers hovering over the keys for maybe a minute. It feels like a betrayal of him, but surely it isn't, for didn't he give her the words?

3

At breakfast, she says, 'Nanny, tell me again, how I came to live with you.'

'Well now, your daddy had been in England, working, and you were born, and then, he brought you here.'

'What about my mammy? Where is she?'

Nanny puts the teapot on the table and sits down. 'God alone knows, child. Didn't your daddy say she deserted you, and he rescued you, and brought you home, to be looked after properly?' The toaster pops and Nanny jumps up, brings the toast, then the marmalade to the table. She sits down and slowly butters a slice of toast, checking she has spread it into each corner. 'Asleep in the back of the car, you were, hugging your little doggy.'

'Soggy doggy?'

'The same. You didn't let go of that little toy for years. Its ears fell off, in the end, from you sucking away at it.'

Roisin knows exactly where that cuddly toy is. 'Did he say anything else about my mammy?'

Nanny chews her toast, and swallows, before speaking. 'I'll never forget the day you arrived, sorrowful little dote that you were.' She tears off a piece of toast and dunks it into her teacup, sucks it, and swallows, every movement slow, while her eyes dart back to Roisin and then fix on something in the distance. 'Anyway, that's a long time ago now, and that's the whole of it so far as I know it, so it's no use asking questions.' She lifts her cup, drinks, then places it back in its saucer with an air of finality.

'So my mother – my birth mother – is she still alive?'

'God only knows, child. What's brought all this on?'

Roisin pushes the newspaper across to Nanny. 'It's talking about a body being found in England. It says it's the boy who kidnapped a little girl, called Rosie. And there's a photo of her, look.'

Nanny is rigid, staring at the photograph.

'Nanny?'

'What? Oh, I'm thinking, I do remember something about... where did you find it?'

'It was in Daddy's drawer. When he spoke to me last, he said, "Your name is Rosie", and said I should find my mother, in England. Nanny, is this anything to do with that?'

'Goodness no, child. That's just an old bit of newspaper.' She taps the photograph. 'Surely, you aren't thinking the child looks like you? Will you look at her? Look at that hair.' She drops the remaining slice of toast onto Roisin's plate. 'Will you get some breakfast down you? And are you going to school today?'

'I've got the week off, compassionate-something. Nanny, where are my photographs? From when I was small?'

'Well, I don't know if I kept any.'

'My school photographs? You didn't keep them?'

'Let me think... Maybe there are some. I'll have a look, later.' Nanny presses her hands on the table to push herself up from her chair and busies herself clearing the pots away.

'It's just that... I found something on the internet, and there was a child called Rosie who was kidnapped from a place called Sheffield, about the time you told me I arrived here.'

Nanny turns on the tap, moves cups and saucers around noisily. 'Is that the truth now? Well, it's a coincidence, you can be sure.'

Roisin wants to believe her. From the article she found in the drawer, she had linked back through Google to get to the archives of several newspapers. She knows the story of a little girl called Rosie Endleby, who was taken hostage during a robbery thirteen years ago; she's read the string of articles about the search for the child. It's not me, she thinks. It's a terrible story, but like Nanny says, it's a coincidence. Surely, Nanny would know if it were true. But Roisin keeps coming back to the photograph of the mother. She has no memory of ever knowing anyone with hair like that, grey with the pale-pink scalp showing through; this woman looks old, worn out; but there's something in those eyes as they look straight at her through the screen of her laptop, that gives her gooseflesh. The article is dated a couple of weeks ago. The headline says:

Mother of missing toddler, Rosie, critical following overdose, and underneath: *Neighbours said tragic Jennifer became depressed and took an overdose on the eighteenth birthday of her daughter, Rosie, who was kidnapped thirteen years ago. Jennifer is in intensive care.*

4

___

Roisin downloads all the newspaper reports and the news videos that she can find on the internet. There's a memorial page on Facebook, with a photo of the little girl, with *Bring Rosie Back* written across it, and it's got over half a million shares, it's been all over the world, going around and around, for years. It's creepy for sure, especially when she comes to the photo of this child as she might look now. The skin on the back of her neck tingles as she looks into the eyes, and the chin with the little dimple in it. But this girl's hair is long and curly, and a kind of gingery blonde, whereas Roisin's is so white no one can believe it's natural; and straight, and very short, in what Pauline, who does the mobile hairdressing, calls a pixie cut. She thinks, it's a me-not-me, this girl, it's like a relative, somebody who shares a gene pool with me, and that's it. Perhaps that's what Daddy was trying to tell her; that something bad had happened to a relative. A person in her mother's family, a cousin, for instance. No, there's nothing here that makes any sense. After all, wouldn't she have memories, if she was four, just a week from being five, when all this is supposed to have happened? Which is another thing. Daddy had been in England for five years; she was four and a bit years old when he brought her home. Her birthday is July fifteenth, the same birthday as Grandpappy who she didn't know because he passed away before she got here. This Rosie in the news would have been eighteen a couple of weeks ago, because, like it says in the paper, the girl's mammy took an overdose on her eighteenth birthday. Whereas Roisin won't be eighteen until next July.

She presses her fingers on her eyelids to concentrate, bringing pictures into her mind of all the things she remembers from being little. Her earliest memory is of being warm and snuggled up, with the smell of the fire which she now knows is from peat and wood; of watching the pictures in the fire as it burns, while Daddy reads her a story. Actually, that might not be the first. She remembers sitting on the back of a sheep, its curly wool scratchy in her fingers, slipping first one way, then another, but not falling off, as Daddy walked them across the yard. Nanny didn't have a camera, and she wouldn't let people take photographs of any of them. Roisin got a school photo every year, and it went on the press for a while, then it disappeared. She asked Daddy once where they went, these photos, and he said he kept them in his secret box with his treasure. Since the funeral, Roisin has looked, but she hasn't found anything in his room except for the newspaper article in his drawer. She must ask Nanny again, to look for them, they will be somewhere. School, friends, the farm... That's her life. Nanny, Daddy, Aodhan, Aunt Anne Marie and Uncle Niall. That's her family.

Once, when she was in primary school she went home with Clodagh for tea. Clodagh's mammy asked her lots of questions: where was her mammy? In England. Did she see her? No. Why not? Because her daddy looked after her. And so on. Before that day, she never thought there was anything unusual about not having a mammy living with her. Later, she repeated the questions to her daddy. He said she didn't need to know anything except he came and took her when her mammy could no longer look after her; and that being with him and Nanny was far better than being with her mammy, and she was not to worry about it. And she hadn't, until last year, when they were studying genetics at school. They were discussing diseases and conditions and so on that might be inherited. Roisin asked Nanny who said there was nothing for her to be afraid of; and she asked Daddy about her mammy's family. He said he didn't know of anything, but then he hadn't known her for very long. She teased him; asked if she'd been a one-night stand. He said, well, it wasn't serious, and eventually admitted they met in a club and it was by chance, years later, that he heard she'd had a child, and went back and found she'd not been looking after her, so he brought her to Ireland.

She asked, 'Why don't I remember her?'

'Probably because it wasn't very nice, back then, and you were happy, when we got here. The good memories might have cancelled out the bad memories.'

'Does she know where I am?'

'No, we thought it best to make a clean break.'

Now, she asks Nanny, 'Do I take after Daddy at all?'

'Well, now, let me think. You don't look like him, but I expect you favour your mammy. After all, you spent nearly four years with her, that would be inevitable. I dread to think what might have happened in those years, but you were terrified of bangs and sudden noises when you were wee, and we had the devil's own job to persuade you to get in the car.' Nanny chuckles and spreads her arms wide. 'Aye, you'd stick out your arms and legs, so you couldn't be put through the door.' She shakes her head and goes back to her crocheting. 'But as you grew up, you took after your daddy more and more. Everything he did, you were on his heels, following him, copying him. If he had ketchup on his chips, you'd have half the bottle. You'd only drink tea,

18

because that's what he drank, and always with the two spoons of sugar.'

'Did you ever think, Nanny, that I wasn't his? That what he said about my mammy wasn't true?'

'No, I never did.'

This is starting to feel like a puzzle her daddy has set for her, to trace a family that's linked to her in some vague way, and she needs to find out how. She tries again to talk to Nanny. She shows her the Facebook page.

Nanny fiddles about, cleaning her glasses, puts them on and glances at the screen. 'You know I can't do computers, Roisin.'

'This little girl who went missing, she has a mammy, and a daddy, and a big brother. I wonder what it was like for him, his sister being kidnapped and never found. Nanny, are you crying?'

Nanny sniffs and pulls her hankie from her sleeve. 'That's a terrible sad story you're telling, Roisin.' She stands up and busies herself switching the kettle on, keeping her hand on it as though that will hurry it up, then refilling the teapot, and pouring them both a fresh cup. She wraps her hands around her own cup and carries it across to the window.

Roisin joins her, watching the wind scudding the leaves around the yard. The freezing rain has given way to a late-afternoon sun which shines low, across the yard, making the fallen leaves glisten gold and red. It's her daddy's favourite time of year. He used to say it was this weather, the middle of autumn, when he came home after being some years in England, that made him fall in love with the place all over again; and then he wondered how he'd ever been able to leave it; and how he'd managed to stay away all those years. *Except I got you, in England,* he'd say, *so it was all worth it.* Roisin has never known anywhere else. Sure, she's never been further than Kilkenny in her... she stops that thought because Nanny just said Daddy brought her from England. Her stomach flutters with panic as she thinks about going away from here. Her teachers have told her she's good enough for university, and even the thought of going to Dublin is scary. She realises that although her Nanny is telling her it's all a coincidence, she's starting to believe there's something to it. Certainly, enough to want to find out more. The thought of having another life, in a different country, is terrifying, but also exciting...

Roisin leaves Nanny at the window and sits at the table, opening her laptop and bringing up one of the articles. It's dated 2006, with the mother and father at a press conference. The father stares at the camera, and Roisin feels his anger spilling down the years into Nanny's parlour. The mother's eyes stare ahead, blank, expressionless. She reminds Roisin of a boy at primary school, who had no use of his facial muscles, and it was hard for anyone to know what he thought. That's what Rosie's mother looks like, as though she's lost the use of her facial muscles and will never smile or frown or laugh again. She scrolls down until she finds the photograph of the little girl, and another, of a little boy; they look like twins.

A short, sharp burst of breath behind her makes her turn to find Nanny staring past her, at the screen, with a hand over her chest. The colour has dropped from her face and her eyes roll up into her head.

'Poor wee dote,' she says. 'Mary forgive us.'

As Roisin stands up from her chair, and turns, with one hand on the table, Nanny stumbles, and Roisin puts out an arm and helps her to the sofa.

5

They agree they definitely won't tell Anne Marie the real reason Roisin is going to England. Nanny says that would be tantamount to putting it in the local newspaper and having it broadcast across the county. And Roisin couldn't bear the gloating, of Anne Marie jumping to the end of the story before she properly knew the beginning, saying, *didn't I tell you so? He was a bad one and haven't I always warned you?* There is probably nothing Anne Marie would enjoy more than thinking Roisin is no blood relative of theirs. She would be absolutely delighted and would be boasting about Aodhan being the only one in line to inherit the farm – if they could stop Nanny selling it, that is. No, they've told Anne Marie the same as everybody else – that Roisin is going to England to visit a friend of her daddy's, from when he lived there, who's invited her over for old times' sake.

Roisin pauses in her packing when Nanny comes into her room with two mugs of tea and perches on the bed. Roisin climbs onto the bed and sits with her back against the headboard. Both wrap their hands tightly around their drinks as if that will give them comfort. Like those cold evenings, when Nanny would bring in a hot drink and perch on the bed, relating a story. Roisin's favourite was always the one about *Fionn mac Cumhaill*, who was challenged to a fight by the Scottish giant *Benandonner*, so he built the giant's causeway where they could meet and fight. Roisin let Nanny carry on telling the story long after she learned that the causeway was a volcanic eruption, because she liked the feel of it: the story of the giant defending Ireland felt like Nanny, keeping them safe on the farm. Such as when Nanny put a padlock on the gate and shut off the footpath that led through the meadow; she fixed barbed wire across it until the hawthorn bushes she'd planted grew big enough to make sure nobody could get through. *Who wants strangers wandering around when you've little children running free, you never know who's wandering about*, she'd say, and nobody challenged her. Nanny was well respected in the village.

Roisin wishes she could climb under the eiderdown and go back in time to that warm place where everything smells of peat and wood and damp wool. It isn't going to happen. Her daddy has set her off on a road where there is no stopping and no turning back. She knows now what people mean when they say something would rock your world. Her world is having a volcanic eruption that is opening up a causeway leading to people and places she can't imagine.

'You know I've got to go, don't you, Nanny?'

'No, Roisin, you don't have to go.' She pats Roisin's arm. 'There may be a lot of unhappiness at the end of this and you don't have to go looking for it.'

'But I do, don't you see?'

'No. Sometimes it doesn't help to go poking into the past. Have you not been happy here? Did we not give you a good life, your daddy and me?'

'Oh, Nanny, you know I have, you did. That's not it.' Roisin wraps an arm around Nanny's thin shoulders. Nanny stands up, letting it fall back on the pillow.

'Will you come back?'

'Course I will, Nanny.' She means it. This is her family, this is home. She pulls Soggy Doggy from beneath her pillow. 'I'll leave him here, so you can be sure I will.'

Nanny smiles as she gathers up the blue cable sweater sitting on top of Roisin's open backpack and presses it against her face. Since the funeral, Nanny has been shrinking. She always seemed strong, unbendable, and now she looks as though a sudden wind might blow her over. Roisin takes the sweater from her hands, gently, tucks it into the backpack, and pulls the cord to close it.

Nanny shakes her head, takes the empty mugs in one hand, stops with the other hand reaching for the door. 'What I wanted to say is... Well, it's this: you must know that you saved his life. Little mite that you were. However it was that you came into his life, you saved it. I know' – she wags a finger at the laptop which is resting on the bedspread, as though it's Roisin's daddy sitting there – 'there was a time when he had the devil in him. Who knows what he got up to, in that godforsaken country. But then he got you. And he brought you into our lives.' She pauses, looking into the middle distance, then shakes her head again. 'He'd have been dead within the year. So thin and sick he was when he came home... he looked like one of those survivors from the concentration camps that you see on TV. Aye, you saved his life all right. And he thought the world of you.'

Roisin jumps up and pulls her into a hug, pressing the mugs in Nanny's hand into their stomachs. 'I know that, Nanny, and I wish I could leave it be, but I have to do this.'

Nanny's head drops almost onto her chest as she turns away and Roisin listens to the back of her slippers flapping against her heels as she goes down the stairs.

6

It's still dark when Roisin comes downstairs in the morning. She peeks into Nanny's bedroom, but the bed is empty, and so is the kitchen. She'll be feeding the calves, saying goodbye to them, too, because Seamus Lewis is collecting them later this morning, taking them to market, for Nanny can't manage the animals on her own. Roisin keeps glancing out of the kitchen window, while she's making and eating her toast and tea, but there's no sign of her. When Niall drives into the yard, she doesn't appear. Roisin takes a few steps towards the calf shed, hesitates: would Nanny want her to see her, upset? She watches the shed door for half a minute, looks at Niall tapping the steering wheel, and decides Nanny must not want to see her leave. She'll be back, soon.

On the drive to Kilkenny, Roisin feels full to bursting with the enormity of what she is doing, with the doubts and the hopes, and all the time, bubbling underneath, is the panic that makes the taste of her toast rise in her throat. She is desperate to talk to somebody, and Niall is here, but what if he told Anne Marie? Although, thinking about it, Roisin might be able to trust him. Last year, she went with Ruari at the dance. Niall was due to pick her up and take her home. He saw them, as he drove into the square, but he sat and waited, with his lights off. He never said a word, until they got to the farm, when he said, *If you should want to go into town of a Saturday night, Roisin, I'd be glad to give you a lift.* As much as saying he'd help her to see Ruari in secret. But she didn't take him up on it. Her daddy was bound to find out, sooner or later, and he was fierce when it came to even the possibility of her dating. No, she didn't think enough of Ruari to risk Daddy getting angry. But it made her think that Niall can probably keep a secret. He senses her staring and looks at her out of the sides of his eyes, smiles.

'Looking forward to your holiday then?'

'Kind of.'

'A big thing, travelling on your own.'

He's a nice man. Roisin can see why he had an affair. He must have wanted a bit of kindness, someone soft, loving, different to Auld Annie Misery, as Daddy used to call her. *Here she comes*, he'd say, *with her face like a slapped arse.* The worst thing for Niall must have been when Anne Marie said she'd not divorce him, despite him carrying on with the woman in Kilkenny. Whispered conversations overheard by Roisin, made her think that Niall might have preferred that Anne Marie did divorce him; but she brought the powers of the church to bear on him and he swore he wouldn't do it again. Even then, he might have gone off with the woman, if Anne Marie hadn't found right then that she was pregnant, after years of trying, and there was no way he could leave her then, could he? Roisin often wonders if he regrets his choice. When he turns and gives her that little smile, he's got sad lines around his mouth.

'So, have you got your passport sorted out?'

'It's what they call a Common Travel Area, Uncle Niall, and doesn't need a passport. I have a Public Services Card.'

'And what's that when it's at home?'

'Like an ID card. I can travel in the EU if I have photographic ID, without a passport.'

'Well, fancy that now. And what will happen when England leaves the EU, will we have to have a passport then?'

'Maybe.'

That's made Roisin think about her birth certificate. She had to produce it to get the card. And earlier, to get her learner driving licence. She asked Nanny, the other day, how come she had a birth certificate, if she wasn't who it said she was? Nanny shrugged. When Nanny got her box down to give Roisin the birth certificate to go into Kilkenny for the card, she felt really nervous as she looked at it. That's when she saw her birth mother's name: Jane Barlow. It put her back into that quandary of thinking all the Rosie business might be just coincidence after all. But she had to know. Perhaps, if she gets through the first bit of this, she'll look for a Jane Barlow.

It's fully daylight by the time they arrive in Kilkenny. Niall pulls into the lay-by near the bus station and looks at his watch.

'Will we catch a cup of coffee? Sure, you've an hour before the bus.'

'The café's not open yet, look.'

'Ah, feck it, I'll take you into Dublin, will that be all right now?'

'But you've got to be at work. I can get the bus, it's no trouble.'

'Ah, now, it's a big day for you and with no daddy to see y'off on your big adventure, I think I ought to see you safely on your way. And for sure, they'll not miss me at the office for one day. Have you the phone on you?' Roisin takes her phone from her bag and holds it out to him. 'Give them a ring. Say you're Anne Marie. Tell them I've got the food poisoning or something.' This is a side of Niall that Roisin hasn't seen before, properly laughing, his eyes twinkling, and the lines around his mouth smoothed out. 'Go on,' he says, and dictates the number.

Sucking in her cheeks and speaking fast, Roisin tells the receptionist, 'Sure now, I'm in a rush, for I have to be getting the boy to school and himself off the lavatory, so I won't wait to speak to the boss, you just tell him Niall might be well enough tomorrow,' and presses disconnect.

Niall guffaws loudly and hits the steering wheel with both hands. 'Fan-feckin-tastic, our Roisin, that was just brilliant. But you gave me the willies. You sounded so much like Auld Annie Misery.' He hoots at the look on her face. 'Did you think I didn't know the nickname Conor gave her?' He winks at her as he turns the key with his other hand and the engine starts. 'Now, let's get you to Dublin.'

It's as if a cork has popped somewhere inside Niall. He puts the radio on and sings along. 'Here, pass me a fag from that tin, under your seat.' The tin is full of humbugs and he says, 'Look underneath,' and sure enough, she finds some cigarettes. He holds out his hand for one, and a Zippo lighter appears from seemingly nowhere. Roisin can't help laughing when she sees him with the window wound right down, his elbow out, drawing on his fag. 'Ah, but that's lovely. Would you like one yourself?' She shakes her head. 'Well, help yourself to a humbug then.' He looks around. 'Ah, now, are you crying? What's the matter? You'll be back home soon enough.'

They pass a sign for a café and he takes the slip road off the motorway. 'Let's get that coffee.' She's crying so hard she can't even think of going where there's people. Niall sees this without her saying anything. He pats her on the shoulder. 'You hang on there, I'll be back in a tick.'

She feels the need to re-centre herself, remember why she's doing this, for otherwise, she'll turn right around and go back home to Nanny. While he's in the café, Roisin reaches for the laptop case from the back seat, opens the lid and flits the cursor around the press reports that she's downloaded. She opens one at random.

28 October 2009: *It's three years today, since little Rosie Endleby was taken hostage and kidnapped, and the police are no nearer to finding her. The body of a man suspected of being one of the kidnappers was found several months later, but there was nothing to lead police to Rosie. Her parents and older brother, pictured below at the press conference at the time, live in hope and police say this is still an active inquiry.*

By the time Niall gets back, with coffees that he places on the floor between their two seats, she's feeling calmer, but her eyes are heavy, as though there are buckets of tears gathered there and ready to spill.

He closes the door, puts the key in the ignition, fiddles with the air conditioning and checks that warm air is circulating. Then, he turns fully towards her. 'Right now, what's the craic?'

She closes the laptop, sniffs. 'How much do you know, about me coming to live here, when I was little?'

'Well now, when we first met you, you was just a little tot, frightened of your own shadow. I think you didn't speak for, oh, a long time, months and months, maybe a year was it? Is that what you mean?'

'Before that. What did you think happened before I came here?'

'I see. Well, your daddy said how he'd found you, alone in the flat where you lived with your mammy, only she'd run off and left you without any food, is that right? It's no wonder you couldn't speak.'

Nobody told her about the not speaking before. She half opens the laptop, pauses. She wants to believe this story, the family version. The story that might not be true, but it's a better story, a story of her daddy rescuing her instead of stealing her. Niall is watching her closely. She has a powerful need to tell him about it, but she remembers what Nanny said about keeping it between them for now, and even though he's being lovely, there's no guarantee that he wouldn't tell Anne Marie. She closes the lid of the laptop, lifts the coffee cup and holds it against her mouth to keep it shut, feeling him watching her. She's scared herself: she was on the brink of telling him. The silence starts to feel awkward, then he swigs back the rest of his coffee, crumples his paper cup, wedges it into the door pocket and starts the engine.

'Would it be that you're thinking of looking her up, this woman who abandoned you all those years ago?' Roisin looks at him, surprised. He gives her a quick smile, taps the side of his nose. 'Worked it out, did I?' He's smirking, pleased with himself, while he manoeuvres the car between the parked lorries and up the slip road back onto the motorway.

Roisin realises he was fishing, and she nearly fell for it. In which case, believing she is going to England to look up the birth mother who abandoned her is not a bad cover story. She says nothing, unwilling to tell an outright lie, trying to think how she can change the subject, but struggling to think what she could talk about.

'Is Aodhan looking forward to his first communion?'

'He is. And hoping you'll be back in time for it. So, you're going to try to find this woman, your mother? What's her name?'

She sees that he is not going to be diverted. 'Jane. Jane Barlow.'

'And is that all you have to go on?'

'I've got my birth certificate. There's an address, so it's some-where to start.' It seems to satisfy him.

'Pass me another fag, will you?' When he's lit up, and has his elbow resting on the open window, he says, 'You know, your Aunt Anne Marie always said that was a fishy story. She never believed your dad. But you're saying it was true?'

'So far as I know.'

He glances at Roisin, who has wrapped herself tighter in her coat, tucking her hands into the opposite sleeves. He flicks the cigarette end out of the window and rolls it up. He switches the fan on full blast. Neither of them speaks for several miles. Every now and then, Niall shakes his head. When the sign for Dublin City Centre comes up, her stomach flips and she starts to shake.

Niall glances at her, pats her on the knee. 'You don't have to do any of this, you know. What will it achieve, do you think? She might be a junkie, or she might be in prison. Jesus, she might even be dead. You never know what you might find over there. Why not come back home, carry on?'

He's echoing her own thoughts. Don't do it. Go home and carry on. Who would be any the wiser? If it is true, then the people that knew her all those years ago must think she's dead. They'll not be expecting her. It could be a bigger shock, if she walks back into their lives. Then there'll be the effect on Nanny. She might be able to fool Niall now, but when it gets out, he'll know the truth, he'll feel cheated, and Anne Marie will know. Given all the media interest in this story, year after year, it'll be a big story. Nanny will be shamed. The police will try to prove Nanny was involved. And the press. Oh my God, the press will be everywhere. She's seen cases like that on the TV, with the paparazzi chasing people. It'll destroy Nanny. Then Roisin thinks about that little boy, at the press conference, in the news video. He reminds her of Aodhan when he was little. Not that the boy will be little now. He'll be a man.

'I have to.'

'Right-oh. Is it the Dublin Port or Dun Laoghaire?'

'Dun Laoghaire. The coach goes from Busárus, all the way to Sheffield. So just drop me there.'

'Ah, no, I'll take you to the terminal. You've got hours yet.'

The road takes them past University College and Niall points and says, 'Don't forget now, we're expecting you to come here and study, next year is it?'

If she gets the grades. Everybody assumes she will. Then she thinks, where will I be, this time next year?

Niall pulls off the coast road, and parks, facing the sea. It's warm through the windscreen. He points. 'See that tiny dot, there, coming towards us? That'll be your ferry.'

It should be exciting, going to the coast, going on a ferry, but that little dot moving slowly towards her is terrifying.

Niall looks at her. 'Nervous?'

She nods.

'Aodhan's going to miss you.'

'I know. I'm missing him already.' She can barely get her voice out, around the lump in her throat.

'I shan't tell Anne Marie the real reason you're going to England. She'll only make a meal of it. No, it stays between you and me. But you've shared a secret with me today, Roisin, and I'll return the compliment.'

She thinks he's going to tell her about the woman from Kilkenny, and she's going to let him because she's fed up of thinking only about herself and what's happening to her, but he says, 'You're not the only one who doesn't know their real mother.' So he is going to tell her his own story, and then he says, 'Aodhan. He's not Anne Marie's flesh and blood.'

Roisin is speechless. He picks up the humbug tin and rummages about until he finds another cigarette. He gets out of the car and walks to the sea wall, where he leans and lights his fag, sheltering the light in his cupped hand. Roisin joins him.

There's a sharp breeze coming off the sea. He takes a long drag, and says, 'Nope. It was all that IVF.'

She doesn't tell him she knew that; but she didn't know he wasn't Anne Marie's.

'You're shocked. We'd been trying for years and it turns out it was Anne Marie, something wrong with the – whatever – you know – and we went in for this IVF.'

'So Aodhan isn't...?'

He shakes his head. 'He's my boy, but, no, he's not Anne Marie's. I'm afraid she's the end of the gene pool.' He laughs, but not in a funny ha-ha way. 'Well, except for you, of course. But that's why she was so bitter with your daddy, that he had a child, and she had to have somebody else's.'

'I'm sorry.' She doesn't know what else to say, except, 'Does Nanny know?' and she knows the answer before he nods.

'She wanted to know why Anne Marie wasn't getting pregnant, and in the end, we told her. It's why she won't leave the farm to Anne Marie, because as she sees it, there's nobody in the family to inherit from Anne Marie.'

'Aodhan is family.'

'Ah, but your Nanny's an old-fashioned woman, and having a child by IVF is the same, in her book, as bringing up somebody else's child.'

'Nanny dotes on Aodhan.'

'No,' says Niall. 'She thinks him a lovely lad, but he's not family, that's her view and she won't give an inch.' He grinds the rest of the cigarette under his shoe. 'And now, now...' He laughs, but again, it doesn't sound as though he means it. 'Our lovely Roisin, it turns out that you're not hanging about waiting to inherit either. What will the old witch make of that?'

'She's selling...' and as soon as the words are out of her mouth, he turns sharply to stare at her and she remembers that he doesn't yet know.

He nods, slowly, claps his hands together. 'So that's how it goes, is it? The old witch is making sure we don't get the farm.' He marches back to the car door. 'Come on, now, we don't want you missing your ferry, do we?'

He says no more, and for the rest of the way, Roisin worries about him telling Anne Marie, and how she will react, her anger... At the ferry terminal, when she leans into the back of the car to get her backpack, Niall says, 'Don't take any notice of me, now. You go careful and come back soon. You're all your nanny's got left of your daddy.'

Roisin isn't so sure; what he said about Nanny not seeing Aodhan as part of the family hit home. IVF or no, she thinks Aodhan has more claim on this family than she does. Watching Niall drive away, her loneliness becomes a sharp pain across her chest.

7

It's a long, long drive on the coach through countryside that Roisin thinks looks every bit like Ireland, except here, the mountain comes right down to the sea. That turns into the biggest motorway and then the bus goes through the middle of Manchester which is dirty and crowded and she's glad when they are back in the countryside, crossing the massive moors. There are not many people on the coach, so she has a seat to herself. And there's Wi-Fi, so she uses her time to catch up with everybody on Facebook, and look at the pictures Clodagh posted on Instagram at her sister's wedding she went to at the weekend. Clodagh has sent her their biology lecture in a PowerPoint attachment that she downloads for later. She repeats all her searches on Rosie Endleby and gets a free search on a directory site. There's a lot of Endlebys in Sheffield, too many to start phoning round. No, the hospital is the best place to start. The coach passes an enormous police building as it comes close to Sheffield, and she thinks of getting off, going in, saying, *I think you've been looking for me.* Then she thinks of Nanny, of her life being turned over and examined by the Gardaí, and being hounded by the media, and she stays on the coach.

Roisin has downloaded a street map of Sheffield and although the hospital is a good walk from the interchange, she wants time to slow down, feeling too close, too soon. She passes a McDonald's and goes in for something to eat. She wonders if the child called Rosie was ever here. Walking on, she imagines living in this town, maybe playing in that swing park, but it triggers nothing for her. No matter how she tries, there is no sense of herself, or of her daddy, in this place. There is no connection at all.

It's gone eight o'clock when she stands in front of the hospital, looking up at rows and rows of lit windows. Inside, there's nobody about and she follows signs to the Intensive Care Unit and reads the names beside the doors until she finds *Jennifer Endleby*. From the open door, she watches the body lying in the bed, just the head and the arms visible above the sheet. Even if she didn't have an oxygen mask over half her face, the woman lying there would look as old as Nanny, with the sucked-in cheeks and wispy, grey hair. Roisin moves closer to the bed, to the weird pumping of air from the machine that sounds like Darth Vader.

'Are you a relative?'

Startled, she finds a nurse standing beside her. 'I think so.'

It takes a few seconds to decipher the nurse's accent and work out that she says, 'It's too late for visiting now. Perhaps in the morning?' Roisin walks away, glancing back to the nurse who is standing in the doorway, watching her.

In the corridor, a woman is coming towards her, head down, shorter than herself, so Roisin is level with the cap of short, curly hair, a coppery colour. She takes in the fluffy pink fleece, and registers that this, and the neat little black lace-up shoes, and smart, pleated black trousers, are all very familiar. The woman senses somebody standing in her way, stops a half metre from Roisin, and looks up. The colour drains from her face and her mouth drops open.

'You,' Roisin says. 'What are you doing here?'

SYLVIA

2006-2008

1

_____

The bell pinged. A car was pulling onto the forecourt. Sylvia swore under her breath. The clocks had gone back the weekend before and it seemed to have been dark ever since. She'd been planning to close up early and catch the ten o'clock bus. She could have been relaxing in a bubble bath with a hot toddy within half an hour. Fat chance.

It was impossible to read the car's registration number through the rain lashing against the window. She sighed, turned to the back cover of her sudoku book and wrote 'dark greenish saloon'. Some toerag had bust the security camera last night. Dave, the area manager, had phoned to say he'd get around to fixing it tomorrow; meantime, she should make a note of all the cars that came onto the forecourt. If she thought anybody was acting suspiciously, she was to hit the lock to close the main door and make them come to the night hatch.

The wind drove the rain horizontally across the forecourt, blowing the hood off the driver's cagoule while he filled up. He was young, with a blond crew cut. Easy on the eye. From the way he moved, he probably worked out. Or had a physical job. He replaced the nozzle and opened the back door of the car. Bodies moved around on the other side of the windscreen. Sylvia watched closely in case he was planning a runner, but two children climbed out. He zipped up their little raincoats. A woman poked her head out of the passenger window and called something to him as he walked away; he acknowledged her with a backwards wave.

The way those two kiddies waddled along behind their dad made Sylvia smile. In their yellow wellington boots and yellow raincoats, running across the forecourt, they looked for all the world like little ducklings. Especially when one of them stopped in the middle of a puddle, stamped hard and laughed as the water splashed up around him. He stamped again. Just like a boy. The other must be a girl, judging by the way she stepped carefully round the deepest puddle. The dad said something, maybe telling them to hurry up or they'd get no sweets, that usually worked with children. The little boy stopped beside every puddle and looked up at the dad before jumping into the middle and stamping his feet. The automatic door swished open and the kiddies stepped inside, blinking in the bright light of the shop. Dad put a hand on each of their heads and slid their hoods back. The one Sylvia had taken for a boy had long, wavy, strawberry-blonde hair. The other was the boy. His hair was short and tousled, making Sylvia think of Dylan's sticky-up hair. The sweets lined up in front of them drew their eyes to the shelves like magnets. They walked along the aisle, picking up first one thing, then another.

Sylvia smiled at the dad. 'Twins?'

He shook his head. 'Everybody thinks that. No, she's younger by nearly a year.'

Sylvia nodded towards the forecourt. 'Foul night for the kiddies to be out so late.'

He glanced at her, as if sensing criticism. 'We're nearly home.' He nodded towards the little girl. 'Birthday girl.'

'Today?'

'Next weekend, but we've been visiting the grandparents today, so she's in the money.'

She might be the younger one, but Sylvia could see she was the boss, from the way she ordered the boy about, telling him what he should choose.

The little girl wagged a finger at her daddy. 'Mummy says, don't forget the milk.'

He laughed and walked towards the fridge. She could obviously wind him around her little finger. Sylvia admired the way he moved: fit, tightly packed with energy, sure of himself. It was a long time since Gerrard's buttocks had been that tight. Come to think of it, when had she last noticed Gerrard's buttocks? Turning from the fridge, a carton of milk in his hand, his eyes met hers and he smirked. He knew exactly what was on her mind. Her face burned.

The automatic door swished open. Relieved to be able to look somewhere else, she focused on two youths standing in the doorway. One wore a hoodie, the other a baseball cap pulled down until the peak rested on his nose. The forecourt bell hadn't pinged. Sylvia looked through the rain-streaked window. Still only one car stood by the petrol pumps, but when she leaned around the cash register, she had a side view of another car, its back end tucked into the car wash, so the number plate was not visible. She cleared her throat, ready to tell the lads that the car wash closed at six o'clock.

The one with the hoodie met her eyes and she froze, the words drying up in her throat. He looked away, watching the children who were examining the chocolate bars, trying to match them up with the prices on the shelf. The other youth walked along the aisle, past the children, glancing left and right as if searching for something. Greasy black hair, curly, poked out from the back of his cap. He walked across to the fridge, passing

Dad, and picked out two cans of beer. He nodded over his shoulder to his friend who shook his head. He beckoned to him, with his thumb, as he came up to the counter and waited behind Dad, who was holding out his cash card to Sylvia. The little girl was explaining to her brother that he couldn't have the crisps that were in his hand, as well as a bar of chocolate. She selected a packet of crisps for herself.

Dad stepped back. 'You go first, mate.' He lifted a road atlas from the display stand and flicked through the pages. The children's voices were getting louder and he called, 'You two, stop arguing or neither of you'll get anything.'

Hoodie joined the curly one at the counter. Sylvia held out a hand for the money. Curly placed his beer cans on the counter, put his hand in a pocket, brought out a gun.

'Empty the till, in a carrier bag. Get a shift on.'

Sylvia, frozen, watched the children moving along the aisle towards the counter, each holding a packet of crisps, their heads together. Dad slowly put down the road atlas. He followed Sylvia's eyes to the girl as she walked into the space between the aisle and the counter.

Curly saw her, and said to the other youth, 'Grab her.'

Hoodie put his hands on her shoulders and held her against him. Her crisps crunched under his foot. She squealed, wriggled, reached for the squashed purple packet that lay on the floor. He pulled her back.

'Daddy?'

Her dad took a step towards her.

Curly swung around, pointing the gun at the father, then at the girl. 'One more move.' Dad froze. The gun swung back to Sylvia. 'Do it. Now.'

The little boy was in the open space and stopped, his eyes meeting those of his sister. He looked from her to his dad, who called to Sylvia, his voice high, 'Do what he says, quickly.'

Hands shaking, she pressed the till override button, pulled a carrier bag from the shelf below and transferred handfuls of twenties, tens, and five-pound notes from the cash drawer into it. Before she could put the bag down, Curly yanked it out of her hand, threw his upper body onto the counter to look over and check the cash drawer, then, waving his gun at each of them in turn, started walking backwards. He bumped into the boy, twisted around and lashed out with the hand holding the gun. The child's feet left the ground and he crashed against the corner of the road atlas display. Dad dropped to his knees and picked the boy up as Curly reached the door and it opened.

'Come on,' Curly beckoned with his head. Hoodie let go of the girl's shoulders. 'Bring her with you.'

As she was steered towards the door, the little girl held out a hand to her father. Her eyes were big and round, her mouth open but not making a sound.

With the boy in his arms, Dad stepped forward. 'It'll be all right, love.'

For several seconds the boy had been stunned by the fall and now he started to scream. Curly pointed the gun at the girl's head, then at Dad, back at the girl. Dad stopped. Curly backed out of the door.

A voice called, 'What the fuck is going on?'

Through the window, Sylvia watched the woman get out of the car as the two lads ran past her, Hoodie carrying the little girl. The child held out a hand towards the woman. Hoodie ran behind the pumps, towards the car wash.

Dad stopped at the door, half-turned to Sylvia, shouted, 'Ring the police,' but her eyes were fixed on the woman running after the youths, reaching out to her daughter . 'Now.'

His shout shocked Sylvia out of her trance. She held one hand in the other to keep it still enough to press the alarm button, then she lifted the phone off its stand, pressed a nine, and again, then harder, until the handset slipped out of her hand and onto the floor.

A car backfired, loudly. The woman fell against a petrol pump and slid down, slowly, one arm raised and twisted like a puppet whose strings had snapped, until her head rested on the fire bucket. The voice from the floor said, *Which service do you require?* The car revved and accelerated out of the car wash, swerving wildly across the forecourt. The baseball cap was in the driving seat and as the car turned towards the exit, she saw Hoodie through the open rear door, holding the girl tightly around the middle, half lying across the back seat. The door closed, the car skidded forward, slewed across the wet tarmac and sped into the road. Dad ran, following the car, the little boy still in his arms. Her head was full of screaming and a voice coming from the handset, saying, '*We've located you, love, we're on our way...*'

2

The police had been there all night, measuring, crawling along the forecourt in the freezing rain, taking photographs, asking questions. Instead of getting the last bus home, Sylvia had been on the first bus, at five-fifteen in the morning. Gerrard was snoring in the armchair where he'd fallen asleep, waiting for her. She took the remote from under his hand and switched the TV to the 24-hour news channel.

The movement disturbed him and he sat up, rubbing his eyes. 'Oh, hello, love. Did you hear the news? Marijohn Wilkin has died.'

Sylvia wondered that the woman's name had been on the news already. She must have looked confused, because he said, 'You know. The country and western songwriter. "One Day at a Time"? Kris Kristofferson?'

While he was speaking, she sat on the sofa, and looked at the TV screen, watching herself duck under the crime-scene tape and walk towards the bus stop. Gerrard looked from the TV to Sylvia. 'What's happened? What time is it?' He looked at the clock on the mantelpiece.

~

Gerrard brought her a mug of hot chocolate into the bathroom. She laced it with brandy from the bottle she kept in the airing cupboard and felt the shaking slow down. Wearing the fleecy onesie he'd bought her for a long-ago birthday, she toyed with the breakfast of eggs and sausage he put in front of her. He wanted to phone the bus depot, tell them he couldn't come in today, but Sylvia promised she'd go to bed and rest if he went to work.

As soon as he'd gone, Sylvia switched on the TV and sat in the reclining armchair, reaching under the lever to find one of her miniatures. She watched the news, then the news update, changed channel to watch it again, had a drink, watched the next update, and the next. She nodded off, dreaming of clouds of strawberry-blonde hair which turned greasy and black, a little hand reaching out, and screamed when a gun exploded.

Gerrard said, 'It's only the door, banging shut in the draught. Your nerves are shot.' He'd brought her fish and chips which he put on a tray that he set on her lap. He changed the television channel and sat on the sofa with his own tray, watching *Top Gear*. The phone rang, and she heard him in the hallway talking to her mother, telling her that Sylvia seemed to have come out of it all right, no harm done. Her mother had waited until Gerrard came home, knowing Sylvia would have put the phone down on her. She reached for the bottle, but Gerrard must have moved it while she was asleep. She changed the channel to *News 24*.

He came back into the room, looked from Sylvia to the television, to her barely touched fish and chips, went into the hallway and she heard him on the phone, speaking to Dave, saying Sylvia wouldn't be coming to work tonight, in fact she wasn't going to work there again. He meant he didn't want her to, they hadn't discussed it, but he was probably right.

'Fair's fair,' he said when he came back. 'Dave said he'll pay you for a week's holiday and fix you up with a job at one of his other places.'

~

If Gerrard was home, and there was cooking and cleaning to do, she could stop thinking about it, but as soon as she sat down, or lay down, it started again, like a film clip on repeat. Gerrard seemed to think the best thing was to act normally, make small talk, not mention it. But it was all that Sylvia could think about.

'What if,' she'd say suddenly, into the silence, or into the middle of some convoluted tale Gerrard was recounting about one of his workmates, or a passenger, 'What if I hadn't been doing sudoku instead of watching the forecourt...' Thinking to herself, *and instead of watching that man's arse*. 'If I'd been doing my job properly, I'd have seen the car coming in, parking out of sight, those lads creeping around... I'd have been suspicious... what if I'd closed the automatic door and made them come to the night hatch...'

Gerrard said, 'They had a gun, they'd have forced you to open the door.'

'What if I'd hit the alarm quicker... phoned the police... hid the children...'

Gerrard sighed. 'The mother was out there, they'd have taken her hostage, they were desperate. Don't dwell on it, let the police get on with their job, there's nothing you could have done.'

He was wrong. Sylvia knew there were many things she could have done, that would have changed the way it turned out. Days had gone by, they hadn't found the car, they didn't know who the robbers were, and there was no sign of the kiddie.

Gerrard patted her on the shoulder. 'The little toerags would have robbed somebody else. If it hadn't been you, it would have been whoever was on duty, or some other petrol station.'

She didn't tell Gerrard that she'd know him, the one with the hood, if she saw him again. She didn't say it to the police either, when they came to take another statement, because what else could she say? It was something she felt, rather than something she could express in words. It would sound ridiculous. She'd answered their questions, as best she could. What colour was his hair? He had a hood, it was up all the time. Did he have any features that you remember – was he spotty, unshaven, did he have facial hair, an earring, a scar, a tattoo...? No. No. No. What about his teeth? He didn't open his mouth. What colour were his eyes? She thought for a moment. No, it couldn't be true. She must be imagining it. She shook her head, no. But she lay awake, thinking about it. Twice, their eyes had met. Just for that second, at the door. And again, when Curly had taken out the gun, the other one had looked straight at her. She'd recognised the shock, the fear. He hadn't expected a gun. He wasn't the instigator, that was Curly. Twice, for a couple of seconds at the most, but it was enough. If she tried to explain this to Gerrard, he'd say she was hallucinating.

She stopped talking to Gerrard. She went into Dylan's room and talked to him. Dylan understood that she was to blame, for everything. She told Dylan about the eyes. Gerrard said she was drinking too much, it made her snore and toss about so he slept in Dylan's room. She felt invaded: Dylan's room was her place. She asked Gerrard to move back into the bedroom, told him she missed him and forced herself to be affectionate; though she couldn't help comparing his lean frame and shock of prematurely grey hair which emphasised the new lines on his face, with the taut youthfulness of the child's father. Gerrard cheered up. He thought everything was getting back to normal, or at least, his idea of normal.

The news was always on. Alone, Sylvia kept the radio in the bedroom and the radio in the kitchen both on and tuned to the local station, and the television in the lounge on *News 24*, so that wherever she was in the flat, she would be listening for updates. Not that most items were really updates, just a repeat of what had already been said, with maybe one new piece of information popped onto the end.

Six days after the robbery, she was in the kitchen when the newsreader announced that the child's mother had been discharged from hospital, and she dashed into the lounge to watch a bent figure, above a red 'Breaking News' banner, limping from the car, past the police officer at the front door. As the camera swung around she saw the street sign, Lacey Gardens. According to the A-Z, it was in the new housing development behind Halfords, not far away. Sylvia studied the street map; there was probably a way round behind the retail park, by the river.

It was longer than the main road, but Sylvia wasn't ready to face the noise of traffic or to run the risk of one of the bus drivers seeing her and reporting back to Gerrard. The path was narrow and muddy. At the sound of a bicycle bell she leapt aside and became tangled in brambles. By the time she got to Lacey Gardens the sun was out, turning the ground a dirty brown where leaves had been trampled into the small patch of lawn by press and television crews surrounding the house. A policewoman stood by the door. Sylvia recognised the little lad pressed against the inside of the window and saw the puzzlement on his face.

The next day, the news had footage and Sylvia recognised Doctor Holden driving up and going into the house. They had the same GP, which meant he would know all about it, she wouldn't have to say much, only that she was there, and he'd know what to do.

'How are you getting on, Sylvia? Yes, I thought that was you, on the news... Of course, I'll give you a prescription, something to sleep, and this will help the anxiety...'

She wasn't about to return to those days of pill-popping, she'd found ways to manage it herself, but she exchanged the prescription and stored the Imovane in the linen cupboard. What she wanted was a sick note, and he signed her off for a month. That would stop Gerrard plotting to get her back to work when she had more important things on her mind.

On the way home from the surgery, Sylvia called in the Co-op and bought one each of the newspapers, a carton of orange juice, and spent the change from a ten-pound note on scratch cards. The assistant with 'Jill' on her name badge said, 'Hi.' Sylvia had seen her around; she lived in their block. Jill asked would Sylvia like to come down to the club on Friday night, with her and the girls? Sylvia said she'd think about it, but knew she wouldn't. As she left the shop, it was going dark and she jogged towards the looming shadows that were the blocks of flats, and in through the entrance. An explosion ripped through her ears and she pinned herself to the wall. A stream of swearing from her next-door neighbour, Mrs Cresswell, echoed from above, down the stairwell, and two youngsters ran down, laughing and pointing at Sylvia as they passed. She realised it was Bonfire Night, another hazard to avoid.

Safely in the flat with the door locked, Sylvia flopped into her chair, still wearing her coat. Taking her glass from where she'd left it on the hearth, she poured herself a long drink of orange juice. She added a generous measure from the new bottle of brandy, tucked the bottle into the recliner mechanism and switched on the television.

The parents had done a press conference. Mum obviously hadn't slept, and he, Dad, was puffy and white. A policewoman sat between them. As though she was keeping them apart; as if they'd had a row. That wouldn't be surprising, would it? If she'd been that kiddie's mummy, Sylvia would want to know why he was so slow on the uptake. Now Sylvia thought about it, how come he stood watching, while they shot his wife and drove off with his daughter? Oh, he ran then, how he ran. Chasing that car into the road. But it was too late, wasn't it? They were well away. It was pouring down and they were going fast. Of course, if Sylvia hadn't stood there like a lemon behind the till, there would have been time to write down the registration number... She poured herself another drink.

The *Sheffield Star* said Dad was a builder, working for Lettertons. It didn't say what Mum did or used to do; presumably she stayed at home with the children. There was a picture of the little boy's school. His name was Jake. The head teacher said Rosie – that was the little girl's name – was in reception class, and everybody loved her, such a lively and intelligent girl. Isn't that what they always say when something happens to a child? She'd only have been there a few weeks; they probably barely knew her name, until this. Or perhaps they have to say something, to make the press go away. Otherwise, those reporters would hang around, picking up scraps to pretend they had news to tease you with, their 'update' this and 'breaking news' that. Jake didn't go to school for a while, but Sylvia listened to the other parents. It was all they talked about, as they stood around the gate, waiting to collect their children from school.

The mother standing next to Sylvia looked her up and down. 'I haven't seen you here before?'

'I'm Dylan's mum,' she said and moved away as the school doors opened.

~

Lettertons was building a new leisure centre in Grenoside. There was a temporary café, in a Portakabin opposite, where the men from the building site went at dinner time. It was all they talked about, too. Rick, that was Dad's name, came back to work after a couple of weeks. Pausing as they passed, one man after another said, 'Ey up, mate?' and moved swiftly on as if he was tainted, as if touching him might bring tragedy to their own families. One did stop, pulled up a chair and said, 'It's Greg's stag weekend, will you come?' Rick shook his head. 'Just for a drink then?' Not even for that. He sat hunched over his dinner, eating a bit, pushing it around the plate, leaving most of it. There was nothing of the jauntiness she'd admired that night. As he left, passing her table without the confident swagger that she remembered so well, he caught Sylvia's eye, paused and frowned, as if he knew her from somewhere but couldn't bring it to mind.

Gerrard said, 'What were you doing, up Grenoside way, today?' One of the other bus drivers had mentioned seeing her. She hated this about his job, that he always knew where she was, as though he had a personal CCTV monitoring her.

'I went to the woods, for a walk, to clear my head.' He raised his eyebrows. He knew she hated the countryside, and walking. 'You did say it wasn't good for me, hanging around the house.'

'I meant perhaps it's time you got back to work. Give Dave a ring. It'll take your mind off it. We can't afford for you not to work. You haven't been there long enough to get sick pay; he was generous to pay you for the first week. When does your sick note finish?'

She recognised his tactics, from that other time. Tough love, he'd called it then. She rang Dave. He needed somebody in reception at his car wash in Parson's Cross. 'I'll work mornings,' she told Gerrard, and could see that he was pleased. He was right, they needed the money. So long as she wasn't out after dark.

Rosie's photograph was in the paper with the headline: **Does she know it's Christmas?** There were heart-shaped balloons, damp teddy bears and plastic ponies with rainbow manes and tails piled on the tiny lawn in front of the house. It was a quiet Christmas, just Sylvia and Gerrard, sharing a turkey thigh at the kitchen table. Without Dylan, there wasn't much point in decorations and so forth. Gerrard probably didn't even notice that the cards – fewer each year – stayed in a heap on the bookcase. She didn't send any. Nobody phoned to ask if they were all right, so presumably her cards hadn't been missed, with her upbeat, newsy paragraphs, sent without fail year after year until they'd moved here.

'Let's go to the pub,' Gerrard said, after they'd cleared away.

'You go, I'd rather stay in.'

When he left, she walked round to Lacey Gardens and put a gift on the doorstep for Jake, with a card, *from a well-wisher*. It was a Lego robot. Sylvia chose it from the box of toys that Dylan had loved most. Reading a few labels as she passed the lawn, she could see everything was for Rosie, which made her glad she'd done something for the little boy.

She was kneeling, rearranging a Sylvanian family that had become scattered, when a car pulled up beside her and Rick got out. He opened the rear door, and Jake slid off the seat onto the kerb and walked towards the house. His father called him back, thumbed towards the car and Jake leaned in, pulled out an enormous Christmas gift bag which she could see was bursting with games and toys. They must have been visiting relatives. Jake dragged the bag along the path to the front door where he waited for his father. The only decoration on view was a paper star hanging from the lampshade, which looked like something Jake had brought home from school. Sylvia thought the mother might have made an effort for the lad. She mouthed *hello* to the little boy and caught Rick's frown. She raised a hand and he nodded, unsmiling.

In the new year, Sylvia started work at Dave's car wash. To avoid the streets, the traffic, the people, she walked the circuitous route along the river and through the new estate, so she passed Lacey Gardens every day. The house was quiet now, the press had lost interest. Often, the little boy would be standing at the window. After a few days, he started to wave back. It couldn't be good for him, stuck at home with his mum all day. There were occasional glimpses of her – Jennifer, according to the newspapers – opening the door to the post or taking in the Asda delivery; enough for Sylvia to see that she hadn't bothered to get dressed and probably not even showered. Then Jake was back at school. Sylvia dilly-dallied after she finished work, so that she could leave in time to be passing by the school as his auntie collected him. He always came out first, crossed the playground alone, stopping, waiting, looking behind him. When he caught sight of Sylvia, he'd pause, look, and sometimes returned her wave.

She overheard another parent speak to the auntie. 'Always in such a rush, Miriam. They're lucky, having you to help out.'

Miriam took Jake by the hand and said over her shoulder,

'My two are at school in Broomhill, so I have to get across there quick as I can.'

It took two buses to get to Broomhill. Sylvia found that if she sat at the back and wore earplugs, she could bear the journey through town, but by the time she got there from work, the schools were closed and quiet.

'I hear you were on Manchester Road today?' Gerrard said.

'There are some good charity shops in Broomhill.'

'Did you find anything?'

Buying second-hand was one of his economy strategies, as he called them. 'Not today, but I might go back, there are a few more to try.'

He nodded and patted her on the shoulder. 'Good for you, getting out and about a bit more, it'll do you good.'

It was the end of February when she saw Miriam in the supermarket. The children were arguing over the sweet shelf, while Jake stood off on one side, looking at his shoes.

She dipped to his level as she passed him, whispered, 'You're remembering, aren't you?'

Miriam looked around sharply. 'Excuse me?'

Sylvia smiled. 'I was saying hello to Jake. It's Miriam, isn't it?'

Miriam frowned. 'Do I know you?'

'Yes of course, I knew you and your sister, Jennifer, when you were growing up. I live near Jennifer now, so I know Jake of course, don't I, Jake?'

Jake looked up at his name. Miriam smiled uncertainly.

Sylvia dropped her voice. 'I can see you're helping the family out, looking after Jake, while his mum... Any news?'

Miriam stepped back. 'No. Excuse me, what did you say your name was?'

'Well, I need to get on. It was nice meeting you.'

Sylvia waggled her fingers at Jake and left the supermarket, putting her earplugs in to dull the noise of traffic. Crossing the road, she saw rather than heard people on the other side yelling at her, felt the rush of air to her right and turned in time to see the grille of a refuse truck bearing down on her. The scream of air brakes penetrated the foam in her ears as she felt herself yanked backwards onto the pavement. Through the throng of people who were helping her up, walking her to a bench, tutting over her torn tights and muddy coat, she saw the *Vacancies* board outside the supermarket. They needed cashiers.

The interview was easy. Sylvia impressed the manager with her list of relevant experience, before, as she explained to him, she had taken time off to bring up a family, and said she could start on Monday, references permitting. When Sylvia phoned Dave, he said it was no problem to leave this week; he'd phone the manager straight away and give her a good reference.

Gerrard brought her flowers and a new sudoku book. 'That's a proper contract and more than the minimum wage. We can increase our payments, pay it off a bit quicker.' He patted her on the knee with one hand, and said 'Mmmm' through a mouthful of seafood pie. He waved his fork at her. 'You're bucking up, how about a bit of a celebration? I could treat you to a new hairdo? A bit of colour? Get your nails done, maybe? We could have a night out at the club? People are asking about you.'

Sylvia imagined the noise of the music and people shouting to make themselves heard. 'I'll have an early night.'

From behind her till, Sylvia saw Miriam often, doing her shopping after school with the children in tow. Little Jake trailed behind his cousins, looking pale and tired. Then came the day that Miriam was at Sylvia's till.

Sylvia said, 'Hello Jake,' and, as Miriam was getting her card from her purse, asked, 'How are things with Jennifer? I hear they found the car?'

Miriam said, 'They're not sure it's the same car.'

'In the dunes, wasn't it, somewhere near Skegness?'

'It was burnt out, no forensic evidence, apparently.'

3

Sylvia went to the community centre, watched the women in pink T-shirts with Rosie's face printed on the front, taking down the names of the volunteers and organising them into the three coaches. Rick was there, and she recognised a number of the men he worked with. It had the feel of those Sunday school outings when she was younger, everybody climbing on board with their packed lunches, heading for the seaside. She could almost smell the egg and tomato that would be squished and crunchy with grains of sand by the time they sat down to picnic beside the sea. Dylan had been terrified of the huge expanse of white-gold beach. He'd wobble frantically in the soft sand, screaming as he lost his balance and ended up crawling behind the windbreak, leaving Gerrard building sandcastles by himself.

Buckets and spades were being packed into the belly of the coach, but not the little plastic ones. This was strictly adults only, with wellington boots and raincoats, woolly hats and scarves. It said on *Look North* that evening that they were given free bed and breakfast by the guest houses in Skegness, and hundreds of locals came out to help. On the television screen, long lines of people of all shapes and sizes probed the beach and the dunes with their fingertips. They found nothing. Rick had been a big lad, that day she'd watched him striding across the forecourt with his two kiddies. She remembered admiring his broad shoulders, his perky arse. But the day she stood with the neighbours outside the community centre, watching them get off the coach, he shuffled along, thin and tired, not reacting when the other volunteers slapped his back as they passed him.

She pulled out more carrier bags and helped Miriam to pack. 'Did I read something in the newspaper about a medium writing to Jennifer to say little Rosie was beside the sea?'

Miriam took a banana from the bunch, opened its top, broke off a section and gave it to her youngest who was sitting in the trolley. 'Mumbo-jumbo. Jennifer wants to believe it, but, you know as well as I do—'

'But if that's where they found the car, don't you think there might be something in it?'

'I'm sure the police had a good look around and there was no sign of anything.'

'Do you want any tokens?'

Miriam nodded, found her saver club card and bent to pick up the discarded banana. As she stood up again she said, 'Thank you, not enough hands.'

'No trouble.' Sylvia stuck the tokens into the club card and handed it back to Miriam.

On Saturday, Sylvia told Gerrard she was working, then going out with the girls from work, so would be late back.

'That's good, you're getting back to normal.'

Normal? Normal Sylvia was Dylan's mum... if she'd been a stay-at-home mum like Miriam, been around for Dylan... no, normal was long gone, she wanted to say to Gerrard, but didn't, for fear of bringing it all up again. If he thought this was normal, it might stop him going on about the alcohol on her breath, and staying in too much.

It was a long journey, with a train to Lincoln, and a bus to Skegness, then a cold and blustery walk along the dunes, before Sylvia found it. A large, darkened circle of sand with a fringe of blackened marram grass marked the spot. She looked around, wondering that the driver had managed to get the car into this position, off a little parking area, behind a row of takeaways, and set fire to it without anyone noticing. She perched on a wooden stump and drank from her thermos.

Walking away from the dunes, along the street towards the bus stop, Sylvia passed a little pub on the corner. Her shoes squelched on the stained carpet and the tables were smeared as if wiped with a dirty cloth, but there was a log fire burning, and the woman behind the bar called a cheery, 'Hello, love, what can I get you?' A couple of elderly men sitting over half pint glasses in one corner watched her as she walked to the bar, then lost interest.

The landlady served her a generous gin from a bottle she took from under the bar. 'We go to Benalmádena every winter, close up here, bring back a few bottles and the brewery's none the wiser.' She followed Sylvia across to the table next to the fire. As she bent to take a log from the basket, she noticed Sylvia's shoes. 'Pop them in front of the fire for a bit, love. It's perishing out there, you wouldn't think it was nearly Easter.'

'I couldn't help noticing there's been a fire or something out there on the dunes.'

The landlady pushed the log into the heart of the fire and perched on a chair. 'Must have happened when everything was shut up for winter. We got back from Benalmádena late and woke up the next morning to find the police everywhere, scouring the dunes, doing a fingertip search, helicopters overhead day after day.' She told Sylvia they'd expected to find a little girl buried there, but if it was the same car, the kidnappers must have dumped it. They'd probably stolen another car and moved on. That's a thought, Sylvia told herself. 'Of course,' said the landlady, 'there's no telling, it could have been any little toerag burning out a car.'

Alone on the top deck of the bus, Sylvia watched row upon row of holiday homes slipping by either side of the road, like travelling through a rainswept ghost town. It was hard to imagine what it would look like a couple of months from now. Then it came to her. What a perfect place to lie low in the winter. Why, they could still be there, living in one of those caravans, and who would know? She thought about it all the way home and, as the train pulled into Sheffield, she was sure she had it. That night was dark, and it would have been late, and they'd have been looking for somewhere to hole up for a while. Call it a sixth sense, if you like.

When Sylvia worked for the bus company, they'd been starting to introduce computers, but that was a long time ago, and Sylvia wouldn't know how to switch one of these modern things on. Now, she saw whenever she went into the office at work, the staff all used computers. She'd heard about search engines.

'We need to get a computer.'

Gerrard said, 'We're not computer people. We've managed

without so far. And, anyway, where would we get the money from? We don't seem to be any better off even with the wages from this new job of yours.'

'It's because we're getting the groceries from work, they're deducting it from my salary so that we get the staff discount.'

He flicked down the top of his Sunday paper and looked over it, his eyebrows raised, but he said nothing. There was a half-empty bottle by his feet and Sylvia realised he'd have found it when he drew the living room curtains.

On Monday, Sylvia left early for work and went into the main police station at West Bar, asked to speak to the high-up who was in charge of the Rosie search, said she had important information. It didn't take long. The fellow didn't look like a proper policeman. In fact, he reminded Sylvia of one of the robbers, with his jeans and hoodie. He took her into a little room with proper armchairs, not like those interview rooms you see on the telly.

'Now then, Mrs Wilton–'

'Sylvia.'

'Sylvia. You told the desk you had some information about the missing girl, Rosie?'

'Yes, I do. I think she's being kept in one of those prefabs, mobile homes, you know, those big caravans in Skegness.'

'The static caravans?'

'Yes.'

'What makes you think she's being kept in a caravan?'

'Well, I read the article about the medium, and it made me think–'

'A medium? You think we should follow the advice of a medium?'

'No, but I have a feeling–'

'A feeling? Do you have a particular caravan in mind, Mrs W – Sylvia?'

'Of course not. Have you searched all the caravans?'

'You want to know if we've searched every caravan in Skegness?'

'Yes.'

'Sylvia, have you any idea of the resources we put into the search for Rosie?'

'Well, officer–'

'Sergeant.'

'Sergeant, I'm sure you did everything you could. But you didn't find her, did you? You found the car she was kidnapped in–'

'Which we suspected she may have been kidnapped in.'

'As you like. But the top and bottom of it is that she was probably taken to Skegness, and they got rid of the car. And where did they go then? Late, dark, got a little girl with them and she would have been drawing attention, say, if she was crying, upset. They would have hidden, wouldn't they? And where would you hide out, around there, in the winter? It's obvious, isn't it? In one of those caravans. That's what I'd do, anyway, if I was in their shoes.'

'Sylvia, I can assure you that all possible resources were mobilised in the search for Rosie. There was a fingertip search of–'

'Yes, yes, of the dunes, and the roads and the verges. But was there a fingertip search of the caravan sites? I don't think so.'

'Well... since you are clearly a member of the public who cares very deeply about this, and because of that, I can tell you that we did take steps to check the caravan sites.'

'Every caravan?'

'Can I ask, exactly what is your interest, Sylvia?'

'It's as you said, I'm a member of the public who cares.'

He took her address and date of birth and left the room. A young officer in uniform came in and handed her a plastic cup of tea. She sipped the powdery machine mixture and spat it back into the cup. The Sergeant returned, said he'd taken a note of her concerns, and they would look into them. She knew a brush-off when she heard one.

He followed her outside and stood on the steps, lit a fag, said, 'You look after yourself.' She stopped at the corner, saw him still watching her, smoking.

The following afternoon, Sylvia was just in from work, taking her coat off, when the bell rang. A man and a woman stood on the doorstep, holding out identity cards. From Operation Check- mate, they said, and one of them added, 'The investigation around Rosie Endleby's disappearance.'

Maybe something was going to get done. 'Is this about Skeg- ness? Come in. Would you like a cup of tea?'

She ushered them into the front room. When she returned with the tray, the woman had on latex gloves and was flicking through the pile of newspapers in the corner, while he was studying a photograph in his hand.

Sylvia was confused. Why were they looking through her things? 'Can I help you? Aren't you supposed to be following up the information I gave you?'

'Mrs Wilton, please sit down. Your name has come up during our investigation...'

Sylvia put the tray on the coffee table and perched on the edge of the sofa. 'Oh, I see. It must be a misunderstanding, offi- cer. I have been trying to help the police.' She leaned forward to pour the tea.

'Mrs Wilton, we have some questions we'd like to ask, if you don't–'

'Not at all. I'm pleased to be of assistance, but please be careful with that photograph.'

He was passing the photograph to the woman. It was the one of little Rosie, that Sylvia had cut out of the newspaper and tucked into the frame that stood on the mantelpiece. A kind of memorial. Like people had pictures of Terry Waite in their windows when he was taken hostage. An act of faith, believing he would come back, when everybody thought he was dead. And it had worked, hadn't it? It just went to show that nobody should give up on Rosie.

He lifted out the cutting of Rosie and studied the photograph below it. It was Dylan's baby picture. She caught a look passing between the two of them. It dawned on her then, that it may not be a misunderstanding. They might not have come to listen to her ideas.

'You won't mind if we have a quick look around the rest of the flat, Mrs Wilton?'

What could she say? The woman was taking books from the shelf of the wall unit, opening each one, checking behind; she lifted out a half-full bottle of brandy, and smirked. Sylvia heard him, opening and closing drawers in the bedroom, then moving to Dylan's bedroom. At the sound of boxes sliding along the wardrobe shelf, and in the tallboy, she shuddered to think of his hands rummaging amongst Dylan's belongings, and jumped up. The woman gestured to her to sit down. She listened to him in the kitchen, then he was in the hallway, going through the airing cupboard. She realised he would find the bottles. There were more than usual because there had been a special offer on spirits at work.

He came back in, nodded at his colleague and sat on the sofa, took out a notebook, flicked through it and wrote something. The woman pulled off her gloves and sat on the armchair, so Sylvia couldn't watch them both at the same time.

'Mrs Wilton, can you tell us why you're so interested in the disappearance of the little girl?'

The clock on the mantelpiece chimed four. Gerrard was due home at four thirty. She needed to get rid of them. Sylvia decided to come to the point. 'Because you don't seem to be doing much to find her.'

'Did you know either of the young men who robbed the petrol station?'

'Of course not. I said all this before, in my witness statement. I am a witness, officer, and I do object to being treated like a suspect.'

'Hmm.' He held her gaze for several seconds then made a note. 'You might want to think carefully before answering this. Had you had any contact with those young men before the events of that evening?'

'How would I know? I couldn't even see them, one with his cap over his eyes, and the other with his hood up. I told you, one was dark and curly, because some hair was sticking out of the back of his cap, but the other one...' She paused, thinking about the one with the hoodie... what was it about him?

'You seem unsure, Mrs Wilton. Thinking about before that night. Had you met them anywhere? Had they come into the shop? It may have been these lads who broke your CCTV cameras the night before, so they'd probably been there. Had you seen them around, maybe, on the street, or–'

'Officer, are you suggesting that I might have known these robbers – kidnappers – and what? That I might have had something to do with it?'

'Did you, Mrs Wilton?'

'Ridiculous.'

The woman spoke. 'Seemingly, you have a considerable

interest in the robbers, and you may have known them, even known what they planned to do? Of course, you didn't expect the family to be in the shop at the time, and I'm sure you didn't expect one of them to be armed. Had you worked it out with them, that you'd just hand over the cash? Then it all went wrong, didn't it, when they took the little girl hostage?'

Sylvia was stunned into silence.

He studied one of the pages in his notebook, then smiled at Sylvia. 'That business a few years ago, Sylvia. 2003, was it...?'

Sylvia knew when it was time to shut up and stop talking. 'No comment.'

Quick as a flash, he said, 'In that case, Mrs Wilton, I suggest we continue this conversation at the station. Are you happy to come with us, to assist with our inquiries, or do I need to arrest you?'

4

———

As she closed the oven door on the steak and ale pie, Sylvia heard Rosie's name and rushed into the living room. On the TV screen was an aerial view of row after row of static caravans: blue-and-white tape surrounded one in the corner. A hedge along two sides separated it from a car park, with a pathway visible between dunes, to a beach, and the sea. A body had been found. Sylvia didn't gloat. She didn't think, *I told you so*. Weighed down by sadness, she moved one of her books on the shelf and pulled out a miniature brandy, drinking straight from the bottle and dropping the empty into her pocket.

A police inspector appeared on the screen, standing in front of the entrance to a caravan park; figures in white overalls moved around behind her. She could confirm that the body of an adult male had been discovered, deceased for some time, but was unable to confirm exactly how long he had been there. Sylvia was sure she'd said 'adult male'. The body had not yet been identified; there would be a full investigation. A reporter off-screen asked whether this death was linked to the kidnapping of Rosie Endleby six months ago? The inspector said there was no evidence of a link at this time. The reporter asked what

Sylvia asked weeks ago: bearing in mind that the caravan park was only a few miles from where the car was found, had the police searched this part of the coast when they were looking for Rosie? The spokeswoman said there had been no evidence of the car being linked to the disappearance of Rosie. But, asked the reporter, given the number of holiday homes unoccupied in the winter... The inspector said, 'Thank you,' and turned away.

The camera switched to a man who was describing how his family had arrived at their caravan for the Easter holiday. The banner on the screen said he was called Colin Standish. The caravan park had been closed for the winter. He'd noticed straight away that the door had been forced, he said. Yes, Sylvia thought, even the most rudimentary search would have discovered a forced door.

Sylvia tried to imagine what it would have been like for the Standishes, walking into their caravan, finding a corpse. This Easter was snowy and cold. The body was probably frozen. She imagined what it would have been like if it had been one of those hot Easters. Though when she thought about it, there had been a bit of a heatwave a few weeks ago, so the body might have decomposed and then frozen, and... Sylvia pulled several books off the shelf before she found a miniature; she didn't bother to look for a glass. Did the Standishes have children? What if the children had run in first? She should feel appalled at the thought; but it was probably nothing beside what Rosie had suffered. Six months. Sylvia felt the vein in her temple throbbing. The police had been so slapdash.

The front door closed, and she jumped up, but didn't reach the kitchen before Gerrard. As he opened the oven door, smoke from the burned pie billowed out.

'Sit down, Ger, I'll put something else in.'

He shook his head and left the room. While she listened to him in the hall, taking off his jacket and boots, then banging around in the shower, she took a fish pie out of the freezer and put it in the oven, and prepared some vegetables. She set the timer. When she heard him breathe out noisily as he sat in the armchair – thinking how he sounded like his father, but he wasn't even forty yet – she made a cup of tea and took it in to him. He had lined up three empty miniature bottles – she didn't remember three – on the coffee table and switched the channel to *Wheeler Dealers*.

She held out the cup to him. 'I was watching the news. They've found a dead body in a caravan near where they found that burned-out car. It might be–'

He sighed, heavily. 'I hope this isn't all going to kick off again.'

'If it's one of the robbers, they'll maybe believe me and try–'

'Sylvia, stop it. It's all supposition. You know nothing except where this got you the other week when you started imagining all sorts of things. In a police cell, if my memory serves me. Let it go, will you? I'm sick of it. Just leave the police to their work. If that little kiddie's alive, whoever's got her will slip up in the end, and they'll find her.'

Sylvia watched Gerrard slurp his tea and thought how much he was getting on her nerves.

There was no further information in the news over the next few days. Sylvia reckoned that if there was anything, they'd tell Rosie's family first. Miriam wasn't in the supermarket at the usual time, probably because it was the school holidays and her routine was different. Once she had Miriam's surname from her saver token card, she'd been able to find the address by phoning all the Osgoods in the Broomhill area and asking for Miriam. When she heard the familiar clipped tone, she didn't even need to ask, just rang off. Miriam's house was a four-storey narrow building in a quiet, residential street. It was quite a walk from the main part of Broomhill. As Sylvia was passing, Rick pulled up in the car and Miriam opened the front door of the house with Jake beside her.

Sylvia called over, 'Miriam, hello dear, how are things?'

Miriam looked startled. She gave Sylvia a tight-lipped smile and said something to Rick as he leaned behind the driver's seat to open the rear passenger door. Jake climbed in, and Rick drove off. Miriam didn't look at Sylvia as she turned and went back into the house.

The body was identified as a Dean Burton. He'd been released from a prison sentence the week before the robbery. Suddenly, there was a link, and it was all over the news again. Dean had been murdered, using a firearm similar to descriptions of the gun used during the robbery, and his death may have occurred shortly afterwards. That's what they said. Which meant the body had been in the caravan since that night, or soon after, just as Sylvia had imagined. They were actively seeking his 'known associates' which included cellmates and people he had previously offended with. Well, that's some progress, thought Sylvia, but if they'd searched the caravan sites at that time... As if she was able to transfer her thoughts by telepathy, the reporter asked exactly that question. It was the chief constable this time. Yes, he agreed, there were lessons to be learned about the way they had worked with the local force to track the offenders and act on information received. That was what he said, 'information received'. That's me, thought Sylvia. They wish they'd listened to me now. Even so, said the chief constable, there was no evidence at this time that the child had been at the caravan.

Then she saw Jake on the television; once the news of the body broke, the press had gathered outside the house again. It was the school holidays, and he was inside that house, penned in by the press, his little face at the window, so forlorn.

The next day, Sylvia told Gerrard she was working a late shift and after he left, turned on *BBC Radio Sheffield* and listened to the update, which was no update, just the same news again, while she went through her collection of cuttings. No sign of the child? She knew what they'd be thinking: the child was dead, somewhere between Sheffield and the coast. They'd be spending millions of pounds of taxpayers' money on searching the verges and areas either side of the route.

Sajid was driving the bus which meant she had to get off at Glossop Road, telling him so that he'd tell Gerrard that she was on her way to work. When he was out of sight, she crossed to the tram stop and took the next tram to the railway station. Within half an hour there was a train to Lincoln. She caught the bus to Skegness. Then another bus along the coast. On her right-hand side, stretches of white sand alternated with short rows of shops, the Butlins metropolis, where she remembered a day trip for Dylan's third birthday; a caravan site. Except for an occasional figure, leaning into the wind, the beach was deserted. After passing through Ingoldmells, the number of caravan sites started to increase, until that was all she could see, on either side, with names like 'Holiday Paradise'.

When she saw a police officer standing beside the entrance to the caravan site, she rang the bell and stood beside the driver's cab. 'How long would it take to walk, from here to Skegness?' she asked him.

'About an hour. But the buses are every hour, so it's not worth–'

'And how long to drive here, from Sheffield?'

'It depends what route you take. There's the motorway, or

going through Lincoln... Let's see, you'd probably take the A57 to Lincoln and–'

'How long?'

The bus had pulled in and the door opened.

'Oh, two, or two and a half, three hours, unless it's holiday traff–'

Sylvia set off walking back along the other side of the road, careful to keep her eyes focused away from the police officer. She passed the entrance, crossed over, and took the side road, signposted '*To the Sea*'. After a hundred yards, she arrived in a car park, with a wooden walkway leading into the dunes. This was the rear boundary of the caravan site. According to the aerial photograph from the news, which was imprinted on her mind, the caravan was on the other side of this hawthorn hedge.

At the end of the car park, the ground became rough, overgrown with thorny shrubs, brambles and rough marram grass. They wouldn't have approached it this way, surely, not at night, in the rain. Sylvia retraced her steps along the boundary hedge and found a gap. On hands and knees, she pushed her shoulders through. It was easily wide enough for a youth, and a child. As she tried to stand, she found her hair and her coat entangled in the hawthorn. She tugged her hair from the thorns and twisted her body to free her coat. Suddenly released, she staggered through, landing on her side. Cursing, she rolled over onto her bottom, and wiped her muddy hands on her coat. Rubbing the sore spot on her head, she looked back at the hedge and saw several strands of her hair attached to the twigs. There was one longer strand, blonde. She yanked it out and looked closely, then got onto her knees, pushed her head back into the gap in the hedge and examined it. Yes, there were several strands of long, blonde hair caught in the hawthorn. She untangled a small clump, clasped it firmly, and sat back, holding her fist to her chest as if that would slow the palpitations. In front of her was the back of a row of static caravans, and the one closest to her, in the corner, had blue crime-scene tape fluttering around it.

She'd dressed for a day at work in the overheated super-market and found she was shivering on the wet grass. There was a tear in the bottom of her coat, muddy handprints on the front, and a hole in the knee of her tights. There was nobody about. Still clutching the blonde hairs, she looked towards the caravan. Her breath stopped when she saw the faint but clear imprint of fingers on the window and imagined Rosie's little hands, leaving a sticky trail. She ran around to the side, ducked under the crime-scene tape, and pulled the door open.

A large patch of muddy brown spread from the carpet, up onto the sofa. The stain was mottled with black dots that started to move, and became flies that she flapped away as they circled her. As the smell reached her open mouth, she dry-retched. She was standing in one longish room divided from a kitchen area by a breakfast bar, then a door into a corridor. When she opened it, she smelled the toilet, and retched again. It was hours since breakfast, so there was no food to bring up. She pulled out her thermos from her bag and took a swig to calm her stomach. Tucking the blonde hairs into the zipped side pocket of her handbag, she held a tissue over her nose as she walked along the narrow corridor. There were two bedrooms, one with two narrow beds for children, with no duvets, and the other with a double bed. There, the bed had been stripped and the duvet was in a heap. She pushed her nose into it, imagining that she could smell the child. Shivering, she sat on the bed and wrapped the duvet around herself. She had a strong sense that Rosie had been here, that she was alive when she was here, and she was alive when she left. Whichever was the dead one – the curly one or the one with the hoodie – the other had taken Rosie. She knew it. The one with the eyes. What was it about the eyes? He was the one. He had Rosie.

If she told Gerrard, once he'd got over his anger that she'd been here, that she hadn't left it alone, he'd probably march her down to the police station, to tell them. What exactly could she tell them that would make a difference? The police were coming in for a lot of stick from the media. The BBC said there was going to be an investigation; not that anything would change, it would just cost a lot of money that would be better spent on catching the robbers. The chief constable said no one had reported a burning vehicle at the time; it was cold, raining, and the thieves must have picked a time when no one was around. When they did find it, the police had assumed the youths wouldn't have walked far with the child, and had only searched the sites nearby. Even Sylvia could work out that they probably brought the child here, and one of them would have stayed with her, while the other took the car somewhere else and got rid of it.

She took the little clump of hairs from her bag and held them up to the light, sure she was looking at Rosie's hair. She examined the fine strands more closely. At first, she had guessed they brought Rosie through the hawthorn hedge, and she had caught her hair on the thorns, just as Sylvia had. If that had been the case, one end would have a root attached. These hairs had been cut.

Would it make a difference, if she showed them to the police? Then she remembered. If they thought she was likely to help them again, after the way they had treated her, they had another thing coming. Her chest burned as she recalled the humiliation of being escorted from her flat by the two officers. Police were always around the estate, usually in *Clement House* which had a reputation for drug dealing; but in *Winston House*, the families were more settled. Sylvia and Gerrard lived on a quiet landing, so it was noticed, especially by Mrs Cresswell, who stood in her doorway, her lips clamped together, watching Sylvia pass.

While one part of Sylvia knew she was in trouble, she also found it laughable; it seemed so much like watching a police interview on television: one of the police officers was all right, the other, the woman, was quite nasty, putting words in Sylvia's mouth. But she didn't laugh. She realised that might make things worse for her.

- *Do you know these lads?*
- *Had they arranged it with you, the robbery?*
- *Aren't you fed up, Sylvia, working for minimum wage? Gerrard can't be earning much as a bus driver, doesn't it get you down, working hard for years and with nothing to show for it?*
- *And what about these County Court Judgements, Sylvia? It must be a struggle, still paying off all those debts? I understand you used to like a little flutter, Sylvia, is that the problem?*
- *When did you and Gerrard last have a good holiday? It must have sounded a good opportunity, to get some extra cash, treat yourself? And no risks? All you had to do was turn a blind eye when they came to bust the camera, then hand over the money when they came in.*
- *Were you planning to meet them later, to take your share? But it all went wrong, didn't it, when that family came in, with the little kiddies. You hadn't planned that, had you, Sylvia? And when they went off with the little girl, you didn't get the handout you were expecting, did you?*
- *Of course, you're upset, I understand that, because you*

*never meant for anybody to be harmed, did you? We
know that. Come on, Sylvia, work with us. Tell us who the
lads are and help us to find them. Help us to find little
Rosie.*

On and on they went, for hours. Sylvia was surprised they
knew so much about her past. They'd been in touch with Dave,
too, and knew she'd been on duty the night before the robbery.

- *So, you could have helped them to damage the cameras, or
even done it yourself, is that how it happened, Sylvia?*

Sylvia pursed her lips. She didn't like this trend for starting
sentences with 'So...' How did they know about the County
Court Judgements, and that she'd fallen behind on the
payments? Gerrard didn't know that, and they promised not to
tell him, if Sylvia helped them. But what could she say? She
tried to explain, again and again, that she'd only been following
the case on the news and thinking about it because she was
upset about the little girl.

- *How did you know about Skegness, Sylvia? Unless you
knew the lads?*
- *How did you know about the caravan?*
- *We know you were in the pub there, the landlady
identified you.*

They had thrust their dirty fingers through her life and her
memories, humiliated her in front of her neighbours, gossiped
about her with the pub landlady, and accused her of the vilest of
actions. The red heat, that she remembered so well but hadn't
felt for years, bubbled and burned its way up from her
diaphragm, ready to burst out in a screaming stream of furious

words. She squeezed her lips together with her fingers to stop the sounds escaping, and looked down, concentrating on a small spot of dirt on her shoe.

A solicitor arrived, saying Gerrard sent him. Later, she learned that Mrs Cresswell had caught Gerrard on his way in from work and told him; he came down to the police station but wasn't allowed to see her, so he'd found a solicitor in the Yellow Pages. They bailed her 'pending investigation'. Gerrard was standing in the lobby, shifting from foot to foot. He thanked the solicitor but didn't speak to Sylvia until they got into the flat. She watched him walking around each room, pulling out bottles, full, half-full, and miniatures, making a show of pouring each one down the sink, and putting the empties in a bag by the front door. He came back, lifted the sofa cushion, took out a handful of scratch cards.

'Time to get back to normal.'

There was that word, again: normal. She tried to explain that she'd done nothing wrong, but he wouldn't listen. Sylvia understood why he was upset. He thought it was happening all over again. The last few years had been hard on them both; but they had settled down. It wasn't the same as having their own home, but it wasn't a bad area. If they had to live in council housing, there were far worse places to live.

Mrs Cresswell stopped speaking to her. Jill at the corner shop hadn't issued any further invitations to join the girls on a night out. Gerrard was hurt on her behalf, but truly, Sylvia didn't mind. It was exhausting, delving for small talk to keep things polite but impersonal. It was much easier not having to bother.

For the next two weeks, Gerrard watched her every move. He even changed his shift pattern, in order to accompany her to work. She felt hemmed in, hardly able to breathe for Gerrard. She tried to get out of visiting his father on Sunday, to get a bit of time to herself, but he insisted. He said his father wanted to see her, but Sylvia knew this wasn't true. His father had told her once that she was a 'drama queen' and ought to start getting over it, to think about Gerrard. They went around in the end, taking a ready-cooked chicken from the supermarket to avoid having to eat his father's speciality, corned beef hash. Pausing outside the door with the plates, she overheard Gerrard saying, '...It's put her back. Let's just say she's very *fragile*–' and his father interrupted loudly with, 'There you are, Sylvia, you are a love, doing all that for me. It looks delicious.'

Sylvia decided to play Gerrard at his own game. She smiled and waited until he stopped being suspicious of her every move. This had been the first day that she'd been able to persuade him to go to the football match with his mates, while she was at work.

It was definitely a no, then. She would not tell the police about finding Rosie's hairs in the hedge. She climbed out of the warm duvet. Her tights were so torn that she pulled them off and stuffed them into her pocket. She forced her feet back into the wet shoes. In the wardrobe, she found clothes that must have belonged to the Standish parents. In the other room, a narrow wardrobe contained children's clothes and toys, books and games. Picking through a few items, she could see they were for boys, two boys probably, of different ages, or one boy, growing up. It was like looking into Dylan's room, with his little jeans, a sweatshirt with mini Transformers marching across, and–

'What the fuck do you think you're doing?' A security officer filled the doorway with his hands on his hips, his arms bulging, whether with muscles or the padding of his jacket, she couldn't tell.

'This is my daughter's caravan.'

He thumbed over his shoulder. 'Didn't you see the signs, and the tape?'

'But they've finished, haven't they, the police? I can't do any harm.'

'We'll go and ask, shall we? The police are just over there, sitting in the office having their break.'

He stopped at the door, waited until she walked past him and stepped out, held up the tape while she ducked underneath, then shepherded her around the next caravan.

'I forgot my gloves, I won't be a minute.' She nipped back behind the caravan and, as soon as he was out of sight, ran across to the hedge and wriggled through the gap. Standing up, yanking her hair free, she hobbled to the left, into the scrub and thorns, crouching down. She inhaled deeply, exhaled slowly, with a hand on her chest, until her heartbeat had slowed down. Minutes passed. When she felt sure nobody had followed her, she limped back to the car park and took the narrow boardwalk through the dunes and onto the beach, dropping her ruined tights into the litter bin. The sea was a long, long way out. Taking off her shoes and carrying them, she made for a stretch of water between two sandbanks and cleaned herself up as best she could with tissues. A bark startled her. A man stood with a dog on the edge of the water, watching her. She smiled, waved, and made as though she was paddling, even though the water was freezing, and she had lost all feeling in her feet and legs. She paddled along, parallel to the beach, carrying her shoes for a long way before taking a narrow lane back to the road and finding a bus stop. While she was waiting, she drank the remaining contents of her thermos. Even so, by the time the bus pulled up beside her, her teeth were chattering and her hands shaking so much that as she opened her purse, the coins fell onto the road. A lad ran towards her and leaned down to pick them up.

'Take your fucking hands off that money or I'll chop them off.'

The boy stopped and stared at her. A woman beside him, who Sylvia hadn't noticed, said, 'Leave the ungrateful bitch alone, love, she's pissed.' While Sylvia stood with her mouth open, the woman pushed her out of the way, to allow the boy to get on the bus. She turned to Sylvia. 'He was only trying to help.'

As Sylvia put her foot on the step, the driver shook his head at her and the door closed, forcing her to remove her foot and watch as the bus drove away.

To try to get warm, she limped, the sand in her wet shoes scratching her cold, bare feet, the wind cutting into her legs, to the next bus stop, muttering to herself about reporting the driver. If Gerrard behaved like that to one of his passengers, he'd lose his job. She decided to ask the driver of the next bus for a complaints form, she knew they all carried them, but by the time one pulled up, she was so cold she could barely speak.

At Lincoln station, she had time to walk to the Tesco Express and buy a little bottle of brandy and an orange juice to thaw herself and try to shift the smell of something stale and rotten that had hung in her nostrils since leaving the caravan. On the train to Sheffield, finally warm, her eyes closed from weariness and also to avoid having to engage with the passengers who filled the seats.

The voice of an exasperated mother came to her from a long way away: 'Yes, you will put your jacket on. It's freezing outside.'

Her eyes snapped open and she watched a little boy doing that passive aggressive thing with his arms, flopping them around so his mother couldn't get them into the sleeves of his coat. That's when it came to her. Of course! He'd have dressed

Rosie in boy's clothes from that wardrobe. They were the right size, she would have looked okay. He could have cut her hair. Disguised her as a boy. Had the police thought of that? she wondered; had they asked questions about a man with a little boy? The kidnapper would have looked like a regular chap, probably, if he'd put on some of those nice clothes from the other bedroom. Had the police changed the description? A well-dressed young man, probably clean shaven, with a little boy? It was nearly six months ago, but somebody might remember something.

Gerrard came out of the living room and watched Sylvia taking off her shoes, hanging up her coat. She felt his eyes on her legs, pausing at the knee with the dried blood, taking in her shoes.

'I tripped over a loose paving stone in the street and landed in a muddy puddle.'

He raised his eyebrows.

'No, I haven't been drinking. I've been at work.' As she passed him to go into the kitchen, her bag knocked against the door jamb and the thermos clanked inside. 'I don't feel too good, after that fall, a bit nauseous.' That much was true. The smell of shit and blood and rotting flesh was stuck in her throat. 'I'll go and have a shower.' He was still watching her as she closed the bathroom door.

Sylvia's mind was spinning too much to allow her to sleep. At half past three, she got up to get started on her idea. From the Yellow Pages and the local free paper, she made a list of portrait artists and illustrators. At five o'clock the alarm went off in the bedroom. Gerrard was on early shift. He charged into the kitchen with a panicked look on his face, worried that she hadn't been in bed; when he found her, wearing her fleecy onesie, cooking him bacon and eggs, he couldn't stop smiling while he ate, and gave her a kiss and a cuddle as he left. Sylvia was irritated by how easily diverted he was.

At eight o'clock, Sylvia phoned in sick and watched the breakfast news, but there was no update. At nine o'clock, she started working through her list. The first two were professionals who quoted prices that made her dizzy. The third was a young woman, Lori, who sounded as though the phone had woken her, but soon perked up when Sylvia said what she wanted. Lori was a fine arts graduate who had advertised in the local paper. She could paint portraits and landscapes from photographs. She sounded excited. She would come round in her lunch hour.

On *BBC Radio Sheffield* at midday, there was an update at last. It repeated the information that the remains, as they called them, had been identified as Dean Burton, and that they had found what they called *paraphernalia* in the caravan confirming that drugs were involved. They also confirmed that the bullet used in his death matched the one lodged in the leg of the other victim, Jennifer Endleby. Because the remains had been there for some time through the winter, it was difficult for the pathologist to estimate time of death. The smell was back in her nostrils and Sylvia retched, but didn't want to miss anything so she thrust a screwed-up piece of kitchen towel into her mouth. The police inspector said they had revised the description of the child. They now knew from the family that jeans and a little blue Puffa jacket were missing from the caravan. There was nothing about short hair. Sylvia opened the back of the photo frame and tucked the strands of Rosie's hair behind Dylan's photo.

Lori was not at all like the art student that Sylvia had spent the morning imagining. Dressed in a pressed trouser suit, hair tied back neatly, she looked more like a plain clothes policewoman as she stood at the door, and it crossed Sylvia's mind that they knew what she was doing and had substituted Lori for an undercover officer. She left Lori in the sitting room and went to make tea. While she was waiting for the kettle to boil, she searched the kitchen and the hall for hidden cameras and checked the phone for bugs, like she'd seen them do on television. Finding nothing, she carried the tea tray into the front room, and even though she knew Lori was observing her with a puzzled frown, she looked at the back of the television, checked around the pictures, until, satisfied, she perched on the armchair and poured the tea.

Lori glanced at her watch. 'This project you spoke about on the telephone...'

'It's private work, if you understand me?' Lori looked blank. Sylvia went on, 'I mean I don't want anybody to know about it, not my husband, not your boyfriend, not even your closest friend.'

'I won't do anything illegal.'

'Oh, it's not illegal. No. On the contrary, it's' – Sylvia leaned towards Lori and dropped her voice – 'private investigation work.' Lori's eyebrows rose. 'To do with a missing person I'm trying to find.'

Lori nodded. 'Sounds interesting. Is it a relative?'

'No. You could say it's a close friend. A child, as it happens. The child of a close friend, yes, that's what it is.'

'Goodness. Aren't the police trying to find him? Or her?'

'The police investigation is not satisfactory. They've bungled it. I've decided to take matters into my own hands. And I need help.' Sylvia passed the plate of fig rolls and Lori shook her head. 'You said on the phone that you were an artist. Can you do portraits?'

'Oh, yes, I'd love to do a portrait of a real person. All I've been getting so far is people who want me to paint a portrait of their pet.'

'This could be an opportunity for you, then?'

Lori put her cup on the table. 'I'm working in a bank in the city centre at the moment. It's just temporary, while I'm looking for work in the arts field. I wanted to stay in Sheffield after my degree, I like it here. And it's easy to get to Manchester, and Leeds, if I find a job. Or, I might go into teaching. This job, it pays the rent, but it's boring.' She points to her trousers. 'And I have to wear this uniform. I wouldn't usually dress like this.'

'I think you look very smart actually. Are you interested in this little bit of work then? How much would you charge?'

Lori shrugged and laughed. 'I don't know, I've not done anything like this before. What would you say to... five pounds an hour?'

It had been a while since Sylvia had any friends and even though she had chosen to keep herself to herself and not try to make new friends, since her old friends had turned away from her, she was enjoying the company of another woman. Especially one who didn't know anything about her and who didn't judge.

Lori scanned Sylvia's file of press cuttings and photos of Rosie. 'Is this the child – isn't it the little girl who–?'

'Yes, which is one reason you need to be completely discreet.'

Lori studied the other photograph, the one Sylvia had taken of Jake, in the park. It was fuzzy because it was taken at a distance, through the play area railings, but it was possible to see the likeness.

'If you cut her hair short and dressed her in boy's clothing, she'd look very similar, don't you think?' Lori nodded. 'Do you think you can draw that?'

Lori nodded again.

Sylvia tossed about, veering between feeling afraid that she had made a wrong decision letting Lori take the photos – she might never see her again, or Lori might go to the police; cursing herself for only having Lori's mobile phone number; and at the same time feeling excited about meeting Lori again, the following lunchtime. Exhausted, she got up with Gerrard at five; they had breakfast together. Sylvia tried to respond to his cheeriness, though she could barely eat for the churning in her stomach. She left the flat two hours early, giving herself time to navigate Broomhill, avoiding the supermarket, as she'd reported sick again this morning, and dodging buses, as she was now on Gerrard's route. She reached the botanical gardens and thought Lori wasn't yet there until she saw a young woman waving to her from one of the benches at the far end. Wearing a crop top and jeans that sat a bit too low on her hips, her hair loose, she was much more the art student. Sylvia sat, and Lori handed her a plastic folder. Sylvia lifted the cover and saw a sketch of Jake. Then realised it wasn't Jake. It was a healthy, happy little boy, but it was Rosie – Rosie, as she was in the shop that night, but with short hair. The next drawing made her breath catch in her throat, as she reared back and smelled, again, the stench of death from the caravan. In the light and dark of her charcoal strokes, Lori had captured the terror in the little face peeking out between the collar of the blue Puffa jacket and a rough crew cut.

5

J ennifer was sitting on a seat beneath the '*Prescriptions*' sign
in Boots. Sylvia saw her in the doctor's waiting room and
followed her here. By walking up the steps towards the
photography department, she could watch Jennifer, and whilst
appearing to examine the digital photo frames, she watched the
pharmacist working behind his counter. She recognised the
small blue capsules he was funnelling into a pill bottle.

If she hadn't seen Jennifer's photo in the newspaper a few
weeks ago, Sylvia might not have recognised Rosie's mother. Her
fingers, thin with overlong, dirty nails, twitched and kept pulling
at her hair which was lank and long, streaked with grey, hanging
over her face. She reminded Sylvia of the kind of stick figure
Dylan had started to draw with a thick wax crayon held in his
fist: a streak of blue under her eyes, splotches of red on her
cheeks, a thin, pink slash where her lips should have been. The
newspaper headline had said: **Will Rosie be home for his birthday?** Jake was seven. Sylvia had cut out the photo of him,
standing at the window, as if he was looking for Rosie, and
tucked it into another corner of the photo frame that Rosie
shared with Dylan.

Lori's little blue Renault pulled up at the agreed time, behind the cathedral. Sylvia appeared from behind the wall and slid into the passenger seat. Lori looked closely at her.

'Are you all right? You look terrible.'

Sylvia didn't say the screeching of Lori's brakes had struck terror into her and she had leapt behind the wall before realising it was her car. It was getting better, but she preferred not to be out in the open if she could help it; no matter how careful she was to watch for danger points, she still got caught out. A car revving or accelerating; a balloon bursting, and the next thing Sylvia knew, she was curled up on the ground... A couple of weeks ago she'd been on the till when she heard a scream... she'd looked up to see a line of customers staring at her and realised where the noise was coming from. A customer, bright red with embarrassment, was trying to pick up the pieces of a bottle she had dropped and smashed, and Dorothy who worked at the next till had come round to help, while Sylvia sat, frozen.

Sylvia's fingers gripped the seat either side of her knees. It felt as though Lori was driving too fast, but when a police car overtook them on the Parkway, she realised it must just be her. It was a long time since she'd been in a car. Three years ago, probably, before they had to sell it. Gerrard had liked to drive them out, into the Peak District on his days off. They took Dylan to the caverns once. He liked the Devil's Arse. He laughed and laughed when he found that he could say the word without being told off. He loved the stories too, about the people who had lived and made rope in the cave: but especially, he asked Gerrard to tell him again and again about the children in Victorian times, who hid in the dark corners of the cavern, making noises to terrify the tourists. That was just before...

'I said, are you okay? Shall we get a coffee?'

Sylvia opened her eyes and saw Lori, too close, staring at her, holding out a pack of tissues. When Sylvia touched a cheek, she felt sticky tracks of tears through her face powder. They were parked in a lay-by. Lori got out and walked across to a dark-green container which had been turned into a café, with a hand-made sandwich board advertising *Tea's and Bacon Bap's*. Two rough-looking characters sat at a table, pushing food into their mouths and slurping from mugs. She scrunched up a few tissues and wiped her cheeks, pulled out her mirror and patted fresh powder onto her face, by which time Lori was calling to her, standing beside a small table outside the café, holding two poly-styrene cups.

Sylvia leaned across and opened the driver's door and waved Lori back to the car. She had no desire to get any closer to the oil-stained men, one of whom was eyeing Lori up and down in a way that made Sylvia feel protective of the girl. Lori plonked her bottom onto the driver's seat and swung her legs into the footwell, passing one of the cups to Sylvia. It was lukewarm, but a nice thought, and Sylvia sipped carefully, trying not to let any of the granules of coffee floating on the surface pass her lips.

Lori twisted herself round and tilted her upper body towards Sylvia. 'You're not all right, are you? It's none of my business, but this little girl – Rosie – I've been looking into it.' Sylvia leaned back into her seat. 'You can't blame me, and it is all over the newspapers, I just didn't put two and two together until the other day. Weren't you the cashier on duty that night, when it happened?'

Sylvia busied herself trying one-handed to pull out a fresh tissue and blow her nose, while not spilling her coffee.

'I thought so. Is that why you want to find her? Because you feel guilty?'

Sylvia sniffed. 'I thought you graduated in fine arts, not in psychology.'

Lori laughed. 'It's funny you should say that. When I was at uni I shared a flat with a guy who was doing psychology. We used to argue all the time. I must have picked up some of his ideas.'

They sat quietly, concentrating on their coffee. The oily men walked past. One paused at the bonnet to stare at Lori while he picked his teeth with a fingernail. His mate called over his shoulder and sniggered as he walked towards a pickup, the back piled high with old washing machines and fridges.

Sylvia blew her nose again. 'You're right, I do feel guilty. I was there, and I didn't do anything. I froze, while they walked off with that little girl.' She held up her hand to stop Lori speaking. 'Before you say anything, of course I should have done something. And now I can. That's why I want to sort it out, to help the family.' She opened her door and poured the rest of the coffee onto the tarmac. 'Shall we go?'

Lori drained her coffee cup, held out her hand for Sylvia's cup, pressed it inside her own, and tossed them both into the footwell behind her seat, where they joined an array of crisp packets, sweet wrappers and empty water bottles.

Lori laughed. 'You've got the same look on your face that my dad gets when he looks in my car.' She started the engine and pulled into the road.

Lincoln was much closer than Sylvia remembered from her train journey, and she felt unprepared when Lori slowed down on a road, looking at numbers, then pulled into a driveway. It was a neat red-brick bungalow surrounded by privet hedges. Sylvia got out of the car and as she approached the door, she felt the skin on her upper arms tightening as if in some kind of premonition.

~

It had taken three months. They had sat side by side in Sylvia's living room, a large road map open on the coffee table, marking the possible routes the kidnapper might have taken to get to a town. Twice, Sylvia had been back to the caravan site, catching buses, speaking to the drivers about travelling times and routes. Lori had placed the picture, and her own mobile phone number, in local newspapers all along those routes.

Sylvia sat beside Lori, watching as she navigated the internet, placing the ads and studying street maps. 'I'd do it myself, but I haven't got a computer, or even a mobile phone.'

Lori's eyes widened. 'How do you manage?'

Sylvia swatted the question away. 'We're not computer people.' She didn't say that the computer and the mobile phones had been the first things to go. 'Oh, I know how to use them, or at least I did, it's been a few years since... But if you could help – you said five pounds an hour?'

Sylvia followed Lori's eyes as they swept the room, taking in the tired furniture, and came back to Sylvia with something like sympathy. 'You don't need to pay me. It sounds really interesting.'

She had flushed with embarrassment. Whenever she raised the question of getting new furniture, Gerrard would nod towards the drawer and say, 'As soon as we have a bit of space in there, when we've paid things off and all the court papers are finished with and we can see a bit of clear blue sky, then we can talk about new furniture.' She'd look for anger, criticism, judgement, but his face was almost expressionless, which was worse somehow.

Lori had placed the ads, and they'd done it again, a few weeks later. They'd had no response. Then, in early August, Lori rang.

'Hello, Lori love, you're sounding chirpy.' Gerrard was smiling as he handed the phone to Sylvia. He hadn't met Lori, but he was pleased that Sylvia had a friend – someone from work, she explained – and was getting out and about.

Lori's voice bubbled with excitement. 'A man called. His mother lives in Lincoln. She sold her car to a young man who had a little boy with him. She recognised the wonky haircut and the Puffa jacket.'

The woman who answered the door was probably in her eighties. She'd seen the photo in her local paper, when she was wrapping bric-a-brac to take to the Oxfam shop. 'I don't read the whole newspaper, it's so full of other people's nonsense. I scan the headlines, the obituaries and the council meetings, then put it in the recycling, so I would have missed it altogether, if it hadn't been for this clear-out. My son is always telling me I should have less stuff. And he's right, of course–'

'And it was definitely them?' Sylvia held up the picture.

'I'd say so. I remember those big eyes, and the haircut! It looked as though the little lad had taken the scissors and cut it himself, you know, like children do.' Laughing, she grabbed a couple of handfuls of her bristly white hair and held them out, to demonstrate. No, she didn't remember how he was dressed, didn't have a name. 'My son told me off, afterwards, said I should have written his name down. Apparently, there's some kind of form I should have filled in and sent off to Swansea, but it was my late husband's car, he dealt with all the paperwork. The young man was in a hurry. He paid cash. He didn't want a receipt.'

They sat in the kitchen drinking tea and eating biscuits while the lady chatted on, but it was all about her son, and there wasn't anything more she could tell them that was useful. Sylvia wondered if she might still have the cash, hidden away somewhere, and if it could be proved that it came from the robbery... but that would be police business. Walking through the house, Sylvia couldn't see a television. It was hard to imagine anyone could have avoided hearing about Rosie, but the woman gave no clue that she knew anything about it. As they waited to pull out of the driveway, onto the main road, a number six bus drove past. Sylvia recognised it as the Skegness bus and smiled to herself. She was beginning to put together a sequence of events that felt more than just imagination. He could have been in a car, but if so, why would he have bought this car? He might have taken a taxi, he had enough money from the robbery, but that would have increased the chances of being recognised. Similarly, a train was very public. There had only been two people on the bus that just passed. Yes, the more she thought about it, the more logical it seemed: he would have been on the bus from Skegness, with Rosie disguised as a boy, when he saw the car for sale outside the house.

Lori said, loudly, making Sylvia think she had said it before, and she hadn't heard, 'Sylvia? What do you think?'

'What?'

'The police. Should we go straight there? Is it Sheffield police?'

'No, of course not.'

'They'll be pleased that you've got new evidence. We have the make and model, the registration number, it could help them. They have cameras, you know, along some of the main roads, they might be able to track where the car went.'

The memory of her last encounter with the police – the arrest, the questions, the humiliation – sent a tremor through Sylvia's body. She couldn't go through that again. 'It's nearly a year ago. Even if they had been on camera, they wouldn't still have it.'

'But, it's important information. The picture, the car–'

Lori's face mirrored the excitement that Sylvia had felt, all those months ago when she thought she could help the police. Lori was an innocent. She considered telling Lori about it, but with her nice, suburban upbringing, Lori probably wouldn't believe her. But now, Sylvia had a quandary. If she refused to go to the police, she needed to make sure Lori wouldn't take it on herself to report it.

'Very well then, but mind you stay with me, won't you?'

At the police station, like the previous time, hardly a minute passed before a police officer appeared at a side door and invited them through, into an interview room. He was young and held his head on one side as Sylvia started to explain about the car. Her hand was in her bag, pulling out the drawings, when the door was flung open and the sergeant she met last year strode in and stood at the other side of the table, his arms folded.

'What is it this time, Sylvia? Wasting more of our time with your cock and bull stories?'

The young officer said, 'Mrs Wilton has information, sir, about a car she thinks one of the robbers escaped in.'

The sergeant put his hands on the table and leaned on them, pushing his face towards Sylvia, making her step back. 'Cops and robbers, is it now?'

Lori put a hand on Sylvia's arm. 'Excuse me, but you're very rude. Mrs Wilton has come here to tell you about—'

'Who are you?'

'I'm a friend.'

Sylvia felt her skin warm beneath Lori's hand. It was a long time since anyone had considered her a friend.

The sergeant addressed Lori. 'You'll know then, that Sylvia is a fantasist? She's well known here for wasting our time.'

Sylvia half heard Lori saying, 'I can't believe you could be so nasty to someone who is trying—' as she barged past the young police officer and trotted along the narrow corridor, casting her eyes left and right until she saw the inquiry desk through a window. She put her shoulder against the door, shoving, trying not to cry. The young officer leaned around her and pressed the button on the wall and Sylvia almost fell into the foyer, where a row of eyes turned to her. She ran out of the open door and stopped, leaning against the railing on the steps outside, breathing deeply. A hand she instinctively knew was Lori's touched her arm.

'I can't believe he was so rude. Now I can see why you were reluctant to involve them.'

Lori's kindness brought the tears to her eyes and she shielded them from Lori and avoided her gaze as they walked away.

By the time they reached the car park in front of Sylvia's block, she'd had enough of Lori's non-stop chatter, with her analysis of the way the police had behaved, and continual protestations that Sylvia was quite right to not trust them. Sylvia needed time to think about her next steps before Gerrard got home. As soon as Lori pulled up, she said goodbye and got out of the car, slamming the door behind her to let Lori know she wasn't invited in. Looking down from the walkway, she saw Lori still sitting, looking up at her through the windscreen. It occurred to her that the girl might be expecting something from her; she had, after all, stood up for Sylvia, and she might need her help again. She forced a smile, a little wave, and watched Lori smile in return and blow her a little kiss, before she started the engine.

Taking the bottle from the laundry basket, she perched on the side of the bath with her drink, replaying the day's events. Something nagged at her memory, just out of reach. Something Lori had said, an idea or a comment in her constant chatter, and it had slipped away before she could think it through. Sylvia replayed their conversations: their coffee break, with the oily men in the lay-by? Something the lady in Lincoln had said? Lori's comments as they left the police station?

Leaving her glass on the windowsill, she went into Dylan's room where she took the box of press cuttings from the wardrobe shelf and started to read through them. The most recent, the one about the dead youth, Dean Burton. What was it about him? Lori said he'd been in Doncaster Prison a short while before the robbery. How did she know that?

That was it. Lori's friend from university, the one who'd studied psychology. Lori had been chattering about him on the drive home. Simon, was it? He wanted to go back to university to do another degree for some reason or another that Sylvia didn't understand, did she say he wanted to be a prison psychologist? Anyway, he needed to save up money, so he'd got a temporary admin job in the prison. He'd told Lori that the police had been in touch about this Dean Burton.

Sylvia was standing in the hallway, dialling Lori's number when the door opened, and Gerrard came in.

'Good day? Where did you get to?' He had remembered she was going out for a drive with Lori. She smiled at him and pointed to the phone as Lori picked up. Gerrard patted her shoulder and carried on into the bathroom. As he closed the door, Sylvia remembered the bottle and glass on the bathroom windowsill.

6

———————

Sylvia devised a route to work that took her past Jake's school and avoided the busy main road. On the late shift, she could pass again during lunchtime play. Usually, she would see Jake standing as near as he could to the door that led into his classroom, watching the other kiddies while they played around him. Once, Sylvia watched as his teacher took him by the hand and brought him into a circle of boys who were kicking a ball about. One of them dribbled the ball to Jake. The ball hit his legs and rolled away. The other boy shrugged, picked up the ball, and ran off to another part of the playground.

When she worked the early shift, Sylvia would walk past the school around home time. Today, she stood on the opposite pavement, waiting for school to finish. If Rick came to pick up Jake, she planned to approach him, tell him what she knew. If it was Miriam, it would depend on what mood Miriam was in; she could be quite sharp at times, when Sylvia was trying to be friendly.

The playground was emptying as the children were quickly absorbed into the group of parents at the gate. Jake came out of the door, walked into the middle of the playground and stopped, looking at his feet. Sylvia watched through the railings for a couple of minutes, then, with no sign of Rick or Miriam, walked through the gates and across the empty playground, and squatted in front of him.

'Hello, Jake.' He looked up at her. 'Do you remember me?'

'Can I help you?' The voice belonged to the young woman, presumably a teacher, who had encouraged Jake to play football.

Sylvia stood. 'I was just passing, Miss, and I see his mummy and daddy haven't collected him yet.'

'And you are?'

'A family friend. I can take him home.'

The teacher picked up Jake's hand. 'We only allow children to leave with named adults. He will stay with me, meantime, won't you, Jake?'

There was a shout from the road, and Miriam jogged through the gate. 'Here I am. I'm so sorry. A misunderstanding. I thought Rick was picking him up.'

'Not a problem. It's helpful if we know who is picking him up, but we know how it is. How is Mummy?'

Taking Jake's hand, Miriam shrugged, and she and the teacher nodded at one another. Sylvia thought, poor Jake, his dad forgetting him and his mother obviously not in a fit state. She turned to go, and the movement caught Miriam's attention.

'Oh, hello, it's–'

'Sylvia.'

The teacher frowned. 'This lady said she was a family friend? She said she could take Jake home. Do you know her?'

'Not really. We've met a couple of times. I think she works at the supermarket in Broomhill.'

The teacher lifted a mobile phone from her pocket.

Sylvia stepped forward and prodded the air in front of the young woman's chest. 'I was trying to help. I saw the little boy on his own, in the playground, no one had collected him. You were nowhere in sight. Anything could have happened.' The teacher had gone pale. 'I was standing beside him, to make sure he was safe, until somebody turned up.' She strode across the playground and out of the gate, without looking back.

After that little contretemps, Sylvia tried to stay away from Jake's school, but as the weeks went by, the thought of the little lad, standing alone and lost in the playground, preyed on her mind. She took to wearing sunglasses and a low-brimmed sun hat, which wasn't odd since the month had started with a heatwave, and she could pass by the school, on the opposite pavement, at the right time.

Then it was the school holidays and Miriam had a different schedule, shopping quite late in the evening, on her own. Sylvia thought Miriam must have a husband who was looking after the children. She missed seeing Jake and decided to alter her own routine, walking up to Lacey Gardens in the morning, usually passing as Rick was setting off to work with Jake in the car, presumably taking him to Miriam's. Rick started acknowledging her; not much, just a hand raised off the steering wheel as he drove past. There was no sign of life in the house after they left; the bedroom curtains remained drawn. It seemed Jake's mother was still incapable of looking after him. What if Rosie was found? Who would be able to care for her, after who knows what she'd been through? Not her mother, and Rick was busy at work, while Miriam had enough on her plate with her own family. It made Sylvia think.

The worst thing about losing her job at the supermarket wasn't losing Gerrard. When Sylvia thought about it, both things came as something of a relief. Living with Gerrard had become a double life. Sylvia felt controlled, watched. Since the incident with the bottle in the bathroom a couple of weeks ago, he had started searching again when he came in at night, opening and closing drawers in every room. He hadn't yet found the little space inside the reclining mechanism of the armchair, but it was surely only a matter of time. Finding a moment to have a drink in peace had become more difficult. Drinking wasn't a problem for Sylvia, but by making such a big deal of it, Gerrard had made it a problem. He wasn't supportive, he didn't understand how a small brandy in the evening loosened everything up, relaxed her. After a couple of drinks, she stopped jumping at every sudden noise: a shout in the courtyard below, or a door slamming in the flat next door, and, if she had another before she went to bed, she was more likely to be able to sleep.

When she told Gerrard she'd lost her job, he shook his head and said, 'That's it.' He picked up the bank statement which she hadn't noticed sitting on the coffee table. He'd drawn a circle with his biro around some of the items, and now he tapped the tip of a finger on them, one by one, drawing her attention to a payment to the *Skegness Standard*, another to the *Lincolnshire Echo*; £25 to BP which she remembered was an extortionate price she'd paid to fill up Lori's car at the services on the M180.

'I thought maybe somebody had stolen your card, but when you came home with the shopping as normal, I could see that hadn't happened. And all these items from around Lincolnshire isn't a coincidence, is it? What's going on, Sylvia?' He picked up a letter and waved it in her face. 'You haven't made the County Court payment this month, have you? I don't need to remind you surely, not after all that we went through, what will happen if the bailiffs come round again. I won't ask my father for another loan. In fact, if they did come and take the furniture, the television, and the microwave, it might do you some good, it might make you realise how easily we could lose everything. As if we haven't lost enough already.'

He dropped the letter onto the table and left the room. She listened to him moving around the flat, opening and closing doors. He came back accompanied by a clinking sound, and stood in the doorway, four of his fingers stuck in the tops of empty bottles that Sylvia had been keeping behind the curtain in Dylan's room until she got the chance to take them to the bottle bank. He placed them carefully on the coffee table next to the bank statement, which he tapped again, as he dropped heavily into the armchair. She felt a sense of injustice. She'd left those letters in the kitchen drawer until she got paid, when she planned to pay the arrears, before Gerrard knew.

He rubbed his face with both hands. 'It's not that I don't care, Syl. I know it's been a tough few years for you, and this business with the missing kiddie, coming on top of it all, no wonder it's knocked you back. I've tried to be understanding. I'd do anything for you, Sylvia, you know that. Well, I think I have. I – well, not to put too fine a point on it, I'm worn out. I just can't do it anymore. I'm calling time. I'm going to move in with my father for a bit.' He rubbed his face again and she thought he might be crying. She knew she should say something, but the main feeling was relief, so, she said nothing. He looked as if he expected her to say something, but she couldn't imagine what, and eventually he stood and went into the bedroom.

One of his mates, she didn't know his name, arrived to give Gerrard a lift with his bags. Sylvia stood on the landing, watching them cross the courtyard below her, the mate saying, 'I don't blame you, pal, nobody does, we're all behind you. You've got the patience of Job.'

Gerrard had left the empty bottles in a box beside the door.

Sylvia picked one up and leaned over the railing, letting it dangle above their heads as they stood beside his mate's car. Gerrard looked up and shook his head and just like that, the urge left her. Then he was gone.

Sylvia sat in the armchair, pressed the recliner button and pushed her hand down between the arm and the cushion to retrieve a miniature. Opening it, she flicked on the television and lay back, sipping from the bottle, enjoying not having to listen to Gerrard's chattering, his endless anecdotes about passengers or workmates. He seemed to think he was doing her a favour by chatting about this petty stuff, and he would look at her out of the corner of his eye while he talked, as if he knew she wasn't really listening. Now, Sylvia could enjoy having time to herself, being able to choose her programmes on television, instead of having to sit through end-to-end documentaries and sports. She flicked through the channels, finding a *Judge Judy* she didn't think she'd seen, sipped and smiled at the thought of not having to watch the clock, not listening for his key in the door; not preparing his meals. She could eat what she liked, when she liked, or not at all if she didn't feel like it. Such as now, when she could enjoy a little brandy in peace, and look forward to a good night's sleep. She wouldn't have to wait for him to go to bed in order to have her nightcap and relax.

All in all then, Gerrard moving out was a good thing. It was losing her job that would affect her most. She couldn't go into Broomhill, wouldn't be able to watch for Miriam and Jake. With the new term starting, they would be back to the routine of after-school shopping. She couldn't risk meeting one of her workmates from the supermarket, and worse still, she might run into that customer. Every time she remembered it, she wanted to curl up and hide away. She had explained to the manager: the little girl was screaming, clearly terrified, the man was dragging her along behind the tills, heading for the door – of course she thought he was kidnapping the child. She'd leapt from her seat, elbowed her way past the customers packing their groceries, got to him just as he reached the door and pushed him into the newspaper stand. He called Sylvia a *fucking nutcase.* Said the child was having a tantrum. The manager gave the customer a voucher, free food for a week, and he agreed not to involve the police. Well, he would, wouldn't he?

'It's not for your benefit, Sylvia,' the manager said, as she stood in front of his desk. 'It would be bad press for the supermarket, if people got to thinking we had nutters working here, attacking the customers.'

As soon as she heard the word 'nutters', she was heading for the door. She hadn't waited to be sacked. Which meant she couldn't claim benefits, and even though Gerrard had said he would pay the rent for a couple of months, she did need to get another job. Dave would be sure to give her a good reference; she could even go back to work for Dave if she got desperate. There was no need to mention the supermarket job on application forms; it had only been a few months; she could say she'd been ill following the robbery. Who would know?

As that first night drew on, Sylvia realised there was another benefit to her freedom. Between work and Gerrard, especially once he started monitoring her every move, she'd not had time to chase up Lori. What was the girl doing? It was days since she'd persuaded her to contact the ex-flatmate. She picked up the phone. The first call went to voicemail and Sylvia rang off and dialled again.

Lori answered, sounding groggy. 'Sylvia, what is it?'

'I wondered how you'd got on, talking to – is it Simon?'

'Sylvia, it's two o'clock in the morning. I'll call you back tomorrow.' Lori cut the call.

Sylvia was in the shower on Sunday evening when she heard the front door closing and was about to scream when Gerrard called out, 'Only me.' The bathroom door opened slightly and even though she was invisible behind the shower curtain, Sylvia put her arms around her body and stood stock still. How dare he walk in as though he still lived here? The bathroom door closed, and she heard him whistling his way to the kitchen. She put on her fluffy dressing gown and found him opening and closing cupboards, peering inside. She leaned against the door jamb and watched for a few seconds before clearing her throat.

'I was looking for the tea bags?'

She pointed to the canister beside the kettle, where the tea had always been, and said nothing while he brewed and handed her a cup.

'Sajid said he saw you on Ecclesall Road yesterday.'

He was still having her watched then. She'd been on her way to meet Lori in Nonna's and came out of a side road onto Ecclesall Road. She pressed the crossing button, and as the green man illuminated, the bus drew up. She turned her face away as she crossed in front of it, but Sajid must have recognised her. Anyway, why should she have to hide? Gerrard had left. What right did he have?

She took a deep breath. 'I want you to give me your key,' and left the room so she didn't see the hurt on his face.

Lori had been full of news. Bless the girl, it turned out she'd been working on Simon for weeks, but it had been worthwhile. Lori ordered a glass of Chardonnay. Sylvia asked for a coffee.

'Simon looked him up. The dead one, Dean Burton, like you said. He had previous for a gun and he'd done time in youth custody for robbery.' A blast from a car horn made them both look out of the window to a man staggering in the road, waving a brown paper bag at the drivers who had come to a standstill.

'You were saying?' Sylvia tapped the side of her coffee cup.

'He says the police wanted the names of all those who'd been released just before that date, and all the ones who'd shared a cell with the dead guy.' She stopped again, watching the activity in the street where one of the drivers had left his car and was trying to persuade the drunk to step onto the pavement.

Sylvia fought back the impulse to shout at her to get on with it. She took several deep breaths, trying to keep a smile on her face. Eventually, she prompted, 'They were asking about cellmates?'

'Mm, yes. There were three of them. One was still inside when it happened. Then there was one called Jase Botham, who came out before this Burton lad, and they followed him up but seemingly he had an alibi. And the third one, a lad called Conor Walsh. He went home to Ireland on the day he came out.'

Sylvia pressed her hand against her chest, in case Lori heard her heart thumping. 'This Conor. What was he in for?'

'Burglary. Simon thinks there was a co-defendant, but he doesn't know who, he doesn't think he was in Doncaster Prison.'

'And he thinks this Conor Walsh went home to Ireland?'

'He definitely did.'

'The same day he got out?'

She nodded. 'I asked him that. There was a report from the Irish police, the Gardaí they call them over there, to say he was living at home with his mother. That he'd gone home the same day.' Lori leaned forward, swishing her wine in the glass. 'But, this bit's interesting–'

'What?'

'Simon phoned me later. He looked on the computer, he shouldn't but then he shouldn't have told me any of that, but in for a penny, in for a pound, as my gran used to say... Anyway, he said this lad hadn't cashed in his travel warrant.' Seeing Sylvia frown, she went on. 'They get a travel warrant to take them home. A lot of them don't bother, especially those who want to get drugs straight away. Simon says the dealers wait for them in the car park and that's most of them back where they started.'

'Was he a druggie then, this Irish lad?'

'Apparently, there's a record of him getting what they call a referral, to go to a drug treatment place. That means they've been taking drugs, and they get an appointment to see a drug worker when they come out.'

'Why did they give him an appointment if he was going home to Ireland the same day?'

Lori shrugged. 'Different departments, I suppose.'

'Tell me about that travel warrant.'

'Simon says...' Lori giggled. 'It's like that game, Simon says...' Sylvia stared at her and Lori's face became serious. 'Okay, sorry, anyway, he explained that cancelled warrants come back to the prison, with an invoice, because they pay for the travel. This one didn't come back. Which means he didn't use it.' She lifted up her empty glass by the stem and waggled it at the waiter, who took it from her.

'So?'

'So, he must have gone to Ireland another way...'

'Or perhaps he didn't go to Ireland at all. He might still be in this country.'

The waiter put the glass in front of Lori and bowed slightly towards Sylvia, pointing to her empty cup. She shook her head. A crash beside her made her scream. Lori giggled and pointed to the window, where the drunk's face was squashed against the glass, his hands splayed. Sylvia felt his eyes boring into her. The waiter waved his arms at the man, while shouting in rapid Italian over his shoulder. Another waiter ran out of the door and Sylvia watched him gesticulate and shout at the drunkard until he staggered away along the pavement, still waving his paper bag. He stopped, turned and looked directly at Sylvia again and she felt the hairs on her arms stand up.

The waiter said to Sylvia, 'You all right, madam?'

'I'll have a brandy and orange.'

He inclined his head and returned to the bar.

'Does he know you?' Lori pointed to the retreating back of the man.

'Of course not.' And she was sure he didn't know her, but she felt as though he'd looked for her, was trying to tell her something, and she felt cold. 'You were saying. These Gardaí. They definitely saw this Conor, in Ireland?'

A splash of wine spilt onto Lori's leg as she waved her arm in the air. She rubbed at the pink spot on her jeans and spread it further. 'Yes, they found him there. But think about this. What if he was the one, and he was at the caravan, and he killed the other guy... Do you see?'

Sylvia saw it perfectly. 'You're thinking it could be him, that he bought the car in Lincoln, and went to Ireland in it? But you said he went back to Ireland the day he left prison?'

'Yes, that's what he told the Gardaí when they followed it up. But they didn't see him that day, did they? He only told them he'd gone straight home. He might be lying.'

The waiter placed a glass in front of Sylvia and she downed half of it in one long gulp. 'Did Simon say where in Ireland this Walsh lad lived? Would he have next of kin on his record by any chance?'

'I couldn't ask him any more questions without making him suspicious. It took three dates to get that much out of him. I had to pretend to be interested in his job and now, he thinks I'm interested in him. He phones me every day, asking me on another date. I'm running out of excuses.' She giggled.

'If you did go out with him again, you could maybe get the next of kin address?'

Lori waved her hand at Sylvia and more wine splashed onto her leg. 'Oops. I don't think so. He really will wonder why I want the information if I ask him something that specific – I've managed to keep all my questions really general so far – and he'll clam up if he thinks I'm using him. And, well, to be honest, he's sooooo boring. And it wouldn't just be a night out. There'd be coming back for coffee, then assuming he'd stay overnight.' She emptied the rest of her wine into her mouth.

Sylvia shrugged. It seemed a small price to pay.

Lori swallowed and leaned towards Sylvia. 'No, listen. I looked the name up on the internet.'

'And?'

'It's a very common name.' She pulled a handful of papers from her backpack and handed them to Sylvia. 'These are just the ones that are on the Register of Electors. That's the same as our electoral roll, in Ireland.'

Sylvia flicked through three pages of names and addresses. She waved her empty glass at a passing waiter. 'Let's celebrate. Except – oh, I didn't bring enough cash out.'

'Don't worry, I'll get it.' Lori held out her empty glass and the waiter took both. 'What's the next step?'

'We'll track down every one of them, until we find him.'

An Irish boy. A green-eyed boy. Green, with yellow flecks that flashed with fear when his friend pulled out the gun. That was what she'd been missing.

7

'Green-Eyed Boy'. Dylan's song. She played it over and over, singing along with Dolly Parton while she cleaned and baked, one eye always on Dylan as he bounced from the swing in the kitchen doorway. It was a game, popping in and out of his line of sight, saying 'Ta-daaah!' making him squeal with laughter. Her very own green-eyed boy. His first word was 'boy': 'boy-boy' was a dog or a cat in the street, and 'boy-boy' was the ducks in the pond. Even Gerrard, before he got 'da-da', would be 'boy-boy', making him hoot with laughter as he lifted Dylan out of his swing and threw him into the air. Her boys, safe at home. Sylvia, keeping them safe. Giving them joy was all that Sylvia desired.

Her first date with Gerrard had been to the cinema, to see *Straight Talk*. It was 1996 and she'd missed the film the first time around because she had no one to go with. Gerrard was sitting at the corner table in the canteen with some other drivers, tucking into something with a mountain of chips smothered in gravy. Sylvia picked at a salad while the girls from the office talked about music. One of them turned to her.

'What's your favourite band, Sylvia? Take That, Boyzone?'

She hadn't heard of either. With her latest pay packet, she'd bought the new Kenny Rogers CD. In her bedroom, dancing in front of the mirror, she imagined herself in a bar in Nashville: she could work as a waitress, call herself Ruby, or Lucille. She hated being called Sylvia. The way her mother said it, putting a sarcastic emphasis on the first syllable: *Syl*via. She grew up to hate the name. One day, her mother let slip that her father had a fancy for a woman called Sylvia. When he'd said, 'Let's call her Sylvia,' her mother had thought it a nice name, until the day they met her in the street, the real Sylvia, who greeted her father warmly. 'She works behind the bar at The Bull,' he said by way of introduction. Her mother suggested that wasn't the only way he'd known Sylvia. From then on, she hated her daughter's name and Sylvia thought her mother had hated her, too.

Her colleagues' laughter had brought her back to the canteen. 'Country and western? Really? My mum goes for that stuff.'

Sylvia had caught Gerrard's eye and he winked. He wasn't joining in the conversation with the other drivers at his table, and certainly not reading the newspaper in front of him. It was upside down, for a start.

Back in the office, the conversation turned to Gerrard. He'd recently arrived with a new intake of trainee drivers. There was speculation about his life, and his past. Sally, in payroll, knew: 'He used to work in the bus depot at Rotherham, he was a mechanic, transferred in as a driver.' 'He's a bit of a looker.' 'Did you see him watching us?' 'Do you think he looks a bit like – what's his name? That new guy in *EastEnders*?' 'Has he said anything about a girlfriend?' She wondered which of her work-mates he was interested in.

A couple of weeks later, Sylvia was clipping along the narrow corridor between the offices and the bus garage, one hand over her mouth to keep out the taste of diesel fumes. She didn't hear him above the noise of reversing buses. When they collided, the pile of clocking-in cards in her other hand concertinaed into the air and scattered across the floor.

He knelt beside her, helping to pick up the cards. '*Straight Talk* at the cinema, Saturday,' he said. Later, she wondered whether he'd been standing in her way deliberately. She looked at him. He handed her the cards. 'D'you want to come?'

'Okay,' was all she could think to say as she squeezed past him, head down to hide her flushed face.

He tapped her on the shoulder. 'You'd better tell me where you live then.'

He was never far from her mind over the next two days, as she sat at her dressing table, fiddling constantly with her untameable hair – *all frizz and flat chest*, her mother always said – wondering what he saw in her. She'd had boyfriends. Several. But as soon as they met her mother, they seemed to melt away. On Saturday, she was seated on the edge of her bed, wearing a new blouse she'd bought that day, watching the clock on her bedside table ticking slowly towards seven, and had decided he wasn't coming when she heard the doorbell. She rushed across the landing to pee, checked her hair in the mirror and dampened the curls at the front, trying to lay them across her forehead. Coming out of the bathroom, she looked down the stairs to the front door where he was standing, in the rain. Her mother had one hand on the door as if he was a travelling salesman and she was about to shut it. He saw Sylvia and waved. Her mother turned, and both of them watched her coming downstairs, her mother's eyes taking in Sylvia's blouse, her damp hair, and her sandals.

'Your feet'll be saturated in seconds wearing those.'

Gerrard held out an umbrella. 'You maybe don't need a coat, though, it's warm.'

Which somehow gave Sylvia the confidence to ignore her mother's face as she picked up her handbag and pulled the door closed behind her.

That was Saturday, and on Sunday they went to Gerrard's local, where he showed her how to play pool, and she met his friends, relieved to find there was no one from the bus company. They started to spend all their spare time together, through a long summer of evening walks by the canal and drinks in country pubs. He insisted on calling for her in his car. Spotlessly clean and polished, she could see he was proud of it, but, 'Isn't it a bit old-fashioned?' she said.

He laughed. 'I should hope so.' He took her elbow and steered her around to the boot and pointed at *Ford Capri* in silver lettering. 'It's a classic.'

She understood that she should be impressed.

A couple of weeks after that first date, Gerrard went onto night shift, and her mother watched Sylvia tackling a pile of ironing.

'Not coming then, your gentleman caller?'

Sylvia just smiled. She was no longer cowed by her mother's sarcasm.

They agreed to keep quiet about their relationship at work. Sylvia didn't know which would get the most gossip: that she was going out with Gerrard Wilton; or that their first date had been to see a Dolly Parton film, and not *Primal Fear*, which they were all talking about. Or that they'd watched the film three times, and by the third occasion, progressed to holding hands. Gerrard said he didn't want his workmates making insinuating comments around Sylvia. If they met in the canteen, in the yard, or in the corridor, he nodded and moved on.

One Saturday, he called in the early afternoon, as he came

off shift. Sylvia was in the bathroom, trying a new hair straightening cream which was thick and greasy, when her mother called up the stairs. Sylvia wondered at what point her mother had stopped calling him her gentleman caller and started using his name. She opened the bathroom door just enough to speak without being seen, and called, 'Go into the kitchen, Gerrard, I'll be there soon.'

She heard her mother huff. 'Well, you'd better come in then.'

When she'd hurriedly washed the cream out of her hair and dressed, she found him in the kitchen, sitting at the table, watching her mother silently and furiously wiping the surfaces.

'Cup of tea?'

He put a bottle of wine on the table. 'Maybe something a bit stronger, help me celebrate? I've passed the driver test.'

'I don't think so, at two o'clock in the afternoon,' her mother said. She put the wine in a cupboard. Sylvia boiled the kettle and mashed the tea, taking cups and saucers from the cupboard, placing the sugar and milk on the table, lifting the biscuit tin from the top of the fridge. Her mother removed and washed beneath each item as soon as Sylvia put it down. It was a well-practised dance that suddenly seemed ludicrous as she noticed Gerrard watching them both, one eyebrow raised. As she poured tea into his cup, he caught her eye and winked. She couldn't help it, the happiness spluttered out of her. He laughed too, and her mother stopped in the act of emptying the teapot that Sylvia had just put down, and stared at them.

'Do you fancy a drive out to Castleton? It's one of my favourite places. I'll show you, if you like.'

She remembered a school trip to the Blue John Mine, but on this sunny, early autumn day, standing on Mam Tor, looking across the valley, it was all new and fresh, and she was enrapt, imagining a different world as he talked about the Iron Age hill fort and the ancient tribes that walked and worked alongside bears that roamed the land.

'We'll go to the museum if you like, you can see the display about it all.'

He took her home, to meet his father.

'Put the kettle on, Sylvia, make yourself at home,' he said, and meant it. Sylvia went to Gerrard's house more often, enjoying his father's easy company, and sometimes meeting an aunt or a cousin who was visiting, but at least once a week, Gerrard would pull out a videotape from his collection of sci-fi films.

His father would say, 'I'll leave you two to it, and have a pint with the lads.'

'He's got a girlfriend,' Gerrard said once, grinning from ear to ear. 'It's about time, it's fifteen years since Mum passed away.'

They watched *ET*, *Back to the Future*, and *Mad Max*.

'What kind of films do you like?' he asked, and when she didn't know, he took her to Blockbuster and showed her where she could rent *Nine to Five* and *A Smoky Mountain Christmas*. She began to feel less guilty when she got home late, and found her mother sitting alone, watching the television.

Sylvia could talk to Gerrard in a way she had never been able to confide in anyone before. Growing up with no friends allowed to visit, no relatives to speak of, just Sylvia and her mother, forever scrubbing and cleaning. Every meal was a rushed affair so that she could get the kitchen clean again. Sylvia thought this obsession had probably started when her father left. As though she was trying to clean away all traces of him. It was never clear to Sylvia, whether he had left, or whether she had thrown him out, or what had caused the schism, but one day he went out and he never returned. She often wondered if he'd actually gone off with her namesake at The Bull. Her life, until Gerrard, had been a stream of implied criticism. So, she listened, astonished and fascinated by the banter between Gerrard and his friends, the way they casually poked fun at one another and obviously didn't mean it.

They went to a country and western club, where local singers and musicians played their favourites in a back room of a pub, throwing something into the kitty so that every now and then they could afford a professional artiste. That's when she heard Dolly Parton again. Well, not Dolly herself of course, but a bottle-blonde woman with a large cleavage whose words transported Sylvia as she leaned against Gerrard, fantasising that she'd call a daughter *Jolene*, and maybe one day they would all go to Nashville, together. She told Gerrard about her fantasy name.

'I'll call you Ruby if you like,' he said. 'But Sylvia's a lovely name. It's from the French, Sylvie, and it means *spirit of the wood*.'

He called her Sylvie, with a fake French accent that made her giggle, and she began to like her name. Gradually, she realised that he simply didn't care about her flat chest and frizzy hair. Once, when Sylvia appeared in a new dress and said, 'What do you think?' her mother said, 'You'll never be an oil painting, our Sylvia.'

And Gerrard said, 'Better than any painting I've ever seen. I think you look lovely.'

Her mother sniffed and left the room.

It was a small gathering at the register office, his father arriving shyly, with his new lady on his arm. They had a mortgage on a small townhouse with a postage-stamp garden, where Sylvia threw herself into cooking and keeping house, doing everything she could think of to spoil the man who had become the centre of her world. She was pregnant within a few months and Dylan was born just before their first anniversary, shortly after her thirtieth birthday, in the spring of 1998.

Gerrard's father visited often, playing with Dylan until his bedtime, then spending the evening with them. They invited her mother, knowing she didn't like to be in their house, finding it nigh on impossible not to pick up scattered toys and wash up the pots that piled in the sink while Sylvia spent her days gazing in wonder as Dylan grew and changed, and her evenings in front of the television, daydreaming with Gerrard about the years ahead.

Standing over Dylan's cot, one hand on his chest to check he was breathing, Sylvia had flashbacks. Lying alone in her cot, crying. Looking over the windowsill, watching the street for her mother to come home… back from school to an empty house, warming a meal from the freezer in the microwave, doing her homework in front of the television. She knew now that her mother had to work in the evenings and had left Sylvia locked in the house.

'Come back to bed, love,' Gerrard would say, hugging her from behind. 'He's fine.'

When he gave her the CD for her birthday, Gerrard said, 'One year, we'll go to America, see her live.'

'One day,' she said, knowing it was a long way off being affordable, especially now, with Gerrard's union pressing for a strike. She went back to work three days a week, they needed the money. Sylvia was promoted to accounts office manager. Her mother looked after Dylan. They couldn't afford a proper childminder.

'Never, ever leave him alone,' Sylvia said.

She often woke in the middle of the night, padded into Dylan's room, looked down on his little question mark of a body, watching him sleeping, dropping an ear to his chest, just to make sure. She would miss her lunch to run all the way to her mother's house, to arrive unexpectedly, invariably finding Dylan and his nana together on the settee watching a Disney video, or

Dylan sitting at his highchair, his face smeared with food. Once, she found the door locked, and there was no response to her frantic knocking. She rattled the letterbox, saw an empty living room through the window, ran out of the gate and almost collided with her mother coming in, with a sleeping Dylan in his pushchair. She realised her mother made a better grand-mother than a mother and gradually began to trust her with her boy.

The girls in the office didn't tease her now; they envied Sylvia her house, her little boy, and her husband who stuck his head around the accounts office door whenever he was passing and winked at her. She had never shared the office banter, but now it was because Dylan occupied her thoughts; she didn't even hear the chatter. As she made up the payroll, she paused to make a note to remind herself to buy nappies or a jar of puréed vegetables on the way home. If she made a mistake, her super-visor laughed it off, joking about hormones. Whenever the office phone rang, and someone called, 'It's for you, Sylvia,' her heart thumped in her chest and she was unable to move her lips until the caller started speaking and she knew it wasn't about her boy. Everything ached for Dylan: her arms, her thoughts, her breasts; there was no relief until she ran into her mother's house and scooped him up, leaving quickly to get home, to have Dylan, and Gerrard, to herself.

Instead of going on strike, Gerrard announced that the union had secured a new pay deal, with back pay. Suddenly, there was money in the bank. Gerrard brought home a brochure for a tour of Nashville.

'Let's go, Dylan will be fine with your mum.'

At JFK, they checked into the airport hotel and booked an alarm call to be sure to make their connection to Nashville. The telephone woke them, and, expecting the receptionist, it took several seconds for Sylvia to recognise her mother's voice. And when she did, befuddled by sleep, Sylvia couldn't understand what her mother was saying. Until she did: Dylan in hospital. Meningitis. Come home. They caught a taxi back to the airport and bought new tickets on the first plane. It was her fault, she shouldn't have left him. She'd been too busy, too excited about the trip to notice that he was ill. She had one job, to keep her green-eyed boy safe, and she had let him down.

8

The two faces had begun to merge behind one pair of green eyes, flecked with yellow. She knew it wasn't Dylan of course; but she started to feel Dylan moving beside her, talking to her. Though she couldn't yet make out the words, she knew he was trying to tell her something important, that if she listened hard enough, he would lead her to the boy called Conor, and she would find Rosie. With Gerrard's constant noise-making, whether it was eating, shouting at the television, singing in the shower, talking; even when he was asleep he'd be popping and grunting and snoring, it was no wonder she hadn't heard Dylan before. Now that she was on her own, she could listen, and hear. And concentrate on searching for the green-eyed boy.

Lori phoned. Sylvia had bought a pack of highlighters from the newsagent's and was going through the Register of Electors, colouring in any Conor Walsh who was born between 1980 and 1990, which she'd agreed with Lori was about the right age range. There were eighteen of them. Lori was chattering on about her friend Simon.

Sylvia cut across her. 'Can't you get an exact date of birth from Simon? That would cut it down.'

'No, that's what I'm saying. I can't ask Simon for anything else. He's been caught accessing unauthorised information and he's got a meeting with HR on Monday morning.'

'HR?'

'Human Resources. He's in trouble, Sylvia.'

Sylvia tutted. 'Oh, for goodness' sake, what's he been doing? I hope he doesn't lose his job.'

'He might. You don't understand. He's in trouble for getting the information that we asked him to get.'

'He must have been very careless then.'

'I don't think so. Their IT section can tell who's been doing what, on the intranet–'

'On the what?'

'Intranet. It's what they call the internal database. They do random sampling to check people don't view information that they don't have the right level of security clearance for. And Simon's still at basic security level. He's only allowed to see information about the current prison population, receptions and discharges and transfers, that kind of thing, that's his job. He isn't authorised to access the history.'

'Ridiculous. Like *Nineteen Eighty-Four*.'

'What?'

'Never mind. I'm sure he could have found a way to do it without them finding out.'

Lori exhaled sharply. 'I don't think so. I think the only thing he did wrong was not to realise that he might get caught on one of their spot checks. Anyway, it doesn't matter, does it? It's not his fault, it's mine. I asked him to do it, so I feel responsible.'

'If you say so. As long as you don't bring me into this.'

There was a silence for a few seconds. 'I'm going to have to tell him.'

'Tell him what?'

'Why we wanted the information. It's only fair, if he's going to take the blame. He says he won't mention me, because that would prove he'd been passing information out of the prison and that would be worse.'

'NO.' Sylvia rubbed her eyes to try to clear the red fog.

'Excuse me?'

Sylvia leaned against the door jamb to stop herself falling, with her hand over the receiver so Lori wouldn't hear her exhaling, slowly, inhaling, slowly, forcing herself to keep breathing.

'Are you still there, Sylvia? Listen, if he gets disciplined, fuck, he might lose his job, and it'll be my fault. Our fault.'

Sylvia let out a long shuddering breath and shook her head, still trying to clear it. 'You're sure he hasn't said anything to them yet, they don't know about you, you're absolutely sure?'

'That's what he said. I said I'd take him out on Saturday night, to make up for it. Of course, it won't make it up to him if he loses his job. Sylvia, I need to tell him so that he can explain to HR why he did it.'

'No, I mean... let's discuss it. You're right. We need to help him. Tell you what, come round in the morning and we'll come up with something that we can say to Simon, that'll get him off the hook.'

'Thanks, Sylvia, I knew you'd be able to help.'

'Just don't say anything until we've talked about it. Not to anyone.'

Lori arrived mid-morning on Saturday. Sylvia had been to the corner shop to pick up a pint of milk and was sitting in the kitchen, scratching the last few cards, when she heard the front door and cursed that she'd forgotten to drop the lock as she came in. She pushed the cards under the bread bin and went through to the living room where Lori was opening her laptop. She took a deep breath, moved Lori's backpack from where she'd dropped it in the middle of the floor, and neatly stacked the papers that Lori had already scattered across the table.

Lori pointed to a book of road maps on the table. 'I brought you the map you wanted. And here's the receipt.'

Sylvia put the receipt on the mantelpiece, picked up the wet jacket Lori had draped across the sofa and took it into the kitchen where she hung it over a chair; brought back a cloth and rubbed at the damp footprints Lori had left from the door to the settee.

Lori pulled her feet out of her trainers and folded herself into a lotus position. 'I was thinking. The woman who sold him the car. She said the child was quiet, that he stood back. He, a boy, she said, but we're thinking it was the girl. She didn't seem to be upset, the girl. You'd have thought she would have been crying for her mother, or frightened, wouldn't you?'

Sylvia picked up Lori's trainers by the heel tabs and wiped the carpet where they had been. 'She'd have been shocked. She might have seen him kill his friend.'

The pictures were clear in Sylvia's head. The child couldn't have avoided it in that small space. Imagine the noise of the gun going off. Anyone hearing it from the road would probably have assumed it was a car backfiring, which is what she'd thought when they shot the child's mother. Or maybe he had a silencer. Where would he get one of those from? But, if he knew where to get a gun, why not a silencer? Sylvia had seen a murder on TV once, where the killer shot through a cushion. Even so, it would have deafened the child in that small space. The little girl she remembered was feisty, sure of herself. The shock could have knocked the stuffing out of her. Sylvia watched CSI on television and knew about blood spatter; that little girl must have been covered with blood.

'That'll be why he had to cut her hair,' she thought aloud.

'What?' Lori started to unfold her legs.

'Oh, nothing.'

Holding the trainers out in front of her, Sylvia went into the hallway and placed them on the shoe mat. In the kitchen, the noise from the tap as she filled the kettle covered the sound of Lori approaching and when she spoke, Sylvia jumped. Her stomach contracted and the taste of the brandy she'd drunk earlier rose in her throat. Lori turned off the tap and took the kettle from her, plugging it in. Sylvia watched her take cups and saucers from the cupboard. The girl was making herself a bit too much at home, taking her for granted, coming in uninvited. Who knew what she might see lying around? And she was talking and talking, on and on about Simon. How he loved his job, he was terrified of being disciplined and never being able to work for the Ministry of Justice again. He might even be prosecuted, since he'd signed the Official Secrets Act, you heard about these things, it would ruin his career.

Sylvia wanted to scream at Lori to shut up, but was afraid to open her mouth because of the lump of bile sitting on her tongue. She swallowed hard, fighting back the nausea as the bitterness slid down her throat. She took the tea canister from Lori. 'Go and sit down, I'll bring the tea through.'

She heard Lori go into the bathroom and leaned over the sink, drinking from the tap, swilling out her mouth. She listened for the flush and the sounds of Lori going back into the living room, then popped into the bathroom for a quick check around and straightened the hand towel.

In the living room, Sylvia handed a cup to Lori who put it on the table. Sylvia found a coaster and put the cup and saucer on it. She perched on the armchair, picked up the road atlas and flicked through to find Ireland.

'Where did he go then, after he bought the car? Probably to Ireland.'

Lori slurped her tea and wrinkled her nose.

'Something wrong?'

'Funny taste.'

'I'm trying out a new sweetener. I've run out of sugar.' Sylvia took a sip of her own tea. 'Mine's okay. It says try it for a few days before deciding. It's supposed to be less chemical.'

'Yuk, I don't think I'll be buying it. More chemical, not less. Look at all these little white powder bits on the top.'

'Even so, give it a try. It's on offer. Just empty that one and I'll make you another cup, I'll put a bit less in.'

Lori hit a few keys on her laptop then turned it towards Sylvia, tapping the map on the screen, showing a route highlighted in a direct line. 'Sheffield to Holyhead is quite straightforward. Ferry to Dublin.'

Sylvia put her finger on Dublin. 'So, he's disguised little Rosie, who now looks like a boy, and he'll have to change her name, won't he? She's shocked and not saying much. But how would he get her into Ireland? She wouldn't have had a passport.'

Lori's fingers flew over her keyboard. 'It says here that you can't fly into Ireland without a passport, it's part of the airport security checks. But it's possible to get in without one on the ferry. It's a risk, though, because they do spot checks. He'd have had a passport, presumably, if he'd come from there in the first place...'

'He could have got her in then, but it would have been a risk, if they'd done a spot check. Why would he have taken her to Ireland, though? Why wouldn't he have just dropped her off, abandoned her, let her be found, he could have done it anywhere on that route.'

'We'd know, if a little girl or boy had been found.'

'Unless he – well, you know...' Sylvia was sure he hadn't harmed the child. Perhaps at the beginning, but she'd started to feel as though she knew this youth. He might have hurt his friend, because he had to, but he wouldn't hurt Rosie. She pinched her lips between her fingers and shook her head.

Lori shrugged. 'Okay, assuming he still had Rosie with him, and wanted to take her to Ireland...' She screwed up her face to show how unlikely she considered this to be. 'Don't people have to register their cars on ferries?'

'Maybe they do, but if he turned up and bought a ticket on the spot, the ferry company may not have a record.'

'The police could get the information. Wouldn't that be the quickest way to find out?' Sylvia glared at Lori. 'Okay, I get that you don't want to involve the police, but it would be a lot quicker and easier, they could ask for the' – she tapped at her laptop for a few moments – 'manifest. That's what they call it. Every ship has a list of cargo and passengers, and I'm sure the police could get hold of one for those few days that we're thinking of, without much trouble. I know they've treated you badly, but surely, if we take the information we've got, about the car, and disguising the child–'

'More tea?'

In the kitchen, Sylvia ground the Imovane more carefully using the back of a spoon and added a spoonful of sugar. When she came back, Lori was keying in the last of the addresses to a Google map of Ireland. She took the cup from Sylvia and pointed to the red flags littering the screen: Cork. Waterford. Kilkenny. Three around Dublin. Two in Ennis. Four scattered across Galway.

'If you want to track down each and every one, it's going to take a bit of time.'

Lori slurped her tea. 'That's better. Maybe I'm getting used to it, like you said. I was thinking, let me go to the police and tell them what we've found. You don't need to come if you don't want to. I can show them everything on the laptop.'

Sylvia took a long slug from her cup. She felt the brandy slide down her throat, calming her, helping her to keep breathing.

'Or,' Lori talked on, 'why don't I bring Simon over, so you can meet him, tell him why it's important to you? Even better...' Lori swung her legs from under her and jumped onto her feet, gesticulating. 'Yes, even better. I'll bring Simon round and if you really won't go to the police, Simon can come with me... perhaps he could say it involved a family friend of his, so he was particularly interested... Yes, and he can say that to the prison, so they understand... Woooo-oh.' She fell back onto the sofa and laughed. 'Feeling dizzy!' She yawned and closed her eyes for a few seconds, then sat up again.

'Burning the candle at both ends?'

Lori laughed. 'It was a 4am finish at The Leadmill. Good group though. But I haven't had much sleep. Do you have any coffee?'

'I've run out of coffee. They say there's caffeine in tea, though. I'll go and make a fresh one.' Sylvia took the cups out and switched the kettle back on.

When she came back, Lori was looking at the screen. Sylvia sat next to her and pointed. 'How far are these distances? How long do you think it would take to drive them? If we went across to Ireland–'

'Wow, are you thinking what I'm thinking? That we could go together?' She bounced on the settee, unfolding and refolding her legs. 'I could take a holiday. But...'

'What?'

'I don't think I could afford a holiday. My parents gave me a loan to get this...' She pointed to the laptop.

'Don't worry about money. It's my idea, I'll pay for it.'

'Really?' Lori yawned. 'That would be mega.'

'You do sound tired. If you don't have to rush off, why not have forty winks?'

Lori giggled. 'Forty winks? That's something my granny would say. But if you don't mind, I will just lie down here...'

Sylvia washed up. Thinking. She peeped around the door of the living room to see Lori lying full stretch on the sofa, her eyes closed. When Sylvia leaned over her, Lori opened her eyes as if sensing the cutting off of the light. She smiled slightly and closed them again. Sylvia watched her; she was a nice girl, but how to stop her talking to this Simon, how to make her listen, to understand? She couldn't let her leave, not while she was determined to get Simon involved.

Sitting at the kitchen table, Sylvia watched the clock, thinking. She took the bottle from behind the curtain, shaking her head at herself for continuing to hide it, even though Gerrard had left. Pouring herself a generous measure, she took it into the hallway and listened to Lori's gentle snoring. In the front room, she sat on the armchair, watching her. She tugged the map from half beneath Lori's legs and spread it on the coffee table, pressing out the creases, nudged the laptop and compared the map on the table with the one on the screen, and emptied her glass. Lori's phone buzzed and vibrated across the coffee table. Lori stirred, mumbled, turned over. Sylvia picked up the phone. A text from Simon was on the screen:

See you later, can't wait to hear the full story.

Under the kitchen sink was a box that Gerrard had left. He'd made a thing of putting together a collection of small DIY tools that he said she might need in the house. He'd gone over each one, explaining how to change a plug or a light bulb, or fix the knob on the cooker that was always coming loose. Sylvia's mind had blanked: she only wanted him to leave. Now, she rummaged through screwdrivers, retractable knives, items she neither recognised nor understood. She lifted the sliding shelf. There was a roll of tape which Sylvia remembered seeing Gerrard use to seal a cracked pipe in their old house. The end of the roll had curled and browned. In the kitchen drawers, Sylvia found the scissors and tried to cut it off, then, the scissors hanging from her fingers, used her teeth. A piece of the broad, sticky black tape came away in her mouth and she gagged and spat. A crash from the living room startled her and she ran through.

One of Lori's arms had swung out and knocked Sylvia's empty glass off the table. It had smashed against the fireplace. Lori seemed to be asleep. On the table, the phone buzzed again. Lori's head turned towards the sound and she muttered. Sylvia watched her lips moving as if she was having a conversation with someone only she could see, and realised, whatever Sylvia said, Lori would tell Simon. And he would probably tell the police. She pulled the end of the tape away from the roll and carefully, experimentally, pressed it against Lori's cheek. Lori's head moved from side to side and her eyes half-opened, then widened as she saw Sylvia's face close to hers. She felt her mouth, grabbed the tape with her fingers and ripped it from her face, yelping as it came away. Sylvia stared, fascinated by the numerous droplets of blood pulsing from a triangular red welt beside Lori's mouth. Lori tried to rise and, lurching forward, Sylvia pressed Lori's upper body down, into the sofa cushions, and spread the strip across her mouth. With her knee in Lori's chest, she pressed the tape firmly against her lips with her thumb, saying, 'Stop it, stop it, just stop talking and listen to me...'

But the sounds kept coming from Lori's closed mouth. Sylvia

climbed off the sofa and took a step back, her legs against the coffee table, watching Lori's fingers frantically tugging at the edges of the tape, while the roll swung from her cheek. Lori wriggled into sitting position and, grabbing Sylvia's cardigan, pulled Sylvia towards her. Sylvia curled her hands into fists and pounded Lori's chest. Lori's eyes became huge and round and rolled up, disappearing into her head while the sounds coming from behind the tape turned to a high-pitched keening. She fell back onto the sofa, the scissor handles sticking out from her chest.

9

The bottle was empty. Sylvia checked the oven, the hall cupboard, the shoe boxes in her wardrobe. She twisted around the living room door, eying the bookcase, sure there was half a bottle behind her collection of Catherine Cookson titles if she could only reach it without looking at the sofa. She walked sideways on the other side of the coffee table, and stepped on the broken glass, looked up and caught sight of the sofa in the mirror, and a small scream escaped her. She pulled a handful of books off the shelf and grabbed the bottle behind, retreating as fast as she could. At the kitchen table, she drank the contents in two long slurps. The clock said half past four. She picked up her coat and purse and slipped out of the door, checking it had clicked and locked behind her, hurried down the stairway and came up short when she found herself facing Lori's little blue Renault which was parked in front of the entrance. She retreated quickly into the doorway, looked around, then rushed past the car, across the asphalt towards the road. Looking back through the rain and gathering dark, she made out the first-floor walkway and the closed curtains of her flat, and the shape of the car. Turning, she trotted down the road to the Co-op, bought two bottles, and walked quickly home, averting her eyes as she passed the car.

'I only wanted to stop you talking. You wanted to tell him. He would have told them. I thought you were on my side, thought you could be trusted. We were in this together. We could have found Rosie. Why didn't you listen to me? I only wanted to make you listen. I thought you were my friend. Now I'm on my own again. If only you'd stopped–' At a rapping on the window Sylvia jumped up and ducked behind the armchair.

Gerrard's voice came through the glass. 'Sylvia, you must be in, because you've drop-locked the door. Open up, love, come on.'

She crawled on all fours into the hallway, along to the door, sat with her back to it. The letter flap opened. 'Sylvia? I heard you talking. I know you're there.'

'I've got flu, Ger. Best not come in. It's vicious.'

'Do you need anything? Have you got some Beechams? Why don't you just open the door, Sylvia?'

'I'm best on my own. I'll give you a ring when I'm feeling better.'

'Well, if you're sure, but your voice is hoarse. It sounds as though it might be on your chest. There's a nasty virus going around, a lot of the lads are off sick with it.'

'I'll be all right, really, I'm going to have an early night, sweat it out.'

He said nothing for several seconds. She heard him sigh. 'All right, if you're sure. Tell you what, I'm on earlies tomorrow so I'll come over in the afternoon, and I'll bring a takeaway, something nice, and you won't have to worry about cooking or anything.'

The letter flap snapped closed. With her ear against the door, she listened until his footsteps had faded along the walkway then jumped to her feet and ran into the living room. For the first time she looked properly at Lori. She could think she was asleep if it weren't for the roll of tape hanging from her mouth, and the scissors.

She brought a blanket from the bedroom and threw it over Lori. As she tucked it in around Lori's legs, she started slapping her. 'Stupid, stupid, stupid girl, just look what you made me do.' Tears were pouring down her face and she fell forward, her head on Lori's knees, rubbing her legs as if this would bring her back. A rapping on the door made her sit up sharply, and Gerrard's voice came through the letter flap.

'Syl, I've been to the shop, here's a few bits to keep you going.' She froze, until she heard him say, 'All right, Sylvie. I'll see you tomorrow.'

When she was sure he'd gone, she cracked the front door open and pulled in the bulging carrier bag. Putting it on the table in the kitchen, she saw the tools still scattered and started to pack them onto their plastic tray. She stopped with the removable shelf in her hands, staring into the empty bottom of the little toolbox. The tape. She went into the living room, climbed carefully over Lori's legs and pulled at the roll of tape. Lori's head came forward. Sylvia jumped backwards, dislodging the blanket which slithered to the floor, revealing the scissors lodged in Lori's chest. She looked from the scissors to the tape, then leaned over and tore off the roll of tape with her finger-nails, leaving Lori's mouth taped shut.

In the kitchen, she put the roll of tape in the bottom of the toolbox, replaced the plastic shelf with its array of screwdrivers and picture hooks, clipped the lid closed and pushed the box underneath the shelf beneath the sink. She put on her Marigolds, gathered cloths and towels, poured a bowl of hot water and emptied a bottle of thick bleach into it. Standing in the front room, once she looked properly, she was surprised how little blood there was, just the broad stain on Lori's T-shirt where blood had seeped out around the scissor handles for a few minutes. If she removed the scissors would blood spurt out? One of the real-crime programmes she'd seen had talked about the heart: had they said that once it stopped beating, the body would stop bleeding? She tugged experimentally at the scissors and staggered backwards as they came loose immediately. No blood followed. She dropped the scissors into the bowl. She pushed the coffee table away to give herself some space. The screen of the laptop came to life. It was the Google page, which she had seen Lori use often. With one finger, she slowly typed in *rigor mortis*. Before she'd finished typing, a list of questions came up. She clicked on *how long before rigor mortis sets in*. A few hours, so any time now. She picked up Lori's legs, touched the cold skin between Lori's jeans and her ankles, and dropped them again. She stood back, feeling dizzy, breathed slowly in and slowly out, then leaned over Lori, and with one hand on her foot and one under her knee, folded each leg in turn. There was a bit of resistance, but she managed to push Lori's knees close to her chest. She moved the coffee table further out of the way, spread the blanket on the floor beside the sofa, then rolled Lori off the sofa and onto it. She was surprised how light the girl was, despite being taller than herself. Tugging the blanket by the corners, she managed to heave it through the door, across the hall, and into Dylan's bedroom. She took his toys and books out of the tallboy, removed the shelf, and rolled and tugged Lori into the cupboard. Though she couldn't see any stains, she carefully washed the sofa, the coffee table, the carpet and the laptop, and removed the broken glass from the fireplace. Everything – bowl, cloths, towels, the cup Lori had drunk from, her jacket, and her trainers, went into a bin bag. As she was collecting up the cushions from the sofa, Lori's phone buzzed and vibrated on the coffee table. Sylvia saw Simon's name on the screen and a text:

Where are you?

She dropped the phone into the bag, took off the Marigolds and threw them after it. She picked up the laptop, thought again, closed it and placed it on the wall unit. The bin bag joined Lori inside Dylan's toy cupboard.

Suddenly ravenous, Sylvia emptied Gerrard's shopping onto the worktop: bread, milk and orange juice, cold meats and several tins of soup. With a mulligatawny soup warming in the microwave, she ripped open the pack of ham, pulled two slices of bread from the packet, and made a rough sandwich, biting off a quarter of it immediately. She suddenly stopped eating, dropped the sandwich onto the floor, stared at her hands, rushed to the sink and held her hands under the hot tap. Pulling everything out of her cleaning cupboard, she chose the bottle of Stardrops and poured the ammonia cleaner onto her hands, scrubbing at her nails and between her fingers until they were red raw and stinging. As she turned off the tap, she heard a phone ringing and froze, recognising it as Lori's ringtone. She followed the sound to Dylan's cupboard. She ran to her bedroom, rummaged in her bedside table drawer until she located earplugs, screwed them into her ears and lay face down on the bed, a pillow over her head.

Sylvia woke to find herself still face down on her bed, fully dressed. In the glow of the light still on in the hallway she could read the clock. It was 3am. Cautiously rolling off the bed, pushing her feet into her slippers, she crept into the kitchen, stopping at the sight of ham and bread scattered across the floor. As she stretched down to pick it up, she felt pain shoot along her fingers and looking at her raw hands, it came back to her. She poured herself a brandy and took it into the living room where she leaned against the wall, staring at the dented cushions on the sofa. She slid down to the floor and sat, bottle in one hand, glass in the other, crying, dropping asleep, falling awake. When she heard the distant ringtone of Lori's phone, she looked at the clock: a quarter to nine. She uncurled from the floor and stood, stiffly stretching, walked to the window, looked around the edge of the curtain and realising it was morning, pulled the curtains back fully and stood watching the rain falling straight down beyond the walkway. As she turned, she caught sight of Lori's laptop on the wall unit, lifted it down, and opened it. The browser appeared, and she had just typed in *Ferries to Ireland*, when the door knocker sounded.

She saw her next-door neighbour through the spyhole. Mrs Cresswell hadn't spoken to her since her arrest. She thought about not answering the door, but if she didn't, the old woman would sit by her window, watching for Sylvia to pass, all day if need be. She opened the door just enough to put her head around it.

'Mrs Cresswell, how are you?'

Mrs Cresswell waved one of her walking sticks towards the stairwell. 'That girl, the one who comes to see you–'

Sylvia's stomach tightened. 'She's not here.'

'Well, I saw her come yesterday and I didn't see her go again so she's not far away. But I don't care where she's got to, only that she's parked her chuffing car on the disabled space again.' She waved the stick in the vague direction of the car park, over the walkway.

'What makes you think it's hers? She's not here, so why would her car be?'

'She always does it. And I know her car. It's that little blue one, isn't it? Anyway, it's no use standing there arguing, it's her car and I saw her yesterday and whyever she left it there is irrelevant but there it is and she needs to move it off the disabled space.'

'But you don't have a car, so why–'

'Not that it's anything to do with you, or with your little friend, whether I have a car or not. I might have, and I might not have. Or I might want a taxi to come and take me somewhere. Or one of those volunteer drivers that takes me to my hospital appointments. They need to be able to park at the bottom of the stairs, so I don't have to walk. Anyway, it's none of your business. I fought with the council for years to get that bleeding disabled space and it's mine. So you can tell your little friend...' The walking stick was now tapping the door next to Sylvia's head.

'I'll tell her, Mrs Cresswell, don't you worry, I'll phone or–'

'Hello, Mrs C.' Gerrard appeared from the stairwell. 'Sylvia. How are you doing? Up and about again, that's good to see.'

Mrs Cresswell turned towards him. 'You've decided to grace us, have you? I was just saying to your missus here–'

'Gerrard, there you are.' Sylvia stepped in front of Mrs Cresswell and grabbed Gerrard by the sleeve. 'Don't worry about a thing, Mrs Cresswell, I'll see to it.' She hurried him inside and shut the door.

Gerrard turned in the hallway and as he did, was facing Dylan's room. 'What's going on in here, Syl?'

'What do you mean?'

He pointed at the piles of toys on the floor. 'Looks as though you're having a clear-out.'

She moved in front of him and closed the door. 'Well, it's time, don't you think?'

He looked at her, held out a hand. 'Sylvie, you didn't have to do this on your own.'

'Yes, I do, I want to.'

She felt herself enfolded in his big arms, her face pressed to his chest, remembered how this had felt, and for a moment was tempted to give herself in to the warmth, his smell... and pulled away. He shrugged and turned towards the kitchen. Sylvia opened the living room door, looked around, checking. She heard water pouring into the kettle and found Gerrard plugging it in. Her eyes darted around the room and stopped at the Marigolds hanging over the side of the bowl in the sink. Had she poured the water away? He followed her eyes, looked down into the sink.

'Had an accident?'

'Cut my finger, it was nothing.' She pushed her hand into her pocket. 'Thing is, Gerrard, it's lovely to see you and thank you for the food yesterday, but really I need to get on.'

'Oh, I thought – couldn't we at least have a cup of tea?' He stopped in the act of taking two mugs out of the cupboard and looked at her.

It was easier to agree. Sylvia sat at the table, checked the scratch cards were out of sight under the bread bin, and watched him making the tea.

'What's going on with next door?'

'Nothing much. She wanted me to get a few bits of shopping for her, that's all.'

'I thought I heard her talking about car parking...?'

'I wasn't really listening, to be honest. You know what she's like, when she gets on her soap box.'

'What did she mean by "your little friend"?'

'Is that what she said? I thought she was talking about her friend?'

'Didn't know she had one. Well, anyway, you're looking better, I must say.'

'I'm still a bit achy and tired, so I'll be getting back to bed before too long. Did you, er, did you call round for anything in particular?'

Gerrard pushed the suitcase to one side and pulled out a chair. 'What's the big case doing out?'

'As you saw, I'm having a clear-out, putting stuff in it to take to the charity shop.'

'You'll never lift it on your own, remember? We practically fitted all my clothes in it, but then we could barely move it.'

She looked at him closely. Was he having a go at her?

'Do you want me to bring the smaller case? We could get rid of this one really, it's not much use being so big.' He took hold of the handle, about to move it.

'Leave it, Gerrard.' He stood back, surprised. 'Just leave it. Thanks for trying to help, but I can manage. I'll take the stuff to the charity shop, leave the case there.'

'But the lift is still out of order. The stairs...'

'It's got wheels, I can bump it down the stairs, I don't have to lift it. Sorry to sound sharp, but really, Gerrard, leave me to it.'

'But I could help.'

'I know, but I don't want you to help. You left, Gerrard, remember? I have to learn to manage on my own.'

His shoulders had dropped but he moved towards the hall. As he opened the door, he turned. 'Syl, you're shaking all over. You need to be in bed.' She nodded, unable to speak. 'Are you all right for money?'

She shrugged, avoiding his eyes. He pulled his wallet from his pocket and took out a wad of notes, which he tucked under the telephone. 'You know where I am.'

After the door closed behind him, she pushed against it, dropped the lock, then went back to the kitchen where she sat at the table, staring at the suitcase.

10

————

Gerrard's words had brought it all back. Life after Dylan, that descent into a very personal hell, where no one could reach her. Only when she drank was Sylvia's brain dull enough to allow her to sleep, to not think, to not bawl and scream and yank lumps from her hair. Only when her fingernail scratched away that gold patch, with its promise of another life, of realising her dreams, did she feel anything, and it was not hope or happiness, it was a hunger deep in her belly that lasted a few brief seconds until, whether there was a prize or not, what was revealed was an emptiness, another deep chasm beneath her feet, so she must go back, again and again, to find that promise, again and again. Through the window of the new Bet365 shop, she watched the screens and wondered if that would help her to feel something. Inside, the smell of desperation coming in waves off the people who sat with paper and pencil in their hands, staring at the galloping horses, made her retch and run outside, dry-heaving, folding herself into the pavement. People paused, leaned over, caught the smell, and walked around her.

Often, when she was in town, Gerrard appeared, alerted by a passing bus driver, to bring her home. Once, Gerrard himself, driving along Penistone Road, abandoned his bus to run through the traffic to the opposite pavement, lifting her, in view of all his passengers. After this, he took her to see Doctor Holden, who offhandedly wrote a prescription for antidepressants and handed her leaflets for Gamblers Anonymous and the Alcohol Counselling Service, then turned to Gerrard.

'You need to rest,' he said, noting that Gerrard was underweight, his cheeks had hollowed, his hair had turned mostly grey and he had developed bald patches.

Then the High Court Sheriff's men came. Curtains twitched, but doors remained closed. Except for Jess who lugged the enormous suitcase across the street, skirting the furniture, and the pile of boxes of videos, books, kitchen equipment, and rolled-up rugs that spilled from the little lawn onto the pavement.

Gerrard took the case and said, 'Thanks, we'll bring it back.'

Jess shook her head. 'Keep it, we don't need it, it's far too big to be of any use,' then coloured, glancing up at Sylvia in the bedroom window, and practically ran back into her house. They'd been good friends once, when both their babies were small. Now, she could barely meet Sylvia's eye.

Sylvia watched Gerrard come out of the door below, his arms full of clothes which he hurriedly crammed into the suitcase. He wedged it into the back of the white van at the kerb, banging the door shut. The High Court Sheriff's men who had been standing by the gate, impassively watching as they waited to secure the house, moved forward. Gerrard said something to them, they looked up at Sylvia, and nodded. His father got into the driving seat, Gerrard got into the passenger seat and the van drew away.

Sylvia leaned forward, through the open window, studying the leaded bay window directly beneath her, thinking, for a long time. It would break her fall, but it might also break her neck. It was a fifty-fifty chance. This is it, she thought, the tipping point.

She lay across the sill and rocked backwards and forwards, testing the idea. There was a shout from below, and then Gerrard was behind her, grabbing her arms, pulling her to him. He half-carried her down the stairs. As they walked along the path, his arm holding her tight so her right leg and his left leg moved together, she was reminded of a three-legged race at school, and giggled. The High Court Sheriff's men looked shocked and stood back to let them pass. She sat in the middle seat at the front of the van, watching through the rear mirror while Gerrard and his father lifted a sofa, an armchair, a television table into the van, then packed boxes and bags around them. Gerrard disappeared into the house, returning with a large piece of paper, she thought it was a strip of wallpaper, which read, *Help Yourself*, and taped it to the remaining items of furniture on the pavement.

His father climbed into the driving seat and Gerrard got in beside her. At the corner of the avenue, the van halted, and Gerrard wound down his window.

Her mother looked in. 'Sylvia?'

Sylvia turned her head away, looking past Gerrard's father, her hands over her ears.

'Let's go,' Gerrard said, and they moved off.

In their new home, Sylvia spent days in the room she declared to be Dylan's bedroom, organising his toys and clothes, recreating the room that he had left. Only when it looked exactly the same, did she help Gerrard to unpack the rest of the furniture.

Gerrard made them a roast dinner. 'Come and sit down. We'll be okay here. A fresh start.'

If he said 'fresh start' one more time, Sylvia would scream.

'I bumped into your mother again today.'

She stared at him. Did he really think she'd believe that was coincidental?

'She blames herself, you know, she just wants to make it right with you.'

'Tell her. Tell her from me that if I ever see her again, I'll kill her.'

Slowly, Sylvia started to eat; she talked; she slept the sleep of the drugged while Gerrard sat up late, working out how much overtime would pay off their County Court debts. When Sylvia announced she had found a job, on the till of a petrol station, he said, 'That's fantastic, Sylvie. We might be seeing the light at the end of the tunnel.'

11

Forty-eight hours. That's what the internet said. Sylvia tried to focus on the complicated words to keep away the image of Lori tapping away, showing her how to use the internet to find information. 'It's easy, Sylvia, you just type your question in here, press the return key – here – and up comes a list of results...' Lori thought it was funny that Sylvia didn't know how to use a computer. The bus company had been talking about installing a system when she left. Gerrard had come home with stories about what these new computers could do; he was impressed and worried at the same time, because it was only a matter of time before the buses would be run by computers and he would be out of a job. She found him looking at magazine articles about personal computers and asked him if he wanted one. 'When things look up,' he said, by which he meant when they'd paid off the debts. If Gerrard saw her now...

A message flashed onto the screen:

```
Low  Battery  5%,  connect  to  a  power
source.
```

In Dylan's room, she opened the cupboard, leaping back when Lori's hand dropped forward. She pulled out the bin bag, closed the door quickly and took the bag into the kitchen, spilling the phone, Lori's jacket and trainers, and the contents of the backpack, onto the table. There was nothing that could be a laptop charger. In Lori's purse she found £50 in notes and put these with the £200 Gerrard had left. She cut up Lori's bank cards and dropped them in the bin, followed by the purse. The phone was dead. Using a screwdriver from her toolbox, she prised the phone apart and put the pieces in her coat pocket.

Where was the car key? She went through the jacket pockets again and checked the rucksack. Nothing. It wasn't behind the sofa, or beneath the cushions. She stood at the tallboy cupboard, breathing heavily, touching the door, stepping back, then forward, finally opening it. Looking through half-closed eyes, avoiding Lori's gaze, she reached three fingers into Lori's jeans pocket. As she caught hold of the key and tugged, Lori's upper body swayed towards her. Sylvia screamed, realised her hand was still in the pocket and pushed the body away from her, back into the cupboard.

It had been years since she'd driven, and she'd never been a confident driver, always leaving it to Gerrard. Sitting behind the wheel of Lori's little blue Renault, she checked all the knobs and switches, put her foot on the clutch and moved the gearstick around. She heard Gerrard's voice: *carefully does it, no need to force it, try to relax*, and remembered the birthday. They'd driven out to Castleton, and over a pub lunch Gerrard handed her an envelope: in it, a huge birthday card, and a pair of 'L' plates. He drove out to the landslide below Mam Tor, parked and ceremonially put the plates on the front and rear of his precious car, then handed her the keys. Patiently, over several weeks, on small country roads, and once on the bus driver training ground, he taught her to drive. On the cold winter day at the beginning of

1997 when she passed her driving test, he took her for a Chinese meal and proposed.

She reversed carefully, parking the car neatly in one of the bays. At the top of the stairwell, she met Mrs Cresswell who was standing on the walkway, leaning on the railing.

'I see you've shifted that blasted car then. I thought you said it belonged to that girl, the one who visits you. Where's she got to then?'

'That's my niece, she's lent me the car for a while.'

'Didn't know you could drive. Anyway, if that's your niece, I'm the Queen of Sheba. I remember your husband telling me you didn't have any brothers or sisters.'

'She's my friend's daughter. She calls me Auntie and I've always thought of her as my niece.'

Mrs Cresswell sniffed, looked Sylvia up and down. 'Well, I've not seen this niece of yours go home, not since she came round yesterday, and I keep my eye on the comings and goings. You never know, round here. There was a burglary over there' – she nodded towards the next block of flats – 'and there's drug taking and all sorts in that so-called play area. That's why I started keeping a list, making sure I–'

'A list?'

'Oh yes.' She inclined her head towards her window. 'I keep a record of who's coming and going, and anything I see that's out of the ordinary. That's how I know that your friend – or your niece – came yesterday and hasn't left.'

'There are two exits you know.' Sylvia pointed at the opposite stairwell.

'Yes, and I can see right along this walkway from my window.'

'It was late, you were probably asleep.'

Mrs Cresswell hobbled towards her door. 'Well, it's funny this so-called niece of yours only visits when your husband isn't around. Then there's all that banging and squealing and up-all-hours doing who-knows-what and keeping me awake the last few days. I might ring the bus depot and have a word with that husband of yours, see what he makes of it.' Crablike, she pushed the door open with her hip, placed both sticks in the entrance, and went inside. She turned and shook her head at Sylvia as she lifted a stick to push the door closed.

Forty-eight hours. The bottles were empty. She ate the last tin of soup from Gerrard's shopping and toasted the remaining slice of stale bread, then pulled on her Marigolds. She opened the cupboard door and closed her eyes while she pulled on the blanket, rolling Lori out and onto the floor. Lori was taller than Sylvia, but skinny, Sylvia could feel her hip bones and her shoulder blades, sharp against her hands as she pressed and pushed until she could fold her into a more compact foetal shape and although she was still a little stiff, Sylvia managed to press her into the suitcase. She bounced on the lid until the zip closed all round, lifted it upright and wheeled it into the hallway. She set the alarm for half past three, but was dressed and ready long before it buzzed. Checking there was no one around, she rolled the case out of the door and along the walkway, pausing at Mrs Cresswell's window. The walkway light behind her threw Sylvia's own shadow into the semi-darkness, but she sensed movement. She pressed her face to the glass and her eyes met the glint of her neighbour's spectacles.

The lift was still out of order and she bumped the suitcase down the steps. Seven steps. Turn. Six steps. At the car, she opened the boot lid and tried to lift the suitcase. It was too heavy. Placing one end on the lip of the boot, she raised the other end and wriggled it until it found purchase and she could turn it lengthwise and slide it into the space. It was a tight fit. She slammed the lid down hard.

Back in the kitchen, she took Mrs Cresswell's spare key from the drawer and let herself into the old lady's flat.

Later that morning, she carefully checked every room, collected her small suitcase from the bedroom, checked her passport was in her handbag, and locked the door behind her.

Queuing to board the ferry, she watched a family, two cars in front of her, walking across to the café with their children: two little girls, holding hands, the smaller one only about three or four. It came to her then, how much easier it would have been to put a child's body in the boot. She imagined Lori bouncing on the passenger seat with excitement, saying, *of course, and he'd probably know how to drug little Rosie wouldn't he, he might even have had drugs on him, so she'd have slept through the journey.*

'Unless,' Sylvia said to Lori, 'Rosie was no longer with him.' But she knew Rosie had been with him, and that they were in Ireland, for she was listening to the voice beside her, which was now sometimes Dylan and sometimes Lori, and the voices told her so. She looked away from the family and turned to Lori.

12

Checking behind her and to the right and left, she let the laptop slide out of her hands. It disappeared into the water without a sound. She'd been on a boat just once before, when she and Gerrard went to Lake Windermere for their honeymoon. Even on the silvery smooth lake, the movement had made her feel sick. Gerrard had said, 'It's all about the inner ear and your balance, keep your eyes on the horizon,' but it hadn't helped then, and it didn't help Sylvia now. The horizon wasn't even visible through the mist and when she looked over the railing, the splash of waves hitting the side of the boat made her coffee rise up her throat as if to join them. Laughter and chatter drifted to her from further along the deck. She swallowed hard, closed her eyes and breathed deeply, inhaling a mouthful of second-hand cigarette smoke from a man walking past, and retched. Hand over mouth, she turned and pushed herself off the railing and forward, her other arm stretched in front of her, aiming for the door. As she reached it, the door opened from the inside and a large man jumped to one side, allowing her to continue in a part stagger and part trot, to the nearest table, where she sat heavily.

'Are you all right?' A woman on the other side of the table leaned towards her.

Sylvia got up and walked through the boat, one hand grasping the backs of chairs, then sidling along the wall for balance. Once out of sight of the sea, she actually felt better; so much for Gerrard's gem of wisdom. She went into the duty-free shop and walked the aisles, scanning the shelves. The prices didn't compare well with the supermarket, but there was an offer on if she bought two litres. With her bag of brandy, she found a toilet and sat on the seat, listening to people coming and going, and nodded off, to be awoken by the announcement telling the drivers to make their way to the car deck. She checked herself in the mirror. As she straightened her clothes, she felt the bump in her coat pocket that was Lori's phone, and dropped the pieces into the bin. The staircase was jammed with people waiting for the car deck to open, and more people pressed down behind her. The jolting, grinding and bumping of the ship made her want to scream and push through. She stopped herself only by biting down hard on her knuckles.

It was rush hour and the traffic crawled, which suited Sylvia as she could drive slowly, watching for signs towards the city centre. She had driven over the large, ornate bridge twice, when she spotted a sign for a car park and followed it, onto a spiral ramp that took her above a shopping centre. She drove around several decks before deciding on a corner bay, with only a few cars parked nearby. She walked across to the barrier: the mist had cleared, and the late afternoon sun sparkled, drawing her attention to the broad river winding below. She could see a number of hotel signs along the far bank.

At the *plink* of a car unlocking, she turned and watched a woman in a business suit stride across from the direction of the lift to a sleek black car. She turned back, watching the view while she listened to the car purring down the ramp. There was no one else in sight. She pulled on her rubber gloves and retrieved a sandwich box from beneath the driver's seat. Taking out a cloth and a small bottle of bleach, she thoroughly wiped the seat, steering wheel, gearstick, dashboard, door handles outside, and door handles inside. She stood back, thought a moment, then leaned in and wiped the mirror, sun visor, and inside the flap to the glovebox. About to walk away, it struck her that she needed to do the same on the passenger door, and the boot handle. She closed and locked the doors with the cloth around her hand and put the cloth and her gloves back in the sandwich box. Taking her case from the back seat, she locked the car and headed for the pedestrian exit. Dropping the sandwich box in the litter bin on the ground floor, she passed through the noisy shopping mall, and crossed the road, onto the bridge, pausing to watch the water for a few seconds. When she was quite sure no one was watching her, she let the car keys slip from her fingers into the water.

The receptionist could see she was shocked by the price she quoted and suggested a smaller hotel. It was more a guesthouse really, a tall, narrow house with five floors, like the one Sylvia and Gerrard had stayed in for a weekend in London. It had been one of Gerrard's attempts to cheer her up, after Dylan. That had been near Kings Cross, though you wouldn't have known for it was a quiet little square. It also hadn't had a lift. The room was cosy, though, with its own minute bathroom, like a plastic unit that somebody had popped into the corner, so they could get an extra star and put the prices up. This guesthouse was perfect for not being noticed; except the young man on reception insisted he had to see her passport, and would she bring it down to him when she found it in her suitcase? She switched on the television, kicked off her shoes, and perched on the bed, studying the Dublin A-Z she'd bought at the newsagent's. She marked the streets she needed and turned down the pages and studied the neighbouring streets until she found the nearest primary schools and circled them with her biro. She carefully wrote the instructions in her notebook.

Sylvia had always thought of Ireland as being an extension of England, with the same sort of landscape and the weather and even the people looking the same until they spoke, and she was taken aback by the strangeness of it all. Her breakfast looked similar but not and she had to ask the waitress to repeat a question three times, then just said, 'Yes, thank you,' to get rid of her. The waitress looked at her a little oddly but went away, bringing back an old-fashioned pottery teapot which she banged down on the table. It was a sludgy, brown tea, thick enough to stand her spoon up in, and one sip glued her tongue to the roof of her mouth, but Sylvia didn't want to go through that performance again, so she made do with a glass of orange juice which was really some kind of squash, and a cup of milk. On the street, she didn't understand the voices that surrounded her. The foreignness of it all was underlined when she passed a shop with hundreds of green dolls on display.

'Leprechauns, for goodness' sake!'

Sylvia realised she'd said that aloud when two passing schoolgirls burst out laughing. She watched them walk on, realising that no one knew her. Here, she was anonymous. Then she noticed the noise of the traffic, and realised that although she'd been aware of it, it was background noise, and it didn't scare her. She put a hand on her wrist to check her pulse wasn't doing its usual racing, then held up her head, and walked quickly, with occasional glances at her street map. It was liberating, to be able to tell the bus driver that she was going to Dundrum, without worrying that he was a friend of Gerrard's. This was a part of her life Gerrard would never know about.

'Sure, that's the bus stop you need,' the driver said, pointing to the opposite pavement. 'Here it comes now.'

The only spare seat was beside an elderly man. A single tooth wobbled in his upper gum as she thought he said, 'How's it going?' and found herself smiling back.

It was a council house, quite well kept, with a neat front garden that reminded Sylvia of her own garden. The one she had been so proud of, where she had a swing set long before Dylan was old enough to sit in it. There was no sign of toys here. She must have been staring because a movement made her refocus and notice a figure at the window, staring back: a middle-aged woman with short, grey hair. Sylvia raised her hand in a little wave and opened the gate. As she approached the door, the woman at the window didn't move, reminding her of the time she and Gerrard had been so desperate for money, they had sold kitchen catalogue products door to door. She remembered the excruciating humiliation of approaching the door, not knowing whether the person would smile and invite you in or close the door in your face. Or invite you in, make a show of studying the catalogue, even offering a cup of tea, but eventually saying, 'I don't think I will, thank you, dear,' because they only wanted some company.

Even after she rang the bell, listening to it tinkle the first line of 'Molly Malone', and only when the last bell had chimed did the woman move. She opened the door and scowled down at Sylvia. Behind her, the living room was neat and clean, with nothing to suggest a child living there. Sylvia held out the teddy she'd bought as an afterthought in the shopping centre next to the bus stop.

'I don't know if I have the right house, but I'm looking for the little girl who dropped this in the street?'

'A little girl, at this house?' The woman looked up and down the street as if she might find a stray small child.

'Somebody at the bus stop' – Sylvia gestured in the general direction of the end of the street – 'said a little girl lived here, about five years old?'

'Try next door. They've got children.' The door closed.

She had to go next door otherwise it would look odd, so she waved to the woman who was now back at her window sentry post and went to the next-door gate. Happily, there was no one home and she retreated swiftly to the end of the street, around the corner and into the shopping centre.

A sign for the Irish Lottery stood outside a stationery shop and deciding it was time for some good luck, she entered the next draw and also bought a few scratch cards. It was already eleven o'clock and as she sat over a pot of tea in a café, studying the routes to the other addresses, Sylvia saw how unrealistic her original plan had been. Even her tiny room on the top floor had cost far more than she expected, which meant she could only afford two nights, and one had gone already. On the back of the menu was the telephone number for a taxi. She gave a false name, and a street a few blocks from the next house on her list.

'Here will be fine, it's the house by the corner. I'll be just a mo, my daughter lives here, and she has the money.' Sylvia slipped around the corner into the next street and walked quickly along until she spotted an alleyway which took her into the backs between two streets of houses. She waited, ten, fifteen minutes, then followed her A-Z to the primary school, checking the streets for any sign of the taxi. Parents were starting to arrive, taking children home for lunch, while the children who were staying were milling around in the play area. She walked around the boundary of the school, pleased to see there were no cameras, and came to a stop by the gate.

Someone said, 'Hello, I haven't seen you here before? Which one is yours?'

'Oh, I forgot, he's not here today, he's poorly.' She rolled her eyes. 'I babysit for his mother, she did tell me and it clean went out of my mind. Senior moment!' The woman looked young enough to assume that Sylvia was that kind of age.

After raising a young man from his bed in a dirty flat above a dry cleaning shop; managing to be outside different primary schools at lunch time, afternoon break and home time; and establishing that one young man had moved to America more than a year ago to join his brother, but his mother showed her a photograph of her dark-haired, brown-eyed son, Sylvia was back in Dundrum as darkness fell. She'd taken the bus, having figured that she shouldn't push her luck with taxi drivers. She made her way through the well-lit streets, back to the first house. The curtains hadn't been closed yet and from the pavement she could see the back of the head of a young man of the right age, seated on the sofa. Remembering the gate had a squeak, she opened it carefully, and stepped across the small grass lawn to the window. With her foot on a plant pot, she gripped the sill and put her face close to the window to get a better view of him. He stood and turned, and their eyes met.

'Mammy,' he shouted. 'There's an old woman looking through the window.'

Forgetting she was standing on a plant pot, she stepped backwards and lost her balance, wobbled and fell onto the lawn. Jumping up and running out of the gate, she heard a shout behind her and turned a corner, and another, and again, making her way back to the shopping centre by a circuitous route. She leaned against the bus stop, panting. She knew for sure. This was not her boy.

Back in her room, tired and aching, she was far from feeling disappointed; Sylvia was buoyant. Every time she had a dead end, she felt the roads to her Conor, to her green-eyed boy, became fewer, and shorter. She was getting closer. She counted her money as she ate a supermarket sandwich. None of the scratch cards yielded any cash and she barely had enough left to pay her fare home.

In reception, she checked the receptionist was a different one and unlikely to ask for her passport again, before approaching. She waited behind a French couple who were inquiring about local restaurants. As they left, she asked the receptionist about the times of the ferries. The young woman was patient, logging her on and bringing up the ferry website, showing her the times. A young man with a rucksack came in and the receptionist turned to deal with him. Sylvia watched from the corner of her eyes as the young woman checked the desk, looking for the twenty euro note the French couple had left on the tip saucer; deciding it may have blown off, she searched around the desk, then shrugged and attended to the new guest.

Sylvia clicked on the Google icon and was delighted to find she could remember how to do a map just as Lori showed her. She copied in the remaining addresses from her notebook. There was one, on the way to Dun Laoghaire. If she was snappy in the morning, probably getting to the primary school before the children started arriving, then checking the remaining house address, she could make it to the two o'clock ferry.

~

The ferry was busy. Sylvia found a seat beside the window. She tried to look away as the couple opposite tucked into pizzas and hot drinks.

'Isn't it terrible?'

The woman was talking to her.

'Mm? What's that?'

'The missing girl.'

The woman pointed behind Sylvia and she twisted around to see a large TV screen on the other side of the seating area. She gasped as she took in Lori's face.

The woman said, 'She's gone missing. Like that other student a while ago. Though she's not a student by all accounts, a bit older. Disappeared into thin air they say, a few days ago. Parents must be frantic. Have you got children?'

Sylvia stood and moved nearer to the screen. She was transported back to that day just over a year ago, when different hollow-eyed parents stared at her from the television. The voice-over was saying Lori's parents lived in Devon; she moved to Sheffield for university and decided her job options were better there, and stayed. It switched to a photo of a young man, and the voice said he was due to meet Lori and when she didn't turn up, he didn't think anything of it and didn't do anything because they weren't serious. It wasn't until Monday, when she'd promised to be in touch, and her phone was dead, that he went to the flat she shared with a friend, and she hadn't been home for two days. There was a photo of the blue Renault Clio with him hanging out of the passenger side, Lori waving from the driver's door, the voice saying they'd been friends since university. The camera switched back to Lori's parents who said, 'If anyone has seen our Lori, since she left home on Saturday morning to visit a friend...'

Feeling her elbow grabbed, she yanked her arm away.

'You forgot this.' It was the woman from the table, holding

out Sylvia's handbag.

She was hungry and exhausted from travelling all night on the ferry, sleeping on the hard chairs at Holyhead terminal and then on the first train, getting home at nine o'clock in the morning. There was a Christmas card on the mat. She recognised her mother's handwriting on the envelope and tore it in half. Beneath it, a note from Gerrard:

> *Syl, this is the second time I've been, and you're out, and I've tried phoning as well. Hope that's a good thing and you're finding plenty to do. Sad news I'm sorry to say, Mrs Cresswell has passed away. Met her daughter here yesterday when I called round. She said her mother went in her sleep, which is a blessing, I always think. She must have dropped off, still sitting at the window, in her chair, which is how we'll always remember her, watching the world go by. No news of the funeral yet. I'll pop in again tomorrow. Gx (PS Her daughter needs the spare key to hand the flat back to the council. Can you pop it through the letterbox since we won't need it again.)*

Shoving her case out of the way, she ran into the kitchen, pulled the bin from under the sink and emptied it onto the floor. On her knees, she scattered tins and scraps until, sagging against a chair, she held the pages of spidery writing between her fingers. Scanning the list of names or descriptions of every visitor to their walkway, the colour and registration numbers of cars, the identity of the owner or 'not known'; along with time in, and time out, Sylvia slapped her hand against her forehead repeatedly, cursing herself for her carelessness. In the bathroom, she ripped the pages one by one, into the smallest of pieces and flushed them down the toilet.

13

Christmas should have been easier this year, without Gerrard persistently trying to cheer her up. But he turned up on Christmas Day and announced that she was invited to his father's for lunch. She refused; politely, because she knew he was trying to help, but firmly, as she didn't want to give him any false hope. She planned to spend the day organising her newspaper cuttings into a new scrapbook; she needed to keep focused, remind herself what was really important, and find a way to get the money to go back to Ireland as soon as possible. Activity helped her thinking. At four o'clock she was in the kitchen, getting a drink, when the bell rang. It would be Gerrard. She popped the bottle in the oven and put the glass back in the cupboard. Gerrard stood at the door holding a tinfoil parcel.

She kept one hand on the door and held out the other. He walked around her, saying, 'I won't take no for an answer, Sylvia, I'm sure you've eaten nothing all day. Look at you, nothing but skin and bone these days.' He touched the radiator in the hallway. 'It's freezing in here; when did you last have the heating on?'

She followed him into the kitchen. 'If you leave it on the table, I'll warm it up later.'

Suddenly remembering, she went into the bedroom, closed the door and gathered up scrapbook, papers, scissors and glue, stacking it all in the wardrobe, swearing as the pile of newspapers slid out of the door and so she pushed them under the bed, yanking the bedspread down to the floor. As she closed the bedroom door behind her, she heard Gerrard in the bathroom. She was fairly sure she'd left nothing lying around in there but shuddered at the thought of the smells he might leave behind, and tasks she'd thought were a thing of the past.

She hovered in the hallway, between the bathroom and the front door, hoping to steer him out of the flat. He came out backwards, turned and jumped in alarm when he found her by his elbow.

'Bloody hell, Sylvia, standing there in the dark. If you can't afford to put the heating and the lights on, you only have to say, you know.'

'Thanks for bringing the dinner round, I'll heat it up later, while I'm watching...'

'I put it in the oven.' He glanced at his watch. 'It'll be ready in another ten minutes. And I wanted a word anyway. You're so hard to pin down these days, always out and never answering the telephone.'

She folded her arms. 'I've got a lot to do, Gerrard.'

'It's Christmas Day, for goodness' sake, Sylvia, how much can you have to do?' He held both hands in front of him. 'Okay, okay, I'll go, but just tell me this, Sajid says he saw you driving a couple of weeks ago?'

'He must be mistaken, you know I can't drive.'

'Not so much "can't", Sylvia, as mustn't drive. Your disqualification isn't up until you have a medical, remember?'

'Do you think I'd ever forget? And don't be ridiculous,

Gerrard, where would I get the money for a car? You saw yourself that I can barely afford to put the heating on.'

'You should have said. I can give you–'

'No,' she shouted.

He stepped back in surprise.

'I don't want your money. I've spoken to Dave and he says he's got a friend who will give me a job. I'll be starting in the new year.'

He held up his open palms. 'Well, that's great, Sylvia. I thought Sajid must be mistaken, but he was sure it was you. A little blue car, he said, stopped at the traffic lights on the Manchester Road.'

Sylvia blinked, felt the beads of sweat running along her upper lip, managed to whisper, 'Not me.' She hoped he couldn't hear the tremble in her voice. 'How can you think it would be me? Don't you trust me?'

'I needed to be sure. I'm not sure I know you these days, Sylvia, I thought things were getting better, then you're up to all sorts of odd things that you won't talk about.'

'As I said, he must have been mistaken.' She forced her legs to move towards the door. 'Now, if–'

A *whoomping* sound made them both turn towards the kitchen. Gerrard was there first, reaching for the fire blanket that had hung unused on the wall for years. He switched off the gas and opened the oven door, but the fire was already almost out. Shards of glass fell onto the floor and an overwhelming smell of brandy filled the room. He took out the dinner plate and opened the bin, paused, reached in, and lifted up a handful of scratch cards. He shook his head and dropped them back into the bin, not looking at Sylvia while he scraped the food off the plate, put the plate in the sink, and turned to leave. As she closed the door behind him, Sylvia felt a deep sense of relief.

∾

Mrs Cresswell's daughter dropped a card in, with information about the funeral. She decided to go, knowing Gerrard would make a thing of it if she didn't.

He was standing outside the crematorium and nodded, walking in with her. Apart from the two of them, there was the old lady's daughter, her husband, and their three teenagers who sat looking bad-tempered.

'She had a good innings,' the husband said into the few seconds' silence between the red curtains closing on the coffin and the music starting.

As they passed the gate of the memorial garden, Gerrard cupped her elbow and led her inside, along the path. Sylvia tried to pull away, but his grip tightened, and they stopped by a small marble stone with a glass teddy bear on top.

'Look at it,' Gerrard said, not unkindly. 'When did you last come here? No, I thought not. Come and sit down.' He kept his hand on her arm while they walked to a nearby bench. 'It might help, you know, if you came and just spent a few minutes with him every now and then. I come every week. You look surprised. Remember I asked you every week for a long time? Then I stopped. But you should try it. Really, it helps to have a place. It makes you think, doesn't it, how many years have gone by...'

Sylvia knows exactly how many years have gone by.

'... And now you've finally faced emptying out his room, well...'

'Here you are.' It was Mrs Cresswell's daughter. 'I'm off but before I go, I just want to say, thank you. I know you were a good friend to my mother.'

Sylvia's eyes were fixed on the teddy bear and she said nothing.

'Well, that's it really, just... thanks.'

As she walked away, Gerrard said, 'You might have been a bit friendlier, Syl, that was really nice of her, and it just goes to show, you're appreciated. Mrs Cresswell must have said nice things about you to her daughter. See, not everybody's out to get you.'

Sylvia jumped up and overtook the daughter on the path. She was halfway to the bus stop before Gerrard caught up with her.

'Slow down, love. I'm sorry, I just thought...'

She stopped, turned to face him and planted her feet. 'You thought what?'

'I thought it might help. That's all. I was trying to help, Sylvia. But you've got me foxed, love. I don't know what to do to get through to you.'

'You don't need to do anything, Gerrard. I don't want you to "get through" as you call it. You left, remember? I'm on my own, and thank you for your concern, but I'm doing all right.'

When she reached the corner of the road, he hadn't moved. He raised a hand. She had tried not to show him how rattled she'd been by the memorial garden. Who had put the glass teddy bear there? Had she done that, and forgotten? And the marble stone, had Gerrard arranged it? She'd felt so positive, when she'd come back from Ireland. She'd known exactly what she was doing, and why. Then Gerrard, today, seemed determined to drag her back onto the edge of the dark pit that was always at the very corner of her consciousness, inviting and enticing her to step forward, just a little further forward... She wouldn't do it. She wouldn't return to that.

On the main road, the traffic was heavy, and cars splashed past, spraying the pavement. A lorry squealed towards her, and she stood, staring, daring it. She wouldn't be afraid any longer. The horn blared angrily and the rush from the speed and the weight of it made her rock forwards, then backwards, on her heels, on the edge of the pavement. Then it was gone, and she was fine, she had survived. She would find Rosie.

At the Co-op, she queued at the counter to pay for a few groceries. There were some new designs in the scratch card cabinet and she waved a woman past her, to give her time to study the odds. A new one called 'Shamrock' had that little Irish saying on it about the wind being forever at your back. Yes, she was sure this was meant for her, it was bound to be a winner. She was irritated to see the woman she'd given way to was still there, chattering to the assistant, tapping a pile of *Sheffield Star* newspapers on the counter. Sylvia sighed noisily, hoping they would take the hint, then saw the photograph.

The woman said, 'I saw it on breakfast television. He was a Santa, working in the grotto at this shopping centre. Imagine, he arrives, and he parks his car, and there he is, getting his Santa kit out of the boot, when he hears a buzzing and he sees this car parked next to his. It's full of flies. Then he smells it. Imagine that.'

The assistant held out her hand for Sylvia's basket, and shrugged when Sylvia didn't respond. Sylvia was transfixed by the photograph.

The woman went on, 'It's that girl, the one who went missing. How'd she get to Dublin? It's that so-called boyfriend of hers, that's what I reckon, anyway the police have got him now. *Helping with their inquiries*, we all know what that means.'

'Excuse me, did you want this stuff?' the assistant called after Sylvia.

Still in her coat, Sylvia pulled the pile of newspapers from the wardrobe and selected the top one, the most recent, the *Star* article from Christmas Eve. Below the *Where is she now?* front page headline, the article reminded readers that it was over a year and the police still had no leads as to Rosie's whereabouts. They'd found the car the kidnappers used, and the caravan they'd hidden in. *The trail has gone cold* it said, as though it was a 1950s detective story. Jennifer wasn't in this photograph, but Rosie's father, Rick, was pictured standing outside their house, holding Jake by the hand. Rick's other hand was held slightly out, as if for an invisible Rosie. The little boy sucked his thumb and leaned against his father's leg, looking younger than the seven-and-a-half years old that the newspaper said he was. She wondered what would happen if she told Rick what she'd discovered. He had a car, they could be in Ireland in a matter of hours. They could look for Conor together. It would be over in no time and Rosie could be back within days, holding that hand for a press photograph.

As she turned the corner into Lacey Gardens, the door opened, and Rick came out. Sylvia stopped and took a step back, so she was half hidden by a vigorous Leylandii hedge. She watched as Jennifer came to the door and stood on the step, hugging her arms around herself. Her dressing gown was filthy; her hair hung down greasily. She looked like death warmed up. Sylvia checked her watch: it was almost teatime, going dark. Rick was carrying a black bin bag in one hand, and a sports bag in the other. He threw them into the boot and went back to the house. Jennifer pinned herself to the door to let him past. He came out, leading Jake by the hand; the boy was holding a plastic water pistol that was as tall as himself. He didn't glance at his mother but his eyes widened at Sylvia as the car passed her. His mother closed the door and Sylvia watched the house and waited until a light went on upstairs, then crossed the lawn, and peeped in. Through the smears she saw dirty plates and cups on every surface; the television on so loud in the empty room that she could hear it from here; there were no Christmas decorations.

She went home. She couldn't tell them, there was no one to tell. The photograph was a fake, pretending there was a family here, waiting for Rosie. There was no family, no home for Rosie to come back to.

14

She passed the school each morning and afternoon for several days, and the following week was outside Miriam's house when she arrived back from the school run, but there was no sign of Jake. In the Portakabin at the building site, she sat through a dinner time, listening to the men joking, talking about their Christmases and New Years. Rick didn't appear. She waited until it emptied, then went up to the counter with her mug and asked for a refill that she didn't want.

The cook, who Sylvia had heard called Florrie, tutted. 'I'm not contracted to serve after two o'clock.'

'Let me help.'

Sylvia started to clear tables, piling dirty crockery and cutlery on the counter. Florrie came round and sat heavily at the first table, keeping up an account of how she was more than ready to retire, but the firm kept asking her to come back to their next site, and to be fair, she'd known most of these men and their families all their lives and there were some tales she could tell if she was so inclined. Sylvia took off her coat and moved the dirty crockery over to the stainless-steel sink unit, piling it on the draining board.

Florrie pulled another chair towards her and lifted her legs up to rest her feet. 'You can switch on the urn if you like, we'll have that cuppa.' Sylvia flicked the switch on the urn and started the washing-up. Florrie nodded approvingly. 'I need a hand up here, as you can see, if you're looking for a bit of work. They want a big breakfast at eight o'clock, then a full dinner at one. My daughter used to help me, but she's got a new baby now...'

Sylvia brought two cups of tea over to the table, speaking as soon as there was a pause in Florrie's tide of gossip. 'They seem a nice lot though, the men who work here?'

'Could be worse. They're not a bad lot. Most of them, anyway.'

'Doesn't he work here, that man whose child was taken?'

'Oh him. Yes, he did work here.' Florrie's lip curled in a *tch* sound.

'He's left?'

'It didn't take him long, is all I'm saying.'

Sylvia tilted her head to one side and waited, not for long.

'He's only set up in business himself. With her.' Sniffing as if she can smell Sylvia's interest in her story, Florrie slurped her tea slowly, pushed the empty cup away, and while Sylvia brought her a fresh cup, carried on talking. 'Her from the office. No better than she ought to be. He announces that they're off, him to start his own building business, and her to do the office for him. But we all know he's been having it away with her most of last year. Not that you can blame him, his wife being the way she is, after... Well, a man needs his comforts, but just before Christmas I hear the lads having a go at him, and I pick up that he's moved in with her, what's her name, Tiffany or some such. Barely out of her teens. Then come New Year he's gone. And they say he took the little lad with him. She's got one of those posh waterside places, you know, the new build? Ugly things if you ask me, and liable to be flooded right there next to the river.

Last I saw of them she was all over the little lad, and I suppose he needed a bit of attention. His mother wasn't taking care of him, by all accounts. Anyway, they moved him to another school. Apparently, she's all for a new start, and he's got plenty of work coming in, he's well known. But I don't know about that little lad, he must wonder whether he's on his arse or his elbow, with all that's happened in the last year or two.' She slurped the remaining tea and put down her empty cup. Her feet met the floor with a thump and she stood. 'I must get home, I spend enough of my life in this tin can. Do you want this job or not?'

'I'll let you know.'

In the end, Sylvia hadn't needed to kowtow to Dave to get the job in his friend's corner shop. In the last week of January, she won a hundred pounds on a scratch card. Together with the hundred that Gerrard had given her the week before, and the forty she'd slipped out of Florrie's cash tin, she might have just enough with her next giro. Then she risked it all on *Rosie's Girl* in the 1420 at Cheltenham. It was as though Rosie was telling her it would win. And it did. A thousand pounds. She briefly considered visiting Florrie to slip the money back, but if Florrie had noticed it was missing, she might recognise her, and if she hadn't noticed, it would draw attention to her. She fretted for days and in the end, spent the whole forty pounds on two oleander shrubs in nice patio pots, which she sent to Florrie at the Portakabin by Interflora. It cheered her up to think of Florrie resting her feet and enjoying the flowers. She hadn't seen Gerrard since Christmas Day. It was his birthday in a few weeks, so she bought a gift card for twenty pounds at the Co-op and put it in a birthday card with a message that she was going away for a week or two, for a break.

15

As she walked out of the ferry terminal and turned towards the train station, she shook her shoulders and felt Gerrard and all that remained of that life, fall away from her. Sylvia felt as though she was coming home. The young woman at the information desk had explained the route and it worked out just as she said. As the bus drove through the city centre, she kept her eyes closed, feeling a sense of something evil like a cloud and wanting to be out of it as quickly as possible. Once the bus was on the motorway, she unfolded the original list that Lori had written and reread it. She could practically recite the addresses, but checked and rechecked it against the road map: she'd already ticked off the Dublin addresses, and tomorrow would be Waterford. From there, she would go to a small village on the road to Kilkenny, then Cork. If those addresses hadn't yielded any results, there was enough cash in her purse to travel across to Ennis and up to Galway. She sat back and spent the rest of the journey enjoying the view. In Waterford, she selected the first hotel she came to and didn't worry about the cost of it. Even though it was late, they made up a table in the hotel restaurant and served her a dinner.

The address was near the town centre and not far from the hotel. It was one of the flats above a row of shops and Sylvia couldn't see the door from road level. She showed the photograph of Rosie, and the portrait of what she would look like with short hair to the staff in the shops below. No one recognised the child. She walked around the back of the shops, through piles of cardboard and plastic bin bags awaiting collection, up the flight of rusted iron stairs and knocked on the door of number 4b. There was no reply. She was at the nearest primary school by morning break time, scouring the playground, and the next at lunchtime, and the third, a little further away, at home time. Her feet felt frozen to the ground and she shivered as she waited in the dark shadows behind the shops. A figure passed her and shortly afterwards, the light finally went on at 4b. She stepped carefully between the bags of rubbish and climbed the iron stairs. The door was yanked back, and she found herself facing a young man in a suit and tie, his hair and short beard well groomed, altogether incongruous with his surroundings.

'Is it Mr Walsh?'

He nodded.

'Conor Walsh?'

'And how may I help you?'

'It's a mistake, I'm sorry to disturb you.' She was walking away when he caught her arm.

'Not so fast now. You asked my name and now you're just walking away? What business have you with me?'

Sylvia tried to pull her arm free and his fingers pinched tighter. She clenched her teeth against the pain. 'It's a mistake, as I said. I was looking for a Conor Walsh but you don't match the description.'

She felt his grip relax slightly and pulled her arm free.

He moved across to bar her way to the steps. 'And for what, might I ask, does an English person want with this Conor Walsh who is me but not me? You wouldn't by any chance be sent by my ex-girlfriend who maintains I'm the father of her child?'

Sylvia shuffled back a step, feeling for a moment that he might be a threat to her. 'No, of course not. As I said, there must be two of you with the same name. It's – he's somebody I knew in England, but... I can see that isn't you.' He gave way when she made to push past him, and she hurried down the stairs. Unable to see the bags of rubbish with the light behind her, she tripped and fell to her knees. As she scrambled to her feet, she looked up and saw his silhouette against the light, still standing at the top of the stairs.

Back at the hotel, the receptionist called to her. 'What have you done to yourself, now, Mrs Wilton?'

Sylvia looked down and saw blood running from a cut on her hand, and her knee was grazed. She made for the lift, aware of the receptionist watching.

The bus weaved its way around little lanes, twisting through quiet villages, suddenly passing over or under the motorway that shocked with its thundering traffic. It passed a school where the shouting and laughing of the children made Sylvia's heart race. For several miles, they followed a tractor that looked as though it should be in the transport museum. When it eventually turned into a muddy gap in the hedge, the bus stopped and the tractor driver jumped down and came to lean his elbows on the open window of the bus cab. The two drivers spoke so fast that Sylvia had no idea what they were saying. She could see through the gateway, past the tractor, to a view of fields, and small, rounded hills, never higher than the smallest hill at home. With the burr of the conversation drifting to her from the cab, and the low February sun warming her through the window, she felt she could sit here forever, soaking up the peace of it all. There was a laugh and a slap on the side of the bus, the tractor driver walked away, and the bus coughed into movement again.

The driver caught her eye in the mirror. 'How's it going? Kilabran, is it? Have you family there?'

'It's a holiday.'

'Holiday is it? Well, I never heard of anybody going to Kilabran for their holiday. Not at this time of year. Sure, it's giving out for snow, didn't you know?' Barely were the words out of his mouth before the first spattering of snow hit the windscreen. 'And here it is,' he said as though he had personally arranged it to give the truth to his words.

The flakes became fatter and heavier, and seemingly within a couple of minutes the fields on either side were covered with a thin white sheet and the bus was surrounded by swirling snow.

Eventually, he said, 'Well, here we are then, Kilabran.'

They had been passing modern bungalows, with landscaped and manicured gardens. Most had a small, grey stone house in their garden, usually next to the road. Some were derelict, but a few had been converted into tiny, perfect little summer houses where Sylvia could imagine herself living, were it not for the hulking great red-brick, or white-rendered dormer bungalow with double garage and sweeping gravel drive, that overshadowed it. They passed an enormous church, its cemetery extending into the fields beyond. The driver turned into a narrow street, with houses on either side, and stopped.

He looked at Sylvia through the mirror. 'Now then. There's just the one guest house in Kilabran, and am I right in thinking that's where you'll be staying?'

The receptionist at the hotel in Waterford had called ahead

and booked her in. She wiped the glass with her arm and saw a small '*Tourism Ireland*' sticker above the name plate, '*Ballybrack House*'.

'Well, here y'are then.' He pipped the horn and a woman appeared at the door. Though well into her sixties, she was slim, wearing a sweatband around her silver hair, a purple tracksuit and trainers, as though she was about to run a half marathon.

The driver stuck his head out of the window. 'Are you expecting a lady from Waterford, Niamh?'

'I certainly am, Patrick.'

'You're looking well, Niamh. How's the family?'

She was at his window. 'Very well, all things considered.'

He turned to Sylvia as she was lifting her case off the rack. 'She's a fine woman, is Niamh, sure you'll be well looked after here. Have yourself a grand holiday.'

'Thank you, you've been very kind, I really appreciate it.'

'Fine woman yourself.' He waved cheerily and pulled away.

Niamh gestured Sylvia into the hallway and took her coat. She held it out of the door and shook the snow off. 'Will it be just the two nights?'

'If I decide to stay longer, would that be all right?'

'Right you are, I expect you're thinking you might get snowed in for a while, if this weather continues? Now, I have no other guests at the moment, so you'll not be disturbed. Though I always say I run a quiet house anyway. So, supper-wise, there's the one pub in the village and they do a very nice meal, but if you prefer, being a woman on your own, I do an option of evening meal and I can bring it up to your room.'

'That would be very nice, thank you.'

'Well, let's call it full board then, which will be thirty euros a night? Good, that's settled. In that case, you go on and unpack, it's that room on the right, there at the top of the stairs, and I'll be warming you up some soup.' She grasped Sylvia's hands in her own. 'Sure, your hands are freezing. Go on and make your-self comfortable.'

⁓

Her tiny room was papered with Anaglypta, sticky to the touch from the many coats of magnolia paint. Chintzy curtains clashed with the coverlet which Sylvia lifted to find real blankets on her single bed, and an electric blanket, although her feet and fingers were tingling as they absorbed the warmth of the house. A small armless chair at the window overlooked the street. The fireplace looked useable although it had a pot of dried flowers in it. There was a smell of wind-dried linen. She opened the one door and found a wardrobe. There was no bathroom.

Sylvia was hanging her clothes in the wardrobe when there was a knock at the door. Niamh came in with a tray. She nodded towards the chair and commanded, 'Sit,' and when Sylvia did so, put the tray on the little table and swivelled the top round. Sylvia felt like an invalid, but it was not a bad feeling, being fussed over.

All the time, Niamh talked. 'Here's a little parsnip soup and some nice bread that I made this morning when they phoned me from Waterford as I thought you were bound to be peckish after that journey with Patrick, he's a good driver but somewhat bumpy, so he is. And you look as though you could manage a piece of chocolate cake which I have to admit I got from the corner shop where Mrs Grady has the best baking in the village, which she gets from a lady up the lane who is blessed with cool fingers. There you go, then.' She stood back, her arms folded, waiting for Sylvia to start eating.

Sylvia was struggling with the contradiction between the woman who dressed as though she was about to go to the gym for a workout, and one who had spent her morning cooking in anticipation of a hungry guest. She lifted her spoon and waited, but still Niamh was hanging around the door.

'So, what brings you to these parts then?'

'I thought I might do a little walking.'

'Walking, in this weather? Patrick said you were from Waterford but you're from England, by the sound of it. You'll have come on the ferry to Wexford then?'

'Dun Laoghaire.'

'Is that right, now? So, you've come to Dun Laoghaire, then to Waterford, and then here. Bit of a round trip then? Have you family here? See, we get a lot of people coming over from America, the U S of A as they call it, looking for their ancestry.' She did the little quote marks around the word with her fingers. 'Oh, yes, they're very keen on their ancestry, the Americans, and you'll have seen no doubt that Waterford is all over the famine, making money hand over fist...' She continued talking through her own questions, which Sylvia realised meant she didn't actually have to answer. She sipped the soup and tried to nod appreciatively. 'Aye, it's a good soup, my mother's recipe, God rest her soul.' She crossed herself and rolled her eyes skyward, taking the opportunity to scan the room and catching sight of Sylvia's partly unpacked suitcase.

'If you don't mind me saying, you don't look well prepared for a walking holiday. We're expecting more of this snow, and these fields might look very tempting, but I can assure you with just a bit of snow, you could lose your way in an instant. We do get walking visitors in the summer, oh yes, lots of them, and even with a compass and all the kit, as soon as the mist comes down, they lose all sense of direction.'

'I don't expect I'll be walking far and mostly on the roads.'

'And you have no family to visit around here? Well, I hope you find enough to do in our little village. Now then, I do have a pair of wellingtons and some thick socks you can borrow, should fit you fine. You'll find them in the back porch, just help yourself.' She looked at her watch. 'Will you look at the time and me standing here yattering. I'll be late for my Pilates class at the church hall. Do you do Pilates?' Sylvia shook her head. 'Well, it's a pity you're not here for longer, or you could come along. Now then, you make yourself at home and I'll see you later.'

'Excuse me,' Sylvia called as Niamh turned. 'The bathroom?'

Niamh pointed along the landing. 'The door next to the stairs. Sometimes it can be a bit of a waiting game, when we have a house full. With only you and me, I expect we'll get along fine.'

Sylvia took the tray of dishes downstairs and found the kitchen, pleased to see it was neat and tidy. She put on the trainers she'd bought from the department store in Waterford and set off to walk around the village. The snow had stopped, leaving a light covering on the roads. There seemed to be only three streets, and within ten minutes she was standing outside the primary school listening to the buzzing of children inside, reminding her of watching a beehive on television.

She found the shop with 'Grady' over the door and bought an Irish lottery entry, and scratch cards with the change from a ten-euro note.

'You'll be the lady who's staying at Niamh's place? Would you be visiting family? No? Funny time of year to be having a holiday?'

'I just needed to get away. You know how it is.'

Mrs Grady nodded. 'I certainly do.' She raised her eyebrows and waited, looking expectantly at Sylvia, and Sylvia wondered if she'd failed to hear something. She let out a long breath as if annoyed. 'Ah well, if there's nothing else you'll be needing today?'

'Thank you.' Sylvia put the scratch cards in her pocket and left.

The village, so quiet when she set out, now seemed to be full of vehicles, turning what had been a clean, white carpet over road and pavement to a grey slush. Land Rovers seemed to be the thing, from tatty old vehicles belching diesel smoke, to flashy new models with bull bars. Vehicles were parked on both sides of the road leading to the school, and a large white car with tinted windows was pulling onto the yellow zigzag marking outside the school gate. Sylvia passed the school and stopped at the corner, from where she could see the gate, and the cars would have to drive past her, without drawing attention to herself. The children came out in a rush. She craned her neck to see among the heads. The sight of a blonde, curly head stopped her breath and as she stepped towards it, brakes squealed, and tyres skidded. Oblivious, she ran in front of the car to the other pavement, stopping short in front of a little boy with shoulder length curls. A small red car, snow and mud obscuring the sides and the back windows, came towards her. Her eyes met those of the driver. Fleetingly, for barely a second. At the end of the street, the brake lights came on, then he was gone.

Her knees felt weak, and her whole body trembled. She hadn't seen a child in the car. It may have been a passing vehicle and nothing to do with the school. Of course, a child wouldn't be in the front of a car, and the back windows had been covered in snow. Apart from the little boy, she was sure she hadn't seen the head of a child that could have been Rosie among the children. But the eyes... Dizzy, she leaned against the wall until all the cars had gone, then made her way back to her room.

Niamh was at her door with the tray at six o'clock. She now had a cardigan over the purple tracksuit bottoms and had lost the sweatband so her permed hair fell about her face, giving her much more the look of an elderly grandmother.

'It's a traditional Irish hotpot, and I'll bring you tea in about half an hour.' She looked around and spotted the scratch cards on the dressing table. 'I see you like a little flutter? I'm not averse myself. Never won anything worth having, mind you. Now, Patrick, who you met of course, the bus driver, well his brother's first wife won fifteen thousand euros on one of those what-do-you-call-it instants? And she never told him, no, she disappeared and wrote to him from England, just a postcard that said she wasn't coming back, and he only found out from the newsagent when he next went in there, that she'd had the winning ticket. What do you think of that? And I gather you met our local news service? Oh, she's all right is Mrs Grady, only likes a bit too much of the – you know' – she mimed drinking – 'since her husband died, so she only lives for the gossip, but she's got a heart of gold.' She realised Sylvia was waiting to eat and put her hand over her mouth. 'Oh, will you listen to me, going on, and you waiting to eat, you must be starving. I'll bring that pot of tea–'

Despite the Imovane, Sylvia lay awake. When she closed her eyes, Rosie's face mingled with Dylan's and she sat up suddenly, her heartbeat racing and her hands clammy. Maybe she dropped off eventually, for she became aware of sounds of pots from the kitchen below and could make out all the details of the little room from the grey light filtering through the curtains. On the landing, the smell of frying drifted up the stairs. She came out of the bathroom to find a tray on her table with a full fried breakfast. The nausea rose in her throat and she emptied it into a carrier bag which she folded and stuffed into her handbag. At half past eight, she slipped silently down the stairs, pulled on her trainers and closed the door behind her. She walked to the school. It was deserted. She walked the block, and back again. The main gate remained closed and locked. Outside Grady's shop, she put her carrier bag in the litter bin and went in, holding out the scratch card that had yielded a five-euro instant prize.

'Well, look at you, bringing some luck with you.' Taking a note from the till she held it out, only so far, so Sylvia had to lean across the counter to reach it, as though the money belonged to Mrs Grady personally.

'I'll have two more of those scratch cards, please, and one lottery draw.'

'Well, good luck to you. Now then, how are you settling in at Niamh's place?'

'It's lovely. It's very quiet in the village today, no school?'

'Ah, no, I heard on the wireless that the schools are closed as they're expecting more snow today. And with it being half-term next week, it's an excuse for the teachers to have an extra holiday if you ask me.'

'Half-term?'

'So it is. Now then, will there be anything else today?'

'Would you happen to have a map of the area? Showing the footpaths?'

'Well, I would, but I'll have put it away, the walking season being over until the summer.' She waited, and when Sylvia didn't move, added, 'But, well, maybe if you wait there, I'll be able to find one.' She disappeared into the back and reappeared within seconds with a box.

Leaving the village streets behind, Sylvia found herself walking ankle deep in slush that was slippery beneath the fresh snow. She wished she'd borrowed the wellingtons offered by Niamh, but going back for them now would waste time. Her feet were squelching. At the junction, she checked her route map and took the right-hand turn. The winding lane became narrower, but she was reassured by the sight of faint car tracks and then, after a hundred or so yards, saw the entrance to the farmyard. The gate was padlocked. A mailbox had been fashioned out of a small barrel. The name, Walsh, was neatly painted above the rectangular hole. There was no sign of movement in the yard, but she could hear the soft bleating of sheep, not far away. The red car was between her and the house. She placed one foot on the bottom bar of the gate, and pulled herself up.

'What do you think you're doing?'

Her foot slipped off the wet bar and she lay winded, her upper body resting on the top of the gate. She saw the child first. White, short, straight hair framed the face she had carried in her mind, through all her waking and sleeping hours for the past fourteen months. The man stood behind the child, his hands on her shoulders as he turned her round and steered her through the doorway. He leaned in and his arm reached for something, then he walked towards her. Sylvia was facing a double-barrelled shotgun. As his green eyes met hers, the yellow flecks sparked and ignited with fear.

CONOR

2006-2007

1

_____

I have to tell you. You have to understand. I was on my way home. I had the plan, I had the ticket and I was on my way to Holyhead, for the ferry. I was desperate to get out of the place. England hadn't worked out. It had been a colossal fecking disaster in fact. Oh yes, I was heading home. Then he was there. Dean. I came out of the gate, and there he was, leaning against a car, with a fag hanging off his gob, grinning like a loon. He'd been released a couple of weeks before me. He said his nana had blown him out, so he'd be going down to London. I never expected to see him again.

Lads had told me they felt such muppets, with nobody meeting them at the gate, having to do the walk across the car park, with all the dealers waiting to give them a lift and relieve them of their discharge grant. I was wondering how I could get past and on to the train station. So it was a relief, really, to have somebody meet me. And Dean had been good to me inside. He'd done a few sentences and he knew the system. It was all new to me. He stood up for me. And we had a bit of the craic, so we did, sharing a cell. When I see him, I'm thinking, maybe we'll go out on the lash. And he'll be bound to have a bag on him. I'd gone on the methadone after he was released because I couldn't get any smack. So there was a bit of a pull and a push going on, and all this was going through my head while I walked towards him and in the end I reckoned, if he'd give me a lift to the station, I'd pay him for the bag, then that'd be it.

That's how I ended up, in the car with Dean. I wound the window down and let the air just blast through me. It cleared my head from the stink of the Big House. He took me out to this place, it was fecking unreal, like a landslide where the road had slid down this hill and it was like something out of *Mad Max*, you know what I mean? You do? It felt like when the world has ended after the big bomb. It was helped, of course, by the funny flour he brought with him, and we shared a needle, and we did have a bit of the craic like old times and sure, it got to be fecking hilarious. We slept for a bit. Then he says he's set a job up, to get some proper money. It's a petrol station, and he knows what time there'll be nobody about, except for this woman who works on her own at night, and there'd be all the day's takings right there in the till. He's been and taken out the cameras in the small hours. I don't know about any of that, I'm still thinking I can get a train and be at Holyhead for the night ferry. I say this to him. He fixes me in the eye and he says, 'How you going to pay me back then, Conor?'

'Pay you back for what?'

'Did you think it was free, all the smack inside? When I came out, I owed people. Now you come out, you owe me.'

Of course, he's right. It's a blur then, but honest, I don't know he's got the gun until right there at the counter, when he pulls it out. And I'm shaking cos I'm coming down and I haven't eaten anything since the prison breakfast and then we're running across to the car and I've barely got my legs in the door when the car speeds forward, and there's the screaming of the engine and the squealing of the tyres and somewhere thinking back I guess there's some screeching going on from the child and her mother, but it's all so fecking mental. I get thrown across the back seat, on top of the kid. Dean straightens the car, and I manage to wriggle into sitting up, with my arm holding onto the kid. When I look over my shoulder, through the back window, I see the bloke who's chased us out of the shop. He's dropping back but he's still running, up the middle of the street, with the other kid in his arms. Dean corners fast and when I sit up and look again, the bloke's gone. Then the windows are steamed up inside and running with rain outside and I can't make anything out of the blur of lights and cars and people. The kid's trampling on me and she puts her foot right on my prick, pressing it into the seat, and it takes my breath away. I pull her foot off me and she stamps on my leg and kicks me in the belly and climbs up me to lean over the back of the seat. Her hand's banging on the back window, and she's shouting, I think she's shouting Daddy, and maybe something like Dakey.

Dean says, 'Keep her away from the fucking window.'

She's wearing some kind of slippery plastic coat and she's slithering in and out of my grip. I get a handful of the coat and pull her down and press her into the gap behind the driver's seat.

I say, 'Dean, pull over. I'll put her on the pavement, she'll get found.'

He says, 'Yeah, like nobody'll notice a little kid being left on the street and the fucking car driving off. Just keep her out of sight.'

'There's a camera. Shouldn't we slow down?'

'Yeah, like we're worried about getting a fucking speeding ticket in the post.'

The kid's head bobs up and she starts yelling for Daddy, Mummy, and this Dakey word. I go to push her back down, and she twists round and bites my hand; I lift my hand to my mouth to suck it, and she's up again and banging on the side window.

Dean yells, 'Get the little bastard down, now.'

As I grab her coat, it comes loose, and her arm whips out of the sleeve and knocks Dean's cap over his eyes. The car swerves across the road and back again. Headlights shine right in my eyes and I'm blinded. I hear the tyres swishing on the wet road and realise the door is opening and she's sliding away. I yank her back and the door comes with her. I force her fingers off the handle, and she swings her arm round and grabs a lump of my face, her fingernails dig in right under my eye. Dean gets the car straight and he's swearing, and she's screaming. I hold her down on the seat with one hand while I put my other hand up to my face, feel the blood.

'Jesus, she's scratched me, I'm bleeding.'

Dean says, 'Ah, diddums.'

'It fecking hurts. And my prick, she stood on it.'

'Well, y'are a prick. Can't control a fucking kid.'

'Dean, pull over, let's put her out.'

'No chance, she's got your blood under her fingernails and they'll trace you.'

She stops screaming and starts panting, like she's run out of breath.

'What are we going to do, Dean?'

'We'll go to the coast,' he says. 'I know a place. Me nana took me, she had a caravan.'

You see, Dean was brought up by his nana after his mammy ran off. He was in the house for days without any food, when his nana found him. We had some long talks, like you do, all those nights after lock-up. He wasn't bothered about seeing his mammy again, he doesn't remember her. But when he got that letter from his nana, saying she wouldn't visit him in prison and she wouldn't have anything to do with him when he got out either, until he could prove he'd got his act together, he lost it then. And I knew, he did care about his mammy leaving him because he said he'd find her and kill her.

I'm thinking all this through, wondering how I got myself into this fecking mess, on the run with a kid, and probably all the police in Yorkshire after us. We stop at the traffic lights next to a petrol station. She must think we've come back to the same place because she slips out from under my arm and presses her face against the window and starts banging on it, shouting for this Dakey, and crying.

Dean yells, 'Shut her the fuck up.'

She stops yelling and stares at the back of his head with her mouth open. Then her face kind of crumples and she starts this waah-ing noise, getting louder. Dean bangs the steering wheel. That's when I come up with the game. I tell her we're hiding; like, it's a joke on her mummy and daddy, they're looking for us, and the longer we hide the more sweeties she'll get. She stares at me, and I smile and say, 'Sure, it is, it's a game, go on.' She crouches down in the space between the front and back seats and lets me put my coat over her. Then her head bobs up.

'I want my crisps.'

'What crisps?'

'My crisps fell on the floor.'

I remember.

'Dean, stop and get some crisps for her.'

'Fuck off.' He revs the engine and the car jumps forward. Every few seconds, her head pops up and she asks if they're here, and I make something up and tell her to get down. We pass a chip shop. With all this talk about crisps, I'm hungry enough to eat the twelve apostles.

I says to Dean, 'Let's get some chips.'

Her head bobs up. Dean grumbles, then he says he needs to buy some fags anyway, and he parks in a side street. As he gets out, he holds the gun out to me, through the gap between the seats.

He says, 'Hold onto that, and if she gives you any trouble, use it.'

I put my feet on the kid to keep her down and study the gun. I'd thought it was a revolver, but the barrel is rough, like it's been filed, maybe, and there's a bit on the back where something has been cut off. Dean comes back with two trays of chips and some cola. He puts his tray on his lap and eats as he drives. I make her stay on the floor and pass the chips to her one by one, blowing on them until they cool down. I pass her the cola.

She pushes it away. 'I'm not allowed that.'

'Well, that's all there is.'

She drinks it. She keeps on with the questions:

'Are we there yet?' 'Will Dakey be there?' 'Where's Dakey now?' 'How will he find me?'

I keep on with the nonsense about this game. After the street lamps end and it's coal black outside of the beam from the head lamps, I think she falls asleep. I have no idea where we are, or where we're going, but Dean knows these roads, and I know not to ask too many questions. He was a good mate, for sure, but he had a quick temper and he didn't like to be *mithered*, as he called it.

It seems like hours but then he stops the car and switches off the lights. I open the door and get out. We're in a little car park. It's cold, but it's not raining anymore. She won't get out of the car, so I tell her this Dakey is waiting and she comes quick then, and we follow Dean, along a footpath between some trees, and he steps over a low, wooden fence and I lift her over, and wriggle underneath some thorny bushes. I can't see a hand in front of my face, so I say, 'Where are you, kid?'

'Rosie, it's Rosie.'

'All right, Rosie, come on.'

She's right behind me and when I step back, she squeals.

Dean's breath is in my face and he hisses, 'Stop pratting around and shut the fuck up.'

My eyes are getting used to the dark, and now it's stopped raining, there's a bit of a moon. In front of us is a row of caravans, those big ones, like mobile homes, all with dark windows. We follow Dean to one in the corner, with hedges on two sides. He tries the door, then takes a screwdriver out of his pocket and prises it open. Like he told me once, he always goes equipped.

It's like climbing into a fridge, it was more freezing than outside.

'It's out of season,' Dean says. 'Nobody'll come here for months. So long as we don't use the lights, we'll be all right.'

He lights up two fags, with his hand round the lighter, and passes me one. When I inhale, the end lights up, and I can see the shapes of a table, chairs, and two sofas. I start to pull a curtain closed.

Dean says, 'If you do that, they'll notice when they do the security check.'

She says, 'I can't see. Switch the light on.'

She's climbed onto the sofa and is feeling along the wall for the light switch. Dean grabs her hand and pulls her onto the floor. She lands in a sitting position. She takes one of those long, shaky breaths that kids do, then starts wailing.

'Be careful, you'll hurt her.'

'Keep her out of my fucking way then. And shut her the fuck up.'

He drops onto one of the sofas and I pull the girl to her feet and take her to the other side of the room where I can make out the shape of a table. I see Dean shine the light from his mobile phone onto a bag, and put his hand into his pocket, and he pulls out a piece of foil that catches the light.

'Where's Dakey? I want to go to the toilet.'

I try a few doors until I find it. I stand outside the door. Dean laughs from the sofa.

'Soft get. You'll make a good dad if somebody can't get away fast enough.'

Back in the living space, she stands in the middle of the room, sniffing and wiping her nose up her sleeve. There's a faint glow from a security light, outside.

'Dakey.'

Dean says, 'Shut her the fuck up and give me the gun.'

I take it out of my pocket and hold it out to him. He takes it in both hands, points it at the girl.

'What's that man doing?'

'I'm going to fucking shoot you, kid, that's what.'

See, that woman, chasing us across the forecourt, the blast, her falling into the petrol pump, sliding down. It had been like something else, something not real, like looking at a film. I'd never seen a gun at close quarters before. But when Dean points the gun at the girl and makes shooting noises, it feels like he'll do it, for the hell of it. I lift the kid up, sit her on the seat, well away from him, and sit down between them, with my hand out.

'Show it to us.'

He passes it to me.

'Taurus LBR revolver,' he says.

'What's happened here?' I point to the rough edge of the barrel.

'It was bought legal. They come with a twelve-inch barrel, and at the back, here, there's a wrist support. Imagine what a prat you'd look, holding up a bank with that, they'd think it was a toy gun.'

'So they shorten it? Does it still work?'

He laughs. 'It stopped her in her tracks, didn't it?'

'Have you used it? Before today?'

'Bit of practice, with Jase.'

He takes it back, polishes it with his sleeve.

'Jase? Is that who you got it from?'

Jase had been the tattoo artist on our wing.

Dean says, 'We need to get up to Hull. Pay him.' He nods towards the carrier bag. 'We can get a different car, do another petrol station, or a post office, get up to Hull, pay Jase off with the rest, get some more ammo.'

He says ammo like he's a gangster, in an old movie. I don't like the way he holds it, rubbing his finger along the barrel, his eyes gleaming. He waves it at the girl.

'One word out of you–'

He puts the gun on the shelf above the window and takes a crisp packet out of his pocket. The girl's bottom lip trembles. I think she's going to cry again. I get hold of her hand and pull her up.

'Come on, let's go and see what's in the other rooms.'

We go into a small bedroom with two narrow beds, worse than any cell I'd seen. She looks around at the shapes that we can see from the little outside light.

'Is Dakey in here?'

'He's gone home, he couldn't find you, he'll come back in the morning.' I know I'm talking rubbish, but it's the first thing that comes into my head, just trying to keep her quiet.

'No, he hasn't. He won't go home without me. He'll be looking for me.'

Before I can stop her, she's running back into the main room, yelling, 'Daaaykey.' I see the shape of Dean coming towards her with his arm raised and I move between them and lift her up, move her out of his way.

I say, 'Let's have a look see if we can find any games.'

I'm surprised when she goes for this.

'Then will Dakey come?'

'Who is Dakey?'

'Not Dakey, stupid. Dake. Dake is my brother.'

I keep her talking and she tells me about her brother, this Dake, her mummy and daddy, and how she's just started going to school, and on and on. I can tell Dean is wound up by her chattering, but at least it stops her screaming. A clock on the side says quarter past three when he stands up and says he has to go out, get rid of the car, before it gets light. While he's gone, I use my lighter in short bursts to get my bearings. I take her round the caravan with me, making it part of the game. We find quilts in the bedrooms and she lets me wrap her in one. Then I tell her the story of Finn McCool the giant, that I remembered from my own mammy.

She says, 'Tell me again,' just like I used to with my mammy. 'Tell me again.' And she says, 'Will you tell Dakey that story when he gets here?'

Four times I have to tell it. At some point she falls asleep. I take one of the quilts into the living area and lay down on a sofa. It's coming light when Dean gets back, stinking of petrol.

He says, 'I had to walk fucking miles.'

I've been thinking how I can get out of this and on to the ferry. I'm not bothered about the money, I'll leave him with that. But every time, it comes back to the girl. I know I can't leave her with him. I need to get her somewhere she can find her way home or somebody can find her without finding us. Dean takes two cans of beer out of his pockets and drops one on my lap.

He says, 'I need to get the taste of petrol out of my mouth.' He takes the crisp packet from his pocket and from it he takes a bag and a syringe.

It's good. Everything starts to slow down. I hold my hand up and it's stopped shaking for the first time since...

He says, 'Together again, eh?'

The warmth moves through me, and I'm heavy, dropping into somewhere glowing, where I know it's going to be good. It's too good to miss, one last blast with Dean, then we'll get rid of the girl, leave her somewhere she'll be found after we're long gone, then that'll be it, I'll be on my way home. I'll phone Mammy and I'll be coming home.

2

────────

The screaming cuts through the cotton wool in my head. The sun is shining in my eyes, and as I sit up it feels as if a flaming sword is splitting my head open. I put my hands over my eyes and when I move them, the shape of Dean has blocked out the sun. He's holding something wriggling that he throws onto me and I see it's the kid.

He says, 'I'll fucking kill you.'

I think he means me. The kid gets up onto her knees and scuttles behind my back. I'm slow and groggy.

'What the feck is going on?'

'I want my mummy. Muuuummmy.' I twist round, grab her, put my hand across her mouth, tell her to shut up.

He says, 'She was almost out of the door, that's what. She'll have us nicked.'

'She's only a kid, she can't do much.'

'She's fucking Satan is what she is.'

Now he's moved, I can see that Dean's eyes are crazy, blood-shot and wide. What else was he on last night? I take my hand off her mouth. She keeps her lips closed and starts this low-level grizzling sound that cuts right into my brain. I roll off the sofa, stand up, pull the duvet round my shoulders, feel a bit dizzy, sit down again. I look around. It's a smart place. Nice furniture. My guts are twisting and my mouth is dry.

'Is there anything to eat?'

'I'm not your fucking mother. Have a look.'

With the duvet wrapped around me, I stand up carefully and when I'm sure I won't fall over, I go across to the kitchen and look in the cupboards. There's a stack of tins. Some long-life milk. The kid stays curled in the corner, her thumb in her mouth, eyes wide, looking from Dean to me. I pour the milk into a cup and hold it out to her. She takes it, drinks some. Her face squashes up and she spits a mouthful of milk onto the duvet. Dean kicks out at her and she pulls her legs back further into the corner. I open a tin of rice pudding and take it over to her, hold some out on a spoon. She presses her lips together and shakes her head. I eat what's on the spoon, dip the spoon in again and press it against her lips. She stops shaking and opens her mouth, tastes it, takes the spoon and starts eating it. Dean sits at the table. I hold out a tin of beans to him and he holds up a palm to push it away. He starts cutting smack with the coke left from yesterday.

She says, 'Is my mummy going to come now?'

'Yes, soon.' To Dean, I say, 'What are we going to do?'

'I don't fucking know, why don't you try coming up with a few ideas, Conor, for a change?'

He's right. I've been waiting for him to come up with all the answers. Like inside, where he was the one who got his girl-friend to bring the smack inside balloons tucked into her mouth, that she passed to him while they were snogging. I'd only done skunk before then, but they do these random drug tests, and you lose privileges if you test positive. Everybody knows cannabis stays in your system for at least a week, but smack goes through you much quicker. That's how I got hooked.

Even thinking about Dean, crouched over the toilet in the corner, straining and pushing it out, didn't put me off; that's how bad it gets inside.

'What the feck–' I drop the duvet, run across to the kid, yank the crisp packet out of her fingers, open it.

'How many bombs were there left?'

'If that little bastard's been at my smack–'

He knocks me out of the way, grabs her jumper at the front and lifts her into the air.

'Have you got something in your mouth? Come on, open it.'

He pushes the fingers of his other hand into her mouth. She gags. I pull at his arm.

'Fecksake, you're choking her.'

He throws her onto the floor and she shunts backwards until she hits the table, where she curls up.

'Get her out of my sight. Put her in there.'

He nods towards the bedrooms. He opens the crisp packet, looks inside, laughs.

'It'll sort one problem out, if she has taken it.'

She makes herself as tiny as she can, pushing her feet against the carpet to press herself back into the corner, covering her face. I pick her up. As I carry her past him, he drops his trousers, getting ready to inject. We open a cupboard in the little bedroom, and find some kids' stuff, books and games. There's a ludo game and I show her how to play.

'Again, again,' she says, as soon as we finish a game. 'When Dakey comes, can he play the ludo?'

'Yes.'

'When is Dake coming?'

'He's your little brother?'

'Noooo. He's bigger than me.'

'Will you keep quiet, if we go into the other room?'

She nods. Dean is asleep on a sofa. I move his paraphernalia to one side and we sit at the table, using the ludo counters to play tiddlywinks.

'I want a Fruit Shoot.'

'What's that, then?'

'It's a Fruit Shoot, silly.'

'Let's go and see what we can find, in the cupboards.'

She recognises the spaghetti hoops which I tell her we'll have for dinner, later. There isn't anything to drink, and she turns her nose up at water.

'I want a cup of tea.'

'I can't make tea, there's no electricity.'

'There's a kettle, there.'

'But no electricity.'

'What's lectris?'

'You need it to switch the kettle on. Just sit there, now, while I go to the toilet.'

When I come out of the toilet she's peeking over the side of the sofa, crying, but not loud, more a low grizzle. She wipes her face with her sleeve and snot spreads into her hair. Dean is fiddling with the net curtains.

'What happened?'

'She was looking out of the fucking window, I thought I told you to keep an eye on her.'

He holds the bag out to me. I shake my head, hold my hand out to the kid and she takes it. She's wet herself. I take her into the bathroom.

'Let's get you cleaned up and see if we can find some clothes.'

'You can't come in with me.'

'I need to help you get washed.'

'I can do it myself. Mummy lets me do it myself.'

The water is freezing cold. I wet the flannel under the tap and then the water stops. I go into the kitchen and turn the tap on. A few drips come out. Back in the bathroom, she's not moved. I hand her the wet flannel.

'Here, take your clothes off and have a wash. Can you do that?'

'Course. But that's too cold.'

'It's all we've got.'

'We've got hot water at home.'

'Well, we haven't got any here.'

'This is like camping. Mummy boils a kettle when we go camping. To get hot water.'

'We don't have a kettle.'

'Yes, you do. I saw it.'

'What I mean is, we don't have any electricity to boil the kettle.'

She stares at me as though I'm an idiot.

'You get washed and I'll look for some clothes.'

In the room with two narrow beds, there's a cupboard with kids' clothes. All boys. I find her a pair of jeans, underpants, socks, and a jumper.

'Are you finished yet?'

'I want some clean knickers.'

I open the door a crack and pass her a pair of underpants.

'These are boys. I'm not wearing boys. Are these for Dake?'

'Your mummy is bringing you some clothes later. Just put those on for now.'

'Is Dake coming later as well? Are the clothes for him?'

'Yes. Put these clothes on now.'

I hand her the jeans and the sweatshirt. When she comes out, she's obviously tried to wipe her face with the flannel, and she's changed her clothes. Her hair is tangled and I can't find a comb. When I come back from the bedroom I realise that if I cut it off, she'll look altogether like a boy and it'll be safer to take her out and leave her somewhere. The kitchen scissors are in a drawer. She sits on a stool in the kitchen but as soon as she realises what I'm going to do she squeals and wriggles off.

'Shut the fuck up,' Dean says from under the duvet.

I pick her up and put her back on the stool. 'You've got to have your hair cut. It's the game.'

'Grandma says I've got hair like an angel. I don't want it cut.'

'It'll grow again. It's a disguise. Like the boys' clothes.'

'Have I got to pretend I'm a boy?'

'That's right.'

I hold up the scissors and she slides off the stool, runs into the bedroom, and slams the door.

'Fucksake.' Dean's voice is muffled.

Her voice comes through the door.

'You're lying, Mummy didn't say to cut my hair. Grandma will be cross. I'm going to tell her.'

'All right then, I won't cut your hair. Come here and put these jeans on.'

She peeps around the door and I hold up the scissors to show her I'm putting them back in the drawer.

'I want to watch telly.'

'We can't. There isn't any electricity.'

'Don't be silly. There's a button.'

She picks up the remote from the table and presses the button. When nothing happens, she presses another, then smacks the remote against the table and the batteries jump out and land on the other side of Dean. Before I can stop her, she's climbing over him to get it. He opens one eye and swings a fist, connecting with her cheek. She falls back, stunned for a moment, then her face crumples. I lift her up and carry her into the little bedroom. Tears are running down her face.

'Would you like some more rice pudding?'

She shakes her head.

'Will we play some games?'

She shakes her head. Her cheek is swelling and there's a patch of red from her mouth to her eye. Snot is smeared across her face. I wipe her face with a corner of the sheet and she grabs my jacket with both hands and puts her face into my neck, sobbing. I rub her back and sing something silly that comes from somewhere deep down in my memory, and, when the crying slows up, I sit her on my knee and tell her the story of the giants again. Gradually, her breathing returns to normal.

'Are you hungry?'

She nods.

'Let's go and find those spaghetti hoops, shall we?'

She holds my hand. As we walk around Dean, she avoids his legs which stick out from under the duvet into the middle of the room. In the kitchen area, I open the tin and hold it out to her, with a spoon. She takes a spoonful then spits it out. She holds up a jelly, and I explain I can't make it without electricity. Her lip wobbles, and she looks on the verge of crying, but just then, she hears Dean's voice, and drops onto the floor between the fridge and the cooker, with her hands over her face as if that makes her invisible.

He says, 'Going to town to score.'

He pulls a handful of notes out of the carrier bag.

'How far's town?'

'Skegness? A couple of miles.'

'Will you get us some milk and a loaf of bread?'

'Anything else?'

'Well, maybe butter, and–'

'Who the fuck d'you think I am, your bastard wife?'

He's shaking his head as he goes out of the door. I watch him through the window. He disappears around the side of the caravan, and reappears by the hedge, wriggling underneath on his belly. The clock on the wall isn't even at one yet. What's happening out there? Are they looking for us? Of course, they will be, the world is probably going mad trying to find the girl. But will they know it's me? How long should we stay here? How long can I keep this going? How could I get her back to her mammy? That must have been her mammy, slumped against the petrol pump...

'Take me to the swings.'

'There are no swings.'

'There are. Look.'

I follow her pointing finger and she's right, we can see the edge of a swing set a few caravans along. She's poked her head under the net curtain and has her face pressed against the window. Shit. I grab her behind and pull her onto the floor. She screams. I put the packet of Oreos that she found in the cupboard, and must have dropped, back into her hand.

'I want to go to the swings.'

'All right, all right.'

I think for a minute.

'See that hedge?'

'Yes.'

'Well, the other side of it, I think might be the sea.'

'The sea? Want to go to the sea.'

She jumps up and down.

'Right you are, if you're good. You've got to be very, very quiet, keep away from the window, and then we'll maybe go to the sea.'

'Now. Want to go to the sea now.'

I'm sure that if we go out, get some fresh air, she'll calm down, maybe even go to sleep and I can get a bit of a break, think straight, work out a plan. Her coat has gone with the car, so she agrees to put on a boy's coat that we find in the wardrobe in the little bedroom. I tie her hair back with an elastic band from one of the kitchen drawers and pull the hood up. There is a scarf, and gloves. I thought she had wellington boots but they seem to have got lost somewhere. I try the different trainers on her and find a pair that isn't too big. We creep out of the door, and stick close to the van as we go around the corner, then run across to the hedge. I show her how to wriggle underneath.

'I know,' she says, giving me that 'you're stupid' look. 'We did this before.'

I can hear the sea now. There is just one car in the car park. A kind of boardwalk leads between the dunes, and there it is, a long way out, dull and brown. She doesn't care. She runs towards it, her arms out, screaming. Someone is walking a dog along the beach. He glances at us, then carries on. She has the trainers off and is paddling before I catch up with her.

'Jesus, you'll catch your death, you can't go paddling.'

'Yes, I can. Look, I'm paddling, so I can. Mummy lets me paddle.'

'Okay, just for a minute though.'

She picks up a handful of shells.

'Not that one, see it still has the crab in it.'

'Can I take it home?'

'No, we have to leave it here, where it can find its way back to the sea.'

'Why can't I take it home?'

'Look, here's a nice shell.'

'I want the crab. Dakey found a crab and Daddy let him take it home. I want it.'

'Okay now, let's pop it in my pocket and we'll put it in water when we get back to the caravan.'

The man with the dog has turned and is coming towards us. I realise what a stupid thing I'm doing. I pick up her trainers and grab her hand.

'Come on, we need to get a move on.'

'Is Daddy coming? Will he be there when we get back?'

'He might be.'

'Let's go back then.'

The man with the dog is about twenty yards from us. I pull her along while she slips, in her bare feet, on the deep sand. As we leave the beach, I look back and he's stopped, watching us. The one car is still in the car park. I check there is nobody about and we wriggle back under the fence. As we get to the van, the door is yanked out of my hand and Dean stands over us.

'Where the fuck have you been?'

'It's all right, nobody saw us.'

'Nobody?'

'Just one bloke on the beach, but he was too far away.'

'You stupid, bastard Irish fuckwit.'

The girl is crouched by the door, her hands over her head. Dean runs around the room, looking out of the windows.

'She's going to have to go.'

'Sure, I'll take her down the town tonight, when it's dark, and leave her somewhere.'

'You fuckwit, it'd take them about ten minutes to find us.'

He reaches up to the shelf above the windows, pulls down the gun.

'What you planning to do with that?'

He kicks her feet.

'Come here. I said, come here. Sit down there.'

He lifts her up by the front of her coat and drops her on the sofa. He picks up a cushion, pushes it over her head. She pushes the cushion away, looks at him, then to me. He wraps the gun into the cushion and holds it to her head.

'Jesus, Dean, don't.'

'We can't keep her with us. We can't travel with her. We can't leave her anywhere. We've got to get rid of her.'

He's going to do it, I swear he is. I throw myself onto his back, and he isn't expecting it, so he falls onto his knees, his elbows on the sofa, and drops the gun. I grab it, get to my feet and point it at him.

He says, 'Don't be a fucking moron, you won't get far without me telling you what to do. Fucking robbery, kidnap, murder. How long d'you think it'll be before you get lifed up?'

He grabs the barrel of the gun and twists it in my hand until it's pointing at the kid. She's wrapped herself into a ball, her eyes peeping over her knees.

He says, 'Go on, press it.'

I let go. He laughs, turns the gun around and points it at her, taking a step towards her, picking up the cushion again. I lunge at him, ramming my head into his side, sending him flying. The gun falls onto the floor. We both reach for it. I elbow him in the face and pick up the gun, lashing out at him as I scramble onto my knees. He falls back. Blood is pouring out of his nose and his mouth. He gets to his feet, staggering, shaking his head, the blood spattering across the carpet. He roars as he lurches towards me. I press the trigger. He jumps into the air, backwards, landing half on, half off the sofa.

There's complete silence. I take a step forward. My foot slips and I fall against him. Pulling myself onto my knees, I'm looking at his eye. Wide-open, surprised, staring at me. Just the one eye.

3

Her white face is spattered with red and grey. Her eyes follow me around the room, like that picture of Jesus that mammy has hanging in the parlour. I find a packet of wet wipes in the bathroom cupboard and wipe my face, using more and more of the tissues as they come away stained pink. I open another packet and use all of them to clean her face. She doesn't move. There is no way I can clean her hair, tangled as it is with pieces of gristle. Her eyes widen when I take the scissors from the drawer, but she doesn't resist as I lift her onto one of the stools. My hands are shaking and I can't cut straight, so it gets shorter and shorter until she has a crew cut of about half an inch all over, and there are some bald bits. I strip her clothes off, and my own, drop them in a pile on the floor. I take her hand. It slides out of mine. I pick her up and carry her into the double bedroom, pop her on the bed. Her eyes still follow me, watching me sort through the clothes in the wardrobe. Whoever stays here is bigger than me and older, judging by the style of the trousers. They are quality though. There's a good shirt, and a jacket. A baseball cap.

When I pick her up, her little body is like a block of ice and her teeth are literally chattering. I wrap the quilt around her and take her into the little bedroom where I sort out more of the boys' clothes and find a Puffa jacket. She's like a rag doll while I dress her. I tell her to stay there and in the living room, I walk around Dean, still lying half on, half off the sofa, but I've covered him up with the quilt. I empty the carrier bag onto the table. About eighteen hundred quid. I separate the notes into smaller bundles and divide it between my pockets, sliding some into the back of my pants.

Back in the bedroom I sort spare clothes for both of us and put them into a holdall that is under the bed. She hasn't moved. The light has pretty much gone now, except for a pale orange glow from the direction of the sea, and Dean's shape has almost disappeared. I wipe the grey spots off the Oreos with my dirty shirt from the pile and put the packet in my pocket. I drain a tin of new potatoes, and open a tin of beans, and take these with the half-empty milk carton back to the bedroom. She hasn't moved. She won't eat or drink anything. We sit there while it goes completely dark. I wrap the quilt around both of us. Not a sound. At some point, I hear her snuffling, and I think her little body is shaking, but it's difficult to tell which of us is trembling more.

When I next look at her, she is quiet, breathing normally, and it's getting light outside. My brain feels clearer. By my watch, it's nearly seven o'clock. I slide out from under the quilt and go into the living area. There are some rubber gloves under the sink. I get a pile of tea towels, and a bleach spray from the bathroom, and rub down everywhere, even places I don't think I touched. I clean the kitchen, the living area, and the bathroom, and by the time I get to the bedroom, she is awake, lying still, watching me, just her eyes above the covers. The revolver is under the table, and I rub it clean and push it into the carrier bag that Dean used for the money, along with the towels, the flannel, and everything else I used, even the half-eaten tins. I check there is nobody around and still with the rubber gloves on, open the door, putting the holdall and the bag of rubbish outside. When I tell her to come along, she slides off the bed and stands in the corner while I strip off the sheet and the duvet cover and wrap them into a bundle, and check around, then she follows me without a word. I stand between her and the shape of Dean until she is out of the door. I zip up her little Puffa jacket, close the door behind us, put the rubber gloves into the rubbish bag and pick it up along with the holdall and the bundle of bedding.

She knows how to wriggle under the hedge. I don't know which way is Skegness, but there's a big dipper ride in the distance, so I reckon we are on the right track. The beach is deserted. All the way along, I keep up a chatter, trying to be normal, talking about the sea, promising her candy floss, toffee apple, all the things I used to like about going to the beach. Her face stays blank and silent and her eyes are enormous, under her spiky hair.

When we reach the town, I put the carrier bag into a litter bin on the pavement, and the bedding in another one, further along. Her little ears are pink and I'm about to go into a shop to buy her a hat when I see the headline on the heap of newspapers on the counter and keep walking. There's a little park and I tell her to sit on a bench. I watch a while from the gate. She's tiny, sitting on her hands, looking straight ahead. People walk past but only one or two glance at her and no one stops. Everyone is buttoned up and focused. I stare at each one, willing somebody to notice the child, alone.

As if the thinking creates the person, a man walks past me, into the park. He's wearing a suit and tie but it's shabby, his shoes were smart once but now they look down at heel, his hair's a comb-over. I watch him circle the little rose garden. He's seen the child. He's looking around, then starts to walk towards her. Something about him makes me panic. He's almost at her bench when I overtake him and hold out my hand. She takes it, and we walk out of the opposite gate, onto the street behind the promenade. To the left is a sign for the train station, and I go towards it. The display says the next train will be in an hour and will take us to Nottingham. The café is open. When I ask her what she wants, she doesn't reply. I order her a hot chocolate, get a coffee for myself and a burger for each of us. The server smiles at her, and back at me. I pull my baseball cap down further and turn to the side where her face is staring out from a row of newspapers on the rack. I tug her out of the door, holding the takeaway bag and the holdall in one hand, and keep walking fast. In a few minutes, we are by the sea, and sit in a shelter. I unpack the bag and tell her we're having a picnic as she stares at me over her hot chocolate. It leaves a foamy smile across her face which gives me the creeps and I lean towards her to wipe it. She flinches. A group of people with Irish wolfhounds are gathering on the beach. I think about leaving her here, just walking away, how long would it be, before she was noticed by them? How quickly could I get out of town? No chance, they'd close the roads for sure.

'Come on,' I say, as soon as she's finished.

We're walking along the street, back past the little park, and I see a bus that says Lincoln on the front. I wave at him and he pulls up.

'You're lucky mate, we're not supposed to stop away from bus stops.'

'Thanks. You going to Lincoln?'

'If that's what it says on the front, that's where I'm going. Single or return?'

'Single.'

'A very good decision, sir. That'll be four pounds fifty. Don't you have anything less?'

He counts out the change for my twenty, we go upstairs and sit on the front seat. There's a heater belting out onto our feet and I start to get warm for what seems like the first time in days. I think she must feel it too, because she falls asleep against me. Every time the bus stops, I watch who is around, getting on, getting off. Nobody sits near us. The roads are straight and wide, which makes me think about the winding country lanes at home. After an hour or so, a big church or maybe a cathedral comes into view in the distance. The bus stops for the traffic lights, and that's when I see a car on the verge with a *For Sale* sign. I nudge her awake and ring the bell.

It's the kind of car a granny would drive, and in fact, while I'm looking around it, an old lady comes out of the house and shouts from the doorstep.

'It's got an MOT and it's a good little runner.'

We go up to the door.

She says, 'It was my late husband's. It's been in the garage for a couple of years, so I thought, somebody might make use of it. Hello, what's your name then?'

'How much will you take for it?'

'A thousand pounds, like it says on the notice. What's he done to his face?'

'Fell over. You know what kids are like. Five hundred?'

She looks at me for a long moment. Then at the kid, and back at me.

'You don't come from round here.'

'We've moved into the area, so I need a car.'

'This is your little boy? Or your brother?'

'Seven fifty?'

'You'd better try it first. Hang on, I'll get the keys.'

She disappears into the house, then her head comes round the door again.

'Would your little boy like a drink?'

'We're in a bit of a hurry actually.'

I count the seconds. Ten. I wonder how fast we could do a runner. Twenty. We're halfway up the path when she calls. I take the ring of keys from her and open the car. The kid climbs in the back door and I strap her in. The engine starts first time and I reverse it off the verge, into the driveway. I could just drive away, but she's right there, and she'd have the police onto me in no time. I walk around the car once more, to make it seem that I'm thinking about it.

'Looks fine to me. Seven fifty then? Cash?'

She nods, watches me closely while I count out some notes from my back pocket, then some more from my zipped jacket pocket. She rolls the money into her hand.

'Sure you won't have a drink? It's perishing out there. Your little boy would like a biscuit, I expect? Doesn't he have a hat? Look at his little ears.'

'No thanks, we'll be on our way.'

'Just hold on a minute, I've got something.'

With one foot on the doorstep and one just inside the door, I listen for voices or sounds that she is on the telephone. Thirty seconds. I'm in the driving seat with the car in first gear when I see her in the mirror, waving a folder.

'You'll find all the documents in here. You've to get insurance, you know. And here's something for the little boy.'

'Thanks.'

She passes me the folder through the window and as I'm about to drive off she opens the back door. She hands a banana to the girl. Then she closes the door and waves and I drive off, towards those spires I can see in the distance. I don't know any of the towns on the signs, but when one road goes towards the city centre, I take the other. At the next roundabout we pass a sign for Sheffield to the right, city centre to the left, so I go straight on. The petrol gauge is flashing and I pull in to a garage and draw up to the pump. Her eyes are wide as she watches me through the window. In the shop, I buy loads of stuff – milkshakes, pasties, crisps, sandwiches, sausage rolls. Next to the till is a display of road atlases and I pick one. I keep my eyes on the car as I queue to pay. She hasn't moved.

'Have you got a points card, love?'

'What?'

'A points card?'

I shake my head and count out three twenties.

'Would you like one?'

'One what?'

She's waving a form at me.

'A points card. You can save up points and get money off your shopping. Or your holidays if you use our travel agent.'

'No.'

She points to a pile of chocolate bars on the counter.

'Can I interest you in any chocolate today? A pound each.'

'No. Feck this, can I just pay?'

'Only asking. That'll be twenty-seven pounds thirty.'

I grab my change and drop it, bend down to pick it up and trip over the feet of the fella behind. Apologising, I scoop up the things that have fallen out of the bag and concentrate on walking, not running, to the car. I put the bag beside her on the back seat and open it so she can see inside, though she doesn't even look.

'See if there's anything you want in there.'

I drop the keys into the footwell and scrabble around to find them, and it seems like a whole minute before I get the right one into the ignition and start the car. My leg is jumping with the nerves and I press the accelerator too hard and the guy who was behind me in the shop is about to cross in front and he leaps back and glares at me. I pull the baseball cap down and then we are out and onto the dual carriageway, trying to go slow enough whatever the limit is, but not too slow to draw attention, all the time looking in the mirror for blue lights and sirens. We are coming into a place called Newark before I stop shaking. I can't stop to study the map, so when I see a sign for London I take it. Every now and then I drop the rear mirror and the girl's eyes meet mine.

After an hour or so, there's a sign for Luton airport and I have a brainwave. I could leave her in the terminal and take a flight and be home by dark.

I park the car in the multi-storey and take her into departures where I study the board and sure enough, there's an EasyJet to Dublin and another one to Belfast. I sit her on a bench, and go up to the customer service desk.

'Yes, sir, there's a seat on the four thirty to Dublin.'

I thought of Mammy and there was nowhere I would rather have been.

'I'll have that.'

'Can I see your passport, sir?'

My fecking passport is at Daryl's place in Leeds.

'I need a passport to travel to Ireland?'

'Airline regulations, sir. If you're an EU citizen with a photo-ID card, that would be acceptable?'

'What about the Belfast flight? Surely, I don't need a passport for a domestic flight?'

'I'm afraid so, sir.'

I look for the girl. She is exactly where I left her.

'Ah, forget it.'

I walk around the departure hall, go to the gents, come back out; she still hasn't moved. Her face is a blank as her eyes follow the people, her thumb in her mouth. I could be well away before they realise she's been abandoned. I'm at the main door when a burly fella in a high-vis jacket grabs my arm.

'Excuse me, sir.'

My breath stops in my throat and I try to pull myself free, but he has me firmly by the arm.

'Only trying to help, sir.'

He is pointing behind me. The girl is pushing her way through the people, towards us. She reaches us, wraps both arms around my leg, doesn't say a thing.

'Saw you come in, see. Easy to lose a little chap like this, in these crowds.'

'Sorry, I couldn't – didn't see her, I was panicking...'

He smiles, pats her on the head. I lift her up, head for the car park, strap her into the back seat and sit behind the wheel, trying to get my breath. Our eyes meet and hold in the mirror. It was a stupid idea. There's probably cameras everywhere, and my fingerprints are all over the car. I look away first, picking up the road atlas from the passenger seat, and studying it. Along here is the M1 and straight up there is Leeds.

4

When I first came to England, I got a job in a bar in Leeds. The money was good. I spent it as fast as I earned it, so I was never any better off, but me and the lads who worked there, we had a good craic. I met Daryl in a club and he told me about the hotel he worked at, where I could train as a chef, which is what I wanted. I'd only been there a few months when I got the sack. Then there was the walking around all day, looking for another job. The room went with the job and who'd take on a dole-ite?

I slept on Daryl's sofa. His girlfriend wasn't too pleased, she wanted me out or paying rent. Daryl still worked in the hotel and I reckon she thought I was a bad influence. She couldn't have been more wrong. I lost my job because the hotel manager did a search and found works in my locker. Not mine. I didn't use, not then. No, I was much further down the road before I used drugs. I was clean, those days. Daryl must have got wind of the search and put them in my locker.

Anyhow, I lost my job and he owed me. When she threw me out, Daryl said he had a mate I could stay with. Lee was on the dole and although I still went looking for work, every day, all they had to do was phone the hotel and as soon as they heard I was dismissed for drugs, they weren't about to employ me. I started to sit around with Lee, watching the telly, and the days melted into one long session of smoking, drinking beer and eating pizza. With no address of my own, I couldn't get benefits, so Lee was subbing me. When he asked me to help him on a job, I knew I owed him. I could have gone back home, course I could, but I hadn't been in touch since everything had gone wrong, for the shame of it. When I left, years before, I'd told Pa in no uncertain terms that there was more to life than the farm, and I wasn't about to go eating humble pie, not then.

I reckon Daryl still owes me, and he might help me. I have money now, I can pay digs, keep my head down for a bit, decide how best to leave the kid somewhere. There's a bit of worry nagging away in the back of my mind, knowing how lively she was, and now she just sits there, watching me with that silence all around her. It's a bit creepy, but at least it means I can drive, and think. When I get hungry, I remember the food on the back seat, so I pull in at the services and park right at the back of the lorry park, where I think there won't be any cameras. When I climb into the back of the car with her she wriggles herself right into the corner.

'I won't hurt you.'

I open a bag of crisps and offer it to her. She eats as though she's starving. She drinks most of a carton of juice.

'Do you want the toilet?'

She nods. I can't risk going into the building, so I hold her while she squats down beside the open door. We set off again, and after a few more miles I see a sign to leave the motorway for Sheffield. I hadn't realised that's where we were, and it starts me shaking again. Then we are past. It's raining, and the swishing of the rain and the rocking of the windscreen wipers risks sending me to sleep, so I turn the radio on, pressing the knobs without looking. 'Naughty Girl' is playing and I hear a noise from behind. In the mirror I see her moving her arms and legs in time to Beyoncé singing. But not a sound comes out of her mouth.

The news comes on. 'South Yorkshire Police say there is no progress in the search for four-year-old Rosie Endleby, who was kidnapped three days ago during a robbery in Sheffield. At a press conference today, Rosie's parents and older brother, Jake–' In the mirror she's stopped moving and looks puzzled. I switch the radio off.

It's full dark and she's fast asleep when I pull up outside Daryl's house. I wait until I see him going in, wait a bit longer, and ring the bell.

He stares at me like he's seen a ghost, looks back into the house over his shoulder.

'You're looking well, Daryl.'

He comes out onto the step, pulling the door nearly closed behind him.

'Just been to Ayia Napa.'

'Where's that when it's at home?'

'Cyprus. What do you want, Conor?'

'Can I stay for a bit? I can pay you.'

'Fuck off, Conor.'

'Have you got my stuff then?'

'What stuff?'

'My big holdall with my phone and my clothes?'

'What makes you think I've got it?'

'Lee's mam said she'd bring it round here, for you to look after, when we got sentenced.'

'Don't know anything about that.'

'That's all my stuff.'

A woman's voice comes from behind him. 'Who is it, Daryl?'

'Look, Conor, I've got a job, it's cool, me and her – we're good – she knows about you and Lee going to prison, and she won't have you here.' He steps back into the house, holds the edge of the door, ready to close it.

'But you know who's to blame for all that, don't you, Daryl?'

'All what?'

'Don't play the innocent. If you'd not set me up and lost me the job in the first place, then not let me stay here–'

'I put you on to Lee, didn't I?'

'Aye, and a mess that turned out, didn't it?'

'Not my fault, Conor, you fucked up all by yourself.'

'What about Lee, is he out?'

'He got into some bother in the nick, got extra time, I think he's out next week. Is that your car?'

I nod.

'Who's that with you?' He points to the outline of the girl, sitting in the back seat.

'It's a friend's car. That's his kid.'

'Sounds as though you're all right then? For somewhere to stay?'

'I'm going to – to London. I'm not stopping around here. Thought I might go to London, head for Germany, get a bar job.'

'Sounds like a plan. Well–' The door is closing. I put my hand out and stop it.

'Daryl?' The woman's voice again.

I can hear cooking noises. Bastard won't even invite me in for a meal.

He calls over his shoulder, 'There in a minute.'

Her voice comes back, 'Who is it?'

'Nobody. About a – a parcel for somebody.' He turns back to me. 'Fuck off, Conor, she'll be here in a minute.'

'Lend us your passport.'

'What?'

'Your passport.'

'I haven't got–'

'You've just been on holiday, I know you've got a passport. I'll send it back to you, just need it for a day or two. Come on, you owe me.'

He glares at me, glances over his shoulder.

'Just a minute.'

He tries to close the door but I have my foot in the gap. He shrugs and goes into the house. I count, wondering if I can trust him, or if I should clear off. Then his hand comes round the door, I grab his passport and run back to the car. I check the map and we're soon on the M62.

I find a music station on the radio and when the rain stops and I can see the shapes of the hills and a sky full of stars, all round me, that's when it starts. Really deep down in my belly, I get this feeling that it's going to be all right. Better than that. It's going to be fecking fantastic. I pull into a lay-by, turn the lights off, get out and walk away from the car and stand, taking it in. Pa said to me one day that wherever I would be in the whole world, there would be Orion's Belt, there would be the Plough, the North Star. There was no getting away from it. Everything would stay the same. It would always be there. He was right. Only me, I would have to change. Walking back to the car, I'm surprised by the outline of the kid's hand, spread across the back window. She's looking for me. She wants me. And that's maybe a first, to think somebody needs me. I know what to do.

'Okay, kid, we're going home. We're going to see your nanny and grandpa.'

5

_____

At Holyhead, I drive around till I find an open-all-hours, buy a bottle of whisky, one of those mobile phones like your granny would get with the big buttons, a SIM card, and a packet of Nytol. They've got these little cuddly toys, shiny things in all colours, in a basket by the door, and I choose one at random. The next ferry is at half past two in the morning. I drive out of town, park in a lay-by. God forgive me, I make her drink that whisky in the rest of her juice, even though she gags; I tell her the pills are sweeties, and sit her on my lap until she falls fast asleep, then I lay her in the boot, wrapped in a picnic blanket that is there. I close her hand around the little multi-coloured dog.

I phone home. Anne Marie answers.

'No, you can't speak to Mammy, she's got enough on her plate.'

I hear Mammy's voice in the background, coming nearer. Then she has the phone.

'Who is that? Is it Conor?'

'Hello, Mammy.'

'Conor, where have you been? We've been trying all sorts to find you. Oh, Conor–'

'What's the matter, Mammy?'

'It's your father, he–'

Her voice breaks and her hand squeaks on the receiver. Then Anne Marie's voice comes back on.

'We've been trying to find you for weeks. Where have you been? Our father's dead–'

'What?'

'That's right, Daddy's passed away and you need to get home and help Mammy run the farm.'

'Daddy – what? What happened, was it an accident?'

'No, Conor, it was a long time coming, while we didn't know where you were. Now, are you coming home?'

'I'm on my way. Tell Mammy I'm coming. I'll be with you tomorrow.'

'Mammy, he says he'll be home tomorrow. Conor, you've missed the funeral, you know that?'

'No, I, I'm-I'm sorry. Tell Mammy I'm sorry.'

'Well, then–'

'And I'm bringing somebody with me.'

'Who? Who're you bringing with you?'

'My daughter.'

'Your daughter? Mammy, he's got a little girl.'

6

The sun is shining and I feel the warmth of it on me as I get out of the car and stand in the farmyard. The cold and the rain and the misery are all in another world where I've been lost, and this is my real life. A new start. Here am I, just off the ferry, come home with my daughter. I lift her out of the back, where she's been quiet as a mouse all the way from Dun Laoghaire, sucking on the ears of that funny little multicoloured dog she's been gripping all the way. Mammy comes to the door and stands, drying her hands on her apron. She looks much older than I remember, but when she sees the kid, she smiles and comes over to us.

'Will you look at the wee dote? What's that on his coat? I thought you said it was a daughter you were bringing.'

'It is, Mammy. She's been a bit travel sick.'

'Bless the child. What's your name? Bring her in, Conor, and we'll get her cleaned up. What's that mark on her face? And who on earth has given her that haircut? Has she been at it herself with the scissors? What's that in her mouth, a little dog?' She tries to pull the toy off her and the kid's face crumples up.

'All right then, you suck your doggy, but look, its ears are all soggy now. And where's

her mammy, Conor?'

Over the biggest breakfast I've seen in years, I tell her how the kid's mammy had gone off, disappeared, how I found the child, on her own in the flat, with no food for who knows how long. It's easy, remembering Dean's story and claiming it for my own. As she goes in and out of the kitchen, her hands always full of more food and tea, and another loaf of her soda bread, Mammy questions me non-stop.

'And is she yours, Conor?'

'She is, Mammy.'

'You're sure, now? This girl, her mammy, then, you and her got together straight after you went to England?'

'That'd be about right, Mammy.'

'How come then that you never mentioned her – what's her name now? – when you phoned home?'

'Well, it wasn't long, Mammy. It was just a few weeks.'

'And she ended up with the little one, here? Well, I hope that's a lesson to you, Conor, to take more care. There's nothing wrong with a proper courtship, and waiting, so that children are born within the sanctity of marriage with the blessing of the Virgin.'

'I know, Mammy.'

'And you've no idea where this girl, or woman I suppose, where she is, now?'

I shake my head.

'And she's been badly treated by the look of her. Well, let's make the best of it. She is a little dote and she'll brighten up our lives here, that's for sure. But will you look at that terrible hair-cut? Sure, you can see her scalp just there. Do you think she had an infestation?'

'It'll grow back.'

'Sure it will. Now then, she's not eaten a thing and she looks as though she's half asleep. Come on, let's get you cleaned up. Now, did you bring her clothes with her. Just that little bag? But will you look, these are boy's clothes. After dinner, we'll get down to town and pick up a few things. Is that your car? So, you've not been doing badly for yourself, then, Conor?'

'Not at all, Mammy. I've saved a bit and if it's okay with you, I'll stay and help you on the farm.'

'That would be grand, Conor. Your room is just the same, and we'll get a bed fixed up for – now, what is her name?'

'I'm sorry, Mammy, not to have been here, when... to have missed the funeral and everything.'

'Ah, well, you're here now, and you've been doing all right even if you haven't been in touch, and if you're going to stay and look after things here, that's as much as your Pa could ever have wanted. He was so sorry, you know, about your arguing. He was saddened when you went off like that.'

'Me too, Mammy. I'm glad to be back. I miss him though.'

Mammy takes the child's hand, slides her off her seat and leads her towards the bathroom at the back of the house.

'Well, we have a new life here, now, haven't we? And you still haven't told me what she's called?'

'Roisin, her name's Roisin. Some call her Rosie.'

The kid turns and looks me dead in the eye.

'Ah, we'll not be having any of those English names here. Sure, Roisin is a fine name. And does she ever say a word?'

'She hasn't spoken since...'

I'm reaching for the teapot but knock it and tea splashes from the spout onto the tablecloth.

'Aye, it'll be the shock of it all. What are you doing there, Conor, will you look at him, Roisin, the clumsy galoot has spilled the tea.'

She leaves the kid in the doorway and fusses about with a

tea towel. I stand, feel a bit dizzy and hold onto the edge of the table. She turns back to the kid.

'Now then, Roisin, will we get you out of those dirty clothes and washed and I think we might crochet you a little hat later today, which will be fine until the hair grows back.'

Walking across to the window, I find I can barely stand, and I practically fall onto the settee.

'Tell the truth, Mammy, I'm feeling a bit the worse for wear. If it's okay with you, I'll stay here with Roisin while you pop into town.'

'Of course, of course, you'll be tired from the travelling. Well, now, I'll stay here with you, and Roisin can help me to get a little bed made up in my room. I'll phone Anne Marie and ask her to pick up a few things and...'

7

_____

Mammy tells me later that I was out of it for a few days. I find her sitting by my bed.

'You've had a good dose of the flu. I called the doctor and he said you likely had the hepatitis. He looked at your arms, and Conor, what have you been doing?'

I tell her the part of it, but only part. I promise I'm finished with all that.

'There certainly won't be any more of it, Conor, you're a father now, you have responsibilities.'

I'd forgotten. I look around, and there she is, stuck to Mammy's skirt like a little limpet. The ear of the little toy is still in her mouth.

'Aye, she's doing grand, so she is, though she won't let that toy alone. Soggy Doggy, we're calling it, aren't we? Your sister's been and got her a few clothes, and books and such like, and she's settling down.'

I sit up then.

'Anne Marie?'

'She'll be down to see you soon as I tell her you're up and about.'

I close my eyes. Anne Marie is the last person I want to see. The last time I saw my sister was the day before I left for England, and we swapped words that have shamed me, ever since. I needn't worry though. When she comes, my sister is bowled over by the kid. I sit, wrapped in one of Mammy's knitted blankets in the armchair by the kitchen range, and watch her showing Roisin games and puzzles that she's picked up in town.

'She's a bright little thing, isn't she? Sure, we'll have you talking in no time, so we will, and what's the betting, we'll soon be wishing you'd stop?'

Mammy places a dish of cakes on the table.

'It won't be long, Anne Marie, before you've got little ones of your own. Come on now, you've not told your brother your news.'

Anne Marie looks annoyed.

'He should have been here, not messing about in England, and he would have known.'

'What is it?'

'Your sister got married, what is it, now, eighteen months ago?'

Anne Marie nods, still glaring at me. I can't feel too enthusiastic but try to keep the heat down.

'Well, congratulations. Niall, is it?'

8

It's remarkable, how fast I come to believe my own story. It's as though there is no other story, just the one about working on the farm, being looked after by Mammy and being a father to Roisin. It feels good. I'm not interested in going down the town on a Saturday, even though my old pals get in touch every now and again and ask me to. Mammy tries to persuade me to go, says there's no harm in a bit of craic. But I worry that if I let Roisin or Mammy out of my sight, it will all disappear, and I'll find myself back in that place, where I go to still, in my nightmares, cold, scared and running. I think although she says I should get myself a social life, Mammy is glad I don't want to leave the farm. She dotes on Roisin and lives in fear of me moving away with her. Roisin follows Mammy everywhere as she moves about the farm, milks the goats, feeds the chickens. She loves the animals, and we make a thing of giving her a kid goat that is born shortly after we arrive. If ever we can't find her, there she'll be, in the shed, feeding it with the little bottle, and once or twice I think I catch the sound of her singing to the thing. Her hair grows back straight, with not a sign of the curls that I vaguely remember, and almost white where it had been what I think they call strawberry blonde. But still there is not a word from her.

∼

It's maybe six months later, just after Easter, when the Gardaí come around. I see their car at the gate – for we have a heavy padlock as I've told Mammy I worry about the security of the farm – and it's like a dream breaking, falling into shards about my feet as I walk towards them. A dream that started breaking the Sunday before, when Mammy went to church and brought back the newspaper from the village. It isn't real, that memory of the caravan. It's as though it happened to somebody else, and I read the page, thinking how upset those people must have been to find a dead body like that, then I tear it out and tuck it under the lining of one of my drawers.

'Dean Burton. Do you know him?'

I shake my head.

'You shared a cell with him in Doncaster Prison, last year.'

There's no sign of Mammy. She must have gone indoors, with Roisin.

'I kind of remember, it's a while ago.'

'You weren't good pals?'

I shake my head again.

'Sorry, I can't really bring him to mind. I know I shared with a guy called Dean. Does he say he's a friend of mine?'

They exchange a look.

'He's dead.'

I cross myself.

'Jesus, I'm sorry to hear that. Was it the drugs? I remember he was terrible with the heroin.'

'What about you, Conor? Do you take drugs?'

'I dabbled a bit, when I was in the prison. You know how it is.

It's hard not to, when it's going round so much, and it makes the time pass. Tell you what, was that the Dean you're talking about? Him that got me onto the heroin that time?'

The younger one looks at his notes.

'You came back to Ireland when, Conor?'

'The day I came out of Doncaster. It was a bad time for me. The local Gardaí will tell you, I've never been in trouble, and it was when I lost my job and had no money and I was persuaded to – well, I'm ashamed of it, that's the truth.'

The older one says, 'It's true. I've known this family all my life. There was never a bad word said against him before he went to England, or since he came back.'

The younger one says, 'So, you don't know this Dean Burton, don't know anything about a robbery the day you were released from Doncaster Prison?'

'No. I'd have been on the train – they give you a travel warrant, you can check with the prison, they'll tell you – and then on the ferry.'

'The prison says you didn't use the travel warrant, Conor.'

'Ah, they may be right, come to think of it. I was so ashamed, I knew people would know where I'd been if I used the prison warrant. No, you're right, I paid out of the money I had, the discharge grant.'

The younger one says, 'Righty-ho,' and makes a note in his book.

The older one says, 'You're not looking too well, young Walsh, trembling, and sweating.'

'Aye, I've been laid up with the flu and it seems to be going on for weeks.'

'Well, you look after yourself.'

As they walk back across the yard to their Land Rover, I hear a squeak above my head and look up, thinking that might be Mammy's hand I see, closing the bedroom window.

A few weeks later, Mammy gets up early and has me take her to the bank in Kilkenny and wait outside. She comes out with a fat envelope that she puts in her bag. She tells me to drop her at the bus stop for the Dublin bus, and to meet her here again that night. After supper, when Roisin is in bed, she takes a paper out of her handbag and slaps it on the table in front of me. It's a birth certificate.

'How'd you do that?'

'Ask no questions, I'll tell you no lies. It had to be done. Mind the child's got a birthday coming up in July. I've made it the same day as your Daddy so we've no trouble remembering. She'll be five, which means she'll be starting the village school in September.'

It's later in the summer when Seamus Lewis visits, to put down the old mare. It's got to the point we spend more in veterinary bills than we can afford. It's a hard decision, though, because she's always been part of my life on the farm. Roisin is standing in the open doorway, watching Seamus as he jumps down from his battered old jeep, pulls his baseball cap over his eyes and lifts his rifle from behind the seat. He cracks it over his arm and strides across the yard. Her eyes are like dinner plates and her body is rigid. I call to her, to come to me, but she doesn't hear. Her mouth opens, her hand comes up and she points to Seamus. I realise something terrible is going to happen and shout for Seamus to stop but he's in the barn by now. Mammy looks up from feeding the chickens and we are running towards Roisin just as the shot explodes. As the sound fades, her scream continues, echoing around the yard, lifting the crows from the trees and carrying on and on. It seems to go on for minutes, until her voice runs out. By that time, Mammy is holding her tight against her and Seamus is standing at the barn door, holding his rifle, looking from one to the other of us. She pulls away from Mammy and grasps me around the neck, squeezing me with her little arms till I can barely breathe.

'Daddy.'

Mammy is looking at us, raising her eyebrows, nodding and smiling. The burst of warmth deep in my belly, and the sheer joy of it is better than my first burst of heroin, and I'm addicted to it.

And so it was, Sylvia, until the day you found us.

ROISIN

2019

1
_____

Mothballs. The smell transports Roisin back to the farm, where she is wrapped in a blanket, lying on the settee in front of the range. The blanket will have lots of little squares, each one a different colour. There's a pile of them, kept in the press on the landing with mothballs in between, brought out for an extra layer on the beds in winter. Nanny is always busy making the next one from odd bits of wool left over whenever she knitted a jumper; or from old jumpers they unravelled beside the fire at night, Roisin holding the hank across her hands while Nanny wound it into balls.

'Rosie?'

It isn't Nanny's voice, nor does she recognise the other sounds, muffled and distant; the bark of a dog, a baby crying fit to burst, an angry voice yelling. Squeezing her eyes shut, she tries to get back to a place where Nanny is singing along with the radio, accompanied by gentle chopping sounds. When a finger touches her cheek, slightly prodding, not quite stroking, she opens one eye, and sees a boy's face, framed by blond hair, shaved around the sides, floppy on top and hanging over his eyes.

She sits up quickly, pulling the blanket up to her chin, staring over it at the boy. Where has she met him before? Something stirs on the edge of her memory.

He laughs, a nice tinkly sound, says, 'I knew you'd come back in the end,' and sits down, cross-legged, his back against an armchair, watching her.

Roisin grips the blanket. Not that she's cold. If anything, she's too hot, sweating. In her peripheral vision she sees stripes. She drags her eyes away from the boy and takes in the bold pattern of alternating wide and narrow stripes in primary colours, marching vertically up the walls. They look like bars, it's as if she's caged in. If she reached out, she could touch two of the walls. Curtains cover almost all of one side of the room, floor to ceiling, and these are in a red tartan. The clashing patterns make her slightly nauseous. There's a fire, not a real one, the logs might be plastic, and the flames are blue, but she can feel the heat from it. A huge picture of a landscape, on the wall above it, looks familiar. If she stands up, she'll fall over the boy, or the coffee table that's between them, or the television that fills one corner, or the two armchairs that take up the rest of the space. It's an oppressive, crowded little room. Or not such a little room, maybe, it's just that there's so much in it. Every piece of furniture is up against the next piece, so the sofa meets a wall unit, which has a smaller table in front of it, and next to it a standard lamp with a frilly pink shade fills the corner completely, and an armchair is up against all that. There is not a centimetre of clear space all around the sides of the room. There's just enough room to walk between the sofa and the coffee table, and between the coffee table and the hearth. All you can do in this room is walk to a seat and sit down. It's as though somebody bought furniture for a big house, got it home and decided to fit it in anyway.

The door opens, and Sylvia comes in with a tray that she sets down on the little table. She kneels on the armchair to draw back the curtains and Roisin sees that the window is actually quite small. There is a heavy lace curtain, so Roisin can only see an oblong of grey daylight and a few vague shapes. The sounds of dogs, children, and now cars, come to her more clearly now. Sylvia fusses a while, gathering the curtains into tie-backs with tassels, straightening the fringes, checking that both are hanging level.

Sylvia stands, smiles at the boy, at Roisin, back at the boy, at Roisin. She carries on smiling, from one to the other, as she navigates the small space between the coffee table and the fire, stepping over the boy's legs which fill most of it. 'I'll let you catch up a bit,' she says, closing the door quietly behind her.

She says it as though this is a pal that Roisin hasn't seen for a while, who's called in for a chat, but Roisin can't make sense of anything. Tossing the blanket off, she swings her legs round to sit up straight. Her throat is dry, and she drinks the cup of tea in one long slurp. It's sugary and weak and there's barely a mouthful in the cup but it gives her a few seconds to think, though more questions are popping up. How did Nanny's blanket get here? Who is this boy? A photograph from one of the articles flashes into her mind. Was she starting to dream it now? What had Sylvia been doing at the hospital?

Come to think of it, she'd asked Sylvia that last night, and she doesn't think she got an answer. Sylvia lives in England, Roisin has always known that, and even though the journey yesterday seemed to take forever, Roisin has no clear idea how big this town is, or how big England is, so perhaps it isn't so unusual to meet somebody you know. When she got over the shock of coming face to face with Sylvia, she'd been relieved to see her, happy to take her up on the offer of a bed instead of having to find a hotel. Sylvia is Nanny's friend. She would phone Nanny but her phone needs charging and the charger is in the bottom of her backpack. She strokes the blanket, sniffs it, yes, mothballs it is. Nanny must have knitted one for Sylvia.

The boy is watching her, still with the little smile on his lips. She knows him, yet she doesn't know him. 'What's your name?'

He passes his hand across his face, replacing the smile with a frown and downturned mouth, like a clown mask. 'You don't know me?'

She thinks about the article and hazards a guess. 'Jake?'

The smile is back.

'How do you know Sylvia then?'

He looks down at his hands. 'She's let me stop here, while I've been–'

'Is she a relative?'

He shrugs. 'No, she's just – well, she's Sylvia. She's always been around. She's a proper fuddy-duddy, but she's all right. She says you were at the hospital, visiting Mum.'

He has the same way of talking as the nurse she met at the hospital, and there's a couple of seconds between him finishing the sentence and her working out what he said. As if he's mirroring her thought, he says, 'Why are you talking like that?'

'Like what?'

'Funny accent.'

'It's just the way I talk. Everybody talks like that.'

'No, they don't. You sound like that programme, *The Young Offenders*. They all talk like you. It's Irish, isn't it?'

'That's not surprising. That's where I live.'

'No shit? You've been in Ireland? Why? Have you been there all the time?'

'If you mean all my life, I suppose so.'

She throws off the blanket and swings her feet to the floor, looks around and locates her backpack by the side of the sofa. She pulls out the laptop, opens it and brings up the photograph of the press conference. She looks from him to the photo, then turns it so that he can see. 'Is this you? Us?'

Jake nods. 'Do you not remember?'

She points to the photograph. 'You think this is definitely me, then?'

'Course. What have you been doing in Ireland?'

'I've always lived there. In a village, called Kilabran. Near Kilkenny. On a farm.'

His mouth drops open and he says again, 'No shit. A farm? That sounds mega. You've been all right, then?'

She feels guilty, as though she should be telling him a horror story, like the ones she's read, of people who have been kept in a cellar for years.

'Last week, when Daddy died–'

'Who?'

She struggles to find another name for the man she calls Daddy. Of course: 'Conor. He's called Conor.' As if changing his name changes her own identity, she is starting to feel Nanny, the farm, her friends, slipping away, becoming part of another world. She stops talking, to try to keep them close. Jake shuffles closer, as though he senses her moving away from him.

'This Conor, how come you lived with him?'

'I only know the story they told me. That he'd been with my mother here, in England, then she abandoned me, and he took me home to his family. I didn't know any other story until last week, when he died.'

He rubs his eyes, glares at her. 'I fucking missed you so much. Didn't you miss me, Dad, Mum?'

'I don't remember.'

He bangs a fist on the coffee table, making the cup jump in its saucer. 'How can you not fucking remember?'

She pulls her feet up under her, curls backwards, lifting the blanket up to her face, smelling it, for comfort. 'I don't remember anything except the farm, Dad– Conor, and Nanny. I've got no memories of' – she waves a hand at the laptop screen – 'before.' She wants to tell him what she senses he wants to hear. She can't say she didn't know he existed until last week, but she can see from the way his shoulders have sagged that he knows. 'This Sylvia. You say she's always been around. Did she tell you she knew me, that she visited us at the farm?'

His eyebrows shoot up under his floppy fringe. 'She told me she met you at the hospital, visiting Mum, last night, and recognised you. Is that not right?'

Yes, that was how she met Sylvia, last night. Sylvia who she's known since she was small, who visits Kilabran every year, is a friend of Nanny's. But, she didn't know Sylvia lived here, in Sheffield, and why didn't Nanny mention it? Does Nanny know, or is it a coincidence? She asked Nanny once, why she had a friend with an English accent. Nanny said they met in the village, years ago: Sylvia was on holiday, and Nanny popped into Mrs Grady's shop with some cakes that she used to bake and sell, for a few euros on the side. They got talking and the very next day, Sylvia was out walking and came up the track to the farm and Nanny recognised her, showed her where the footpath was closed off and said she had to go back around the road. She made her a cup of tea, though, because it was such cold weather. Sylvia came every year after that, stayed in the guest room. She brought Roisin presents, sent her birthday cards. Every year.

She says all this to Jake.

'That's like, one massive fucking coincidence,' he says. 'Knowing us, and knowing you, and not realising you were the missing kid.'

Probably because so many strange things have happened in the last week, Roisin isn't sure of anything. She has always thought Sylvia was odd, with her bright, darting eyes watching everything; and she knew Conor didn't like her visiting; he always seemed on edge when she was around, and it was better, when she left again. Now, in Sylvia's oppressive little home, she feels as though she has bought a second-hand jigsaw puzzle at the St Vincent's shop and found too many missing pieces to put it all together.

She hears movements outside the door and thumbs towards it, then presses her fingers to her lips and drops her voice. 'How do you know Sylvia?'

'She works for Dad.'

Roisin's mind is swirling with racing, clashing thoughts and feelings, and she shakes her head, to try to clear it.

'She's worked in his office for years. As long as I can remember. He has a building firm. Anyway, I had a row with Dad, he said I couldn't stay at his anymore, he said I was upsetting his new bird.' He saw Roisin's frown. 'He's got married again. She's pregnant. That's not the worst of it though. The worst is that I went to fucking school with her. She was two years above me. It's disgusting.'

It all means nothing to Roisin, who is still puzzling over Sylvia's relationship with both Jake, here, and Nanny, in Ireland.

Sylvia comes in at that moment. She puts another little cup and saucer in front of Roisin, pats her shoulder awkwardly and picks up the TV remote from the coffee table. She looks from one to the other of them.

'Sorry, so sorry,' she says. 'It's Jennifer. Your mum. She passed, in the night.'

Passed where? Sylvia points to the screen where the news has come up and a young woman muffled into a hairy scarf and a high-collared coat stands outside the hospital which Roisin recognises from last night. *Breaking*, it says, in a red band across the bottom of the screen.

... mother never regained consciousness after taking an overdose on the eighteenth birthday of her daughter who was kidnapped thirteen years...

'It isn't my eighteenth birthday.' This detail stands out. A flicker of hope runs through her, until Jake's face extinguishes it. She tosses the blanket aside, slides off the sofa and lands beside him, putting her arm around his shoulders. There's a feeling of disconnect, like the clocks going back but for a very long time, but finally she understands. Her name is Rosie.

2
_____

J ake shakes her off. 'She died that day.' He jumps up and slams the door on his way out.

Sylvia says, 'You mustn't blame yourself.'

'I wasn't going to. What does he mean, she died that day?'

'She didn't get over losing you. I suppose that's what he means.'

'Did you know my mother?'

Sylvia is fiddling with the lace curtains, peeping out. 'Only the same as everybody, I was aware of what had happened, it was all in the news.'

'And when you came to Ireland, did you know who I was?'

Sylvia taps on the window, says, 'Psssht! Look at that cat again, in my window box,' then turns back to Roisin with a perky smile. 'Look at my manners, you must be starving. There's plenty of hot water and towels in the bathroom, so you have a shower if you want to, and I'll be in the kitchen when you're ready.' She's gone.

∽

As she steps out of the shower, Roisin hears crying, banging about, swearing. She towels herself dry and dresses quickly, then listens at the door next to the bathroom. It's gone quiet. She knocks softly and goes in. It's a weird room, a bit like Aodhan's when he was a few years younger, with toys and books, but Aodhan would have those toys all over the place. This room is too tidy for a boy. Jake is lying on the single bed that has a duvet cover with–

'*SpongeBob SquarePants.*' Where did that come from? She didn't know she knew this weird little cartoon character.

Jake's hands drop from his face and he looks at her. 'What?'

'Is that called *SpongeBob SquarePants?*'

Jake sits up and studies the duvet cover as if he hasn't seen it before, and shrugs.

'Why do I know that?'

'Because it was like your favourite thing?'

'Was it?'

'Yep. You were going to have a party the week after you – your fifth birthday. It was going to be a *SpongeBob* party.'

'Do you remember that?'

He shrugs. 'You kept on and on about it, it would be hard to forget.'

She sits on the bed, rubs her hands on the duvet cover, smoothing it, feeling the corner of a memory lifting. But there's nothing beyond the name of the curious cartoon character.

Jake swings his legs around and stands. 'Let's go and have some breakfast.'

Sylvia is scrubbing the kitchen counter as though her life depends on it. Everything, everywhere, is sparkling clean. She stops, smiles from one to the other of them, pulls off her Marigolds. She takes Roisin's phone and charger from her and plugs it in. 'Sit yourselves down. Now then, Roisin, porridge? Good, I've got some cherry-flavoured porridge sachets, would that be all right? And toast? And do you prefer marmalade? Or honey? And what about yoghurt? I've got apricot, or strawberry, or natural. Why don't I put them all on the table and you can choose?' As she talks, she's darting around the kitchen, dropping bread into the toaster, opening cupboards, taking out jars, brewing tea, piling items on the little table between Roisin and Jake: butter, a six-pack of yoghurts, jam pots galore, until there's barely any room left for a plate. Before they have finished eating or drinking, Sylvia whips away the cup or plate, reappearing between them with a clean plate or another cup of tea. Roisin is stuffed. Jake is steadily ploughing through a *Jenga* tower of toast.

Every time Roisin opens her mouth to ask a question, Sylvia offers her something else and chatters about whatever it is, the flavour of the jam, which shop she got it from, and so on, until Roisin feels as though, if she eats any more or listens to any more, she'll throw up. When Sylvia is finally convinced that Roisin really doesn't want anything else, she picks up the Marigolds from the draining board and heads out of the door. Within seconds there are swooshing sounds from the bathroom, and Roisin realises she's cleaning it, which is a bit embarrassing as she thought she'd left it nice and tidy.

Through a mouthful of toast, Jake says, 'She's like that. Always scrubbing and cleaning. Take no notice.'

'I'm sorry about your – our – mother.'

He shrugs, this is something he does; that, and lifting the corner of his upper lip into a kind of sneer, as though he doesn't care.

'You said you'd had a row with your... dad. You didn't live with... our mother?'

He shakes his head. 'Mum fell apart after you went. At least, that's what they said. I don't remember how she was before, but people said she'd been a brilliant mum. Dad left her in the end, then he came back and took me with him. She wasn't capable of looking after herself, never mind me. He had a fling with this girl out of the office, Tiffany she was called. That didn't last long. Then we lived with Granny while Dad built his own place. It's grand, it's out on the Manchester Road, huge place, with a swimming pool, games room, cinema room...'

'Sounds nice. You were okay then.'

The sneer. 'Tch. I fucking wish. I had all this stuff and nobody to share it with. Dad was at work all the time, making money hand over fist. And when he wasn't at work he was bringing one woman after another home, and they all thought they'd be the next Super Mother to me.' He does his *tch* thing, and the lip, again. 'I was in the last year when he started going out with Emma. She came to work in his office after she left school.' He rubs his face roughly and his voice breaks when he says, 'Why did you go, Rosie?'

'I didn't do it on purpose.'

'Didn't you even try to escape?' He's thrusting his face across the table, close to hers, challenging, making her think, didn't she ever guess that things weren't right? No, she doesn't think she did.

'I didn't know there was anything unusual, not until Dad, Conor, not until Conor died, last week. I had no idea, honest.'

He shrugs, lifts the lip. Then he's on his feet, pacing, slapping the back of one hand into the palm of the other, pushing his hands through his hair, letting it flop back, breathing out noisily. She doesn't feel he's angry, more like desperate. A phone buzzes and he pulls his mobile from a pocket, studies it.

Roisin stands up and leans over the sink to lift the slats of the window blind. To the left and right are two more blocks, so she is at the bottom of a U-shape, and this looks like the back, a service area, lined with rows of bins, most with numbers on them, some clumsily painted, one or two covered with patterns of flowers or leaves. A bottle bank sits in a sea of smashed glass, and a supermarket trolley lies on its side. It's raining, and everything is grey, wet, miserable. Behind her, the tiny kitchen, beyond that, the bedroom with the boy's things that look as though they've never been touched, and the overwarm living room that's too small to swing a cat in... Roisin needs fresh air.

'Let's go for a walk.'

He pulls her hand away from the blind and it drops with a clatter. 'I can't go out.' He sees the question on her face. 'Some people, they're looking for me.'

Sylvia sticks her head around the door. 'Anybody need anything? Cup of tea? Coca-Cola? Cake?'

'I don't think I can eat another thing, thanks. Sylvia?'

She's gone.

To Jake, Roisin asks, 'Who's looking for you? Dad?'

The sneer. 'Tch. You think? He couldn't give a fuck what's happening with me or where I am, or even if I'm alive.'

Roisin leans against the sink, and while she's trying to think what she can say, he starts talking.

'See, he took me with him because Mum couldn't look after me, but then he didn't want to. All they ever banged on about was you. Everything was about you. Every fucking year, the photographers, the newspapers. Neither of them gave a fuck about me.' He lowers his chin to his chest and pushes his face towards hers. She steps back, shocked by his hostility. 'Go on, fuck off again, I know you want to. Get back to your precious nanny and your farm and your... I've done without you all this time, I don't need any of you.' He stamps out of the door of the kitchen and she hears his bedroom door slam.

Sylvia bustles in. 'Is everything all right?'

'I'm going out for a walk.' She unplugs her phone from the charger. In the hallway, she finds her coat, and her trainers, stuffed with newspaper.

'They were a bit wet,' says Sylvia, behind her.

Roisin remembers walking seemingly miles with Sylvia through the pouring rain. As she reaches for the door, Sylvia's hand covers hers.

'If you should see anybody hanging around, give them a wide berth. And should anyone ask you about Jake, you don't know him.' She keeps her hand on Roisin's until she looks at her. 'That's important.'

3

It had been dark when she arrived, and now through the drizzle she can see this is one of three blocks of flats, to her right and left, in the same style, with a car park taking up the space in between them, and a play area straight ahead. At the end of the concrete walkway, she goes down two short flights of stone stairs and out of the entrance, looking back to see *Winston House* written over it. The two blocks on either side are called *Harold House* and *Clement House*. She supposes these must be famous English people. With her phone she takes photos of the sign over the entrance door, of the play area as she walks along the tarmac path beside it, and the bus stop, to be sure to find her way back again. When the first bus pulls up, she asks the driver how to get to the Hallamshire Hospital.

'I haven't seen you around here before,' he says. He's smiley and kind, explaining that she can take this bus into town and another one out again, or she can get off somewhere he'll show her, and get the tram, and then walk. It sounds complicated. His name badge says *Gerrard Wilton*.

'That's funny,' she says, 'You have the same name as–'

He's turned to the person behind her. Roisin finds a seat and watches the smeary drizzle. A WhatsApp pings:

Clodagh. *Is it true ur in England? What you doin?*

She replies with:

Tell you soon, big story.

When she sees McDonald's ahead, she gets off the bus and buys a macchiato to take away the sweet, milky taste of Sylvia's tea. She remembers the way to the hospital from the night before. She doesn't know why she needs to be there, something to do with wanting to prove it, perhaps. Her maths teacher's voice suddenly comes to her, telling her to validate; that's it, check out everything from now on, to be sure of what is true and what is not.

The nurse is coming out of the room. 'You were here last night, weren't you? I'm so sorry, are you one of the family? Has someone been in touch with you?'

Roisin looks round her at the bed, empty, made up nice and neat.

'The rest of your family are with the doctor.' The nurse points along the corridor. 'Here they come now.'

She recognises the man immediately: an older version of Jake, muscly with a similar haircut, though he's probably more fashionable than Jake, who looks as though he buys his clothes from the St Vincent's one-euro rail. This man is wearing checked trousers with a short, elastic-waist jacket and Vans. The younger woman hanging onto his arm must be Emma. Two other women are with him, one with her arm around the shoulder of an old lady who is crying. They're coming towards her.

Roisin looks around. She could slip back into the room, but the nurse is still in there. There isn't time to get round the corner of the corridor. She sits on one of the blue chairs and holds a magazine in front of her face, watching their feet walking past. The old lady is sniffing, and says to the other woman, 'It's maybe a blessing, Miriam, she won't suffer any longer.'

She watches them from behind, thinking, 'Say something. Anything. It's my family. All I have to do is stand up. They'll turn around and they'll recognise me.'

The small group stops at the lift. He presses the button. Roisin drops the magazine on the chair as she stands. The young woman half-turns and looks at Roisin; her eyes go down to her feet, up again. Their eyes meet. Seconds pass.

'If you felt anything for me, you'd see me, you'd know me.' Roisin thinks she has spoken out loud. Maybe she has, and her voice was hidden beneath the squealing of the trolley the nurse is wheeling from the empty room. Maybe the words stay inside her head.

The lift pings, the door opens, and they get in. Roisin walks quickly, getting to the lift as the door closes. There is time. She can run down the stairs.

She remembers Nanny. She thinks about Jake. Thinks of the Gardaí...

She walks around the town for hours, marvelling at the size of it, thinking it's maybe as big as Dublin. The hills in the distance remind her of home. The shops go on for streets and streets, and when it starts to pour again, she dips into an indoor market. There's a stall with all the handicraft stuff that Nanny would die for, and looking at the wools and the yarns, and touching the tassels and ribbons, makes her desperate to be back there. Sitting on a bench, she phones Nanny.

'Well now, you oughtn't to be using your money on phoning me all that way,' is the first thing Nanny says, but Roisin can tell she's pleased.

'Ah, Nanny, it's the EU roaming, it costs the same as calling you from Kilkenny.'

'Is that so? Well, and how are things, over there?' She says 'over there' as if she'd like to add, 'in hell's kitchen' which is one of her favourite phrases for anything that's chaotic and ungodly.

Roisin tells her about finding Jennifer and her dying. Does she imagine that Nanny sounds relieved even while she's saying, 'Ah, that's a tragedy, so it is, the poor woman.'

She tells her about Jake. Then, 'Nanny, that Sylvia, your friend who comes for the holidays? She lives here, did you know that?'

There's a long pause before Nanny says, 'I'm not altogether familiar with the names of the places in England, so I'm not sure that I would have remembered that.'

Roisin feels a flush of heat to her face, and wants to repeat Jake's words, 'It's a massive fucking coincidence though, isn't it?' Instead, she just says, 'Aye, fancy that, Nanny. Sylvia knowing us and at the same time living in the city I was born in. And knowing Jake.'

'Sure, Roisin, it's a small world, isn't that what they say?'

Nanny probably thinks England is the size of County Kilkenny. She tells Roisin that Anne Marie has been giving her hell about selling the farm. She doesn't have a go at Roisin for telling Niall about that, though she must know where Anne Marie got the information. Roisin was right, then, not to trust Niall.

'I'll call you again, Nanny.'

There's no goodbye, Nanny just puts the phone down.

Roisin goes back to the handicraft stall and buys Nanny a new rag rugging tool. As she clutches the brown paper bag, she says, 'So I'll be going home then?' and feels a smile lifting her face.

She walks back to Sylvia's flat, which isn't so far out of town. It doesn't matter that it's raining off and on, it gives her time to think. She's crossing the courtyard in front of the flats when a voice says, 'Oi.'

It's a guy hanging out of the open window of a big silver car, one of those new four-wheel drive things that her dad– Conor used to moan about, because they took up the width of the lanes. The guy beckons her over. He looks decent enough, smart, good haircut, like a businessman until he speaks. He waves his index finger around, taking in the three blocks of flats.

'You live round here? Which one?' He talks like Jake.

Now she's close to him, he's giving her the creeps, so she points at *Clement House*.

'Seen a new lad round here? Blond hair, spiky, shaved round the sides.'

She pretends to think for a moment and then shakes her head.

He rolls up the window. The car doesn't move, so she walks across to the *Clement House* entrance, up the steps, onto the first landing. The car is still there. She curses that she doesn't have a phone number for Jake or for Sylvia. There's a service entrance, where the bins are kept, and she can go out of there, and round to the service entrance of Sylvia's block, and get onto the stairs at the opposite end of the walkway. Before she touches the door, it opens and Sylvia pulls her inside.

She peeps out, up and down the landing, then closes the door and leans against it, breathing heavily. 'Did anybody follow you?'

'If you mean the guy with the fancy car and a description of Jake, no.'

Jake appears from the sitting room. 'You've been gone hours. We thought you might be kidnapped – I mean, by the fella who's looking for me.'

She takes her coat off and Sylvia holds out her hand to take it, tuts over it being wet and goes into the kitchen, returning with a towel. As Roisin rubs her hair, Jake beckons her with his head, into the sitting room. There are sandwiches and cakes on plates on the table. Despite thinking her breakfast would keep her full for a week, Roisin is actually quite peckish after all the walking, and it's starting to go dark outside. She feels bad that they've been worried about her.

Her bedding, which she left neatly folded on the sofa, has gone, and there's a row of little cushions, perfectly lined up in overlapping diamond shapes. The room smells of something chemical. She helps herself to a sandwich. Sylvia appears with tea – she seems to live on it – and puts a plate on Roisin's lap beneath the sandwich. She drops a couple of packs of crisps on the table.

Roisin picks up the purple pack, turns it over. 'Crisps.'

'Yes, crisps,' Jake says. 'Don't you have them in Ireland?'

'Of course. But not these. *Walley's* crisps? Why do I know this packet?'

Sylvia has stopped in the doorway.

Jake says, 'You had a packet of crisps when it happened.'

Roisin puts her hands over her ears. 'Did you just hear somebody yelling for crisps? It was really clear, and now it's gone again.' She shivers. 'Was it raining?'

Sylvia says, 'It was like today, rainy, dark. It was the same time of year.'

'I might have just read it, though, it might not be real memory. I read a lot in the newspapers.'

She describes the guy in the car and Jake nods.

'Sean. He couldn't do enough for me when I was working for him. But when he reckoned I'd done him over, he turned into a fucking psycho.'

'Can't Dad help?'

'Dad's too tied up with his new family.'

She nibbles at a piece of cake. 'This is interesting, what is it?'

'Lardy cake.'

'Lard? As in fat-lard? Pig fat? Is that why it's so full of sugar, so you don't know what you're eating?' She spits it onto her plate.

He says, 'We always had lardy cake at home when we were kids. I know you said you didn't remember anything about that night you were taken. But you remembered *SpongeBob Square-Pants*. And the crisps. And the dark, and the yelling.'

'It's like it's coming back in bits, like little threads floating around and every now and then one comes near me and I grab hold of it, and I get a glimpse of something, then nothing until another thread drifts past and I can catch it. Mostly they're just out of my reach and I can't catch one.'

He's disappointed, she can tell. They must have shared nearly five years, did a lot of things together. But she can't give him anything. She wishes she could.

He sits on the sofa and reaches for a sandwich. 'I don't think I'll ever forget that night. The gun, the man grabbing you, pulling you out of the door – Dad picked me up, ran after them, Mum got shot–'

'Was she badly hurt?'

'There was a lot of blood, I think it was her leg or something. But I don't think it was too bad. She only stayed in hospital for a day or so. That wasn't the problem...'

'What then?'

'She hated me, after that.'

'Sure she didn't. Whatever makes you think that?'

'She blamed Dad, for grabbing me, instead of chasing after you. She couldn't bear me being around. Auntie Miriam looked after me, picked me up from school, kept me until Dad finished work. Mum wouldn't take me to school. Wouldn't come to parents' evenings. I think she was glad when Dad took me away.'

'Did she – Mum – did she get married again?'

'No, she wasn't interested in anything. She was in hospital at one point, sectioned, I think. She took a kid who looked a bit like you, from the playground.'

'Poor Mum.'

'Yep. Poor fucking Mum. Poor fucking Dad.'

'Oh, Jakey. Poor you. You lost your sister, then your Mum, and then your Dad by the sound of it.'

'Did you just say Jakey? You called me that all the time. Well, Dakey, cos you couldn't talk properly.'

'Really? It just came out like that.'

He roughly swipes his arm across his eyes. 'You were such a pain, such a bossy kid.'

She starts to laugh, and he joins in, laughing and crying, and she punches him on the shoulder. He picks her up and drops her on the carpet in a half nelson. She screams. Sylvia rushes in, her eyes wide, but he's already started tickling Roisin whose screams turn to squeals and helpless giggles. Sylvia perches on the arm of the sofa, watching and smiling.

Roisin and Jake have swapped so she has the bedroom and he sleeps on the sofa. She dreams of shadows moving about the room, whispering to her, and when she comes out in the morning, she finds Sylvia walking up and down the hallway, biting her lower lip.

'Is he with you?'

'Jake? No.'

'He's gone.'

4

Her phone pings: *Meet me dads office S knows where it is.*

The tinted car is not in the car park, but as they pass the play area, Sylvia whispers, 'On your left, don't let him see you looking.' A lad, wearing a beanie hat, jeans and a football shirt, scruffy, is leaning against a wall.

When they are on the main road, Roisin says, 'Tell me everything you know, about these guys that are following Jake.'

'Your brother's in a bit of trouble.'

'What kind of trouble?'

'Drugs. He owes this – whatever his name is or pretends to be – they say he owes them money.'

Sylvia flags down the bus. The driver acknowledges her by name. When they sit down, Roisin says, 'It's like home, where everybody seems to know everybody else.'

Sylvia says, 'That's not necessarily a good thing.'

At the bus station they walk along a covered walkway, across the road and in through the high stone arches to the railway station. Sylvia hooks her arm into Roisin's to lead her onto the platform, then out through the exit, and into the first black cab in the queue.

'Malin Bridge.'

When Roisin tries to talk, Sylvia shushes her, and except to whisper, 'He's taking us the long way round, but we don't want to draw attention,' they are silent.

The taxi driver stops beside a tram terminus and as Sylvia is paying, Roisin watches a tram pass with '*via Interchange*' on the front and wonders what that was all about. She follows Sylvia a hundred metres along a road and down a short gravel lane, to a single-storey, red-brick building. Around the back, between large white bags and piles of slates, Sylvia takes a key from her pocket and unlocks a door. Jake's head appears from a doorway in the short corridor, and they follow him into an office, with a large desk and chair and two fake leather settees facing one another across a low table.

Jake goes to the window and peers between the slats of the blind until he's satisfied and turns to them. 'You're sure you weren't followed?'

Roisin looks from one to the other. 'What is this place?'

Jake waves his arm around. 'Dad's.'

She turns to Sylvia. 'You have a key?'

'I work for your father. In the office. I cut another one for Jake, for an emergency.'

'But these guys who are after you? Surely they know about this place?'

Jake shrugs, curls his lip. 'Sure. They've done the place over. That's when Dad said he'd had enough and kicked me out. He found out about the drugs. They thought he'd pay my debt, but he refused. So I reckon they know he won't hide me. But I can't stay here long. He'll be here in the morning.'

Of course, it's Sunday. Roisin curls onto the little settee and looks from Sylvia to Jake. 'You need to tell me everything, both of you. Creepy guys stopping me in the street and asking if I know you, and here you are hiding out. I need to know. Are you taking drugs?'

'Course not. I'm not stupid. I was just delivering them for some guy, around the estate.'

'You're supplying?'

'It's not like that. These are people who are already using.'

'What's the difference?'

'I'm not getting people into drugs. I wouldn't do that.'

'I'm not sure I think it's different. But why is this guy after you?'

Sylvia takes a foil-wrapped parcel out of her large bag and hands it to Jake, who rips it open and eats the toast hungrily.

'I'll make tea for us,' she says.

With his mouth full, Jake says, 'He reckons I paid him short. I didn't. But he went to the customer and he said he'd paid me the proper amount, and he hadn't.'

'How much?'

'Five thousand.'

'Jesusmary, that's a lot of drugs.'

'They reckoned they could shift the blame onto me. That worked.'

'And you've no hope of paying it off?'

'Tch. No chance. And it goes up every day. It was seven thousand last time I saw him.'

'This guy, Sean. Can we negotiate with him?'

'Pfff.' He splutters crumbs and wipes them from his front with his spare hand. 'The guy who said he'd paid me, he was three fingers short already.'

Roisin feels as though she's walked into a crime serial. She's seen the stories, heard the words, but between the farm and Kilkenny hasn't known anybody like this before. 'Where does Sylvia come into this?'

The shrug. 'She was in the hospital. Mum took the overdose,

on your birthday, and I found her – it was horrible, coming home and... anyway, I called the ambulance and I went with her, to the hospital. It was the early hours when I got back to our street and spotted one of his stooges parked up, watching the house. So I go back to the hospital, sleep outside the intensive care place. She – Sylvia – she was there, and she said I could come home with her. She went and got some clothes for me, I think she said they were things from her ex-husband, old bloke's stuff' – he waved a hand at his own clothes – 'but hey, it meant I could get out of the hospital without being seen.'

'So, whose bedroom is that, where you've been sleeping?'

He looks surprised, as though he's never thought of it before. 'Don't know, maybe she's got a kid, but she hasn't mentioned it. I think only she lives there.'

Roisin's phone pings with a WhatsApp.

Clodagh: *saw yr Nanny at church, says ur coming back, when?*

Sylvia comes in with tea and a tin of biscuits. They are all silent for several minutes. Roisin fiddles with her phone.

'Right,' Roisin says eventually. 'Can you get into town and meet me tonight? Nanny gave me the money for a hotel and I haven't used it, so...' She waves her phone. 'I've booked into somewhere you can stay for a few days. While we think about it.'

The hotel is along a narrow lane, just off the high street. Roisin reckons there's a few ways of getting out in a hurry if needs be: a fire escape and several little alleyways. She's booked in under her own name and has to show her ID and fill in a registration form. Jake, hidden beneath the hard hat and big yellow hi-vis coat and work boots that he's been wearing since he left his father's office, wanders through reception while Sylvia keeps the receptionist occupied by discussing the attraction leaflets on the display. The room is on the fifth floor and reminds Roisin of Sylvia's sitting room, so crowded is it. There's a Sainsbury's on the high street and Roisin brings Jake sandwiches and drinks.

'Give me your phone.' She flicks through his texts and WhatsApps, skimming the ever-increasing threats from Sean. 'Who's Adam? He seems friendly, wants to help.'

'Don't believe it. He was my best pal, when we were working together, but now he's with them, he's just trying to find out where I am.'

She opens his phone, takes out the battery, and the SIM card, puts them into separate pockets, wondering briefly how she knows this stuff. Too much TV, her daddy would say.

'How will I get in touch without my phone?'

'I'll contact you.' She nods towards the phone beside the bed and smiles when he looks shocked. 'Through reception. If that rings, it'll be me.'

The door to the flat is ajar. Roisin presses a finger against it, and it swings fully open. The drawer from the hall table is upside down on the carpet, its contents scattered. Sylvia rushes past Roisin and into her bedroom, closing the door. Roisin listens for a while then opens the bedroom door. Sylvia is kneeling on the floor holding a CD, rocking, her shoulders shaking. Roisin tries to take the broken CD from Sylvia, but she's gripping it tightly. Dolly Parton? Nanny likes her, too. Such a mess: the wardrobe doors are open, clothes flung around, newspapers and photographs all over the floor. One photograph catches her eye: herself, maybe seven or eight years old, standing between Nanny and Conor, at the door of the farmhouse.

5

The yellow sodium light on the walkway shines through the open curtains and reflects orange on the photographs around her. Like the rest of the flat, Sylvia's room looks scrubbed, smells faintly chemical, and is overstuffed with furniture. The carpet is an old-fashioned shag pile, a reminder of Anne Marie who has this same style all through her upstairs. Roisin gathers up the photographs that have been scattered across the carpet and spreads them out, roughly in date order. She follows herself from one side of the room, as a short-haired, wide-eyed elfin, past the bright, blue-eyed, laughing child in the middle, to the window, where her image is that of the sulky teenager. Sylvia hasn't moved.

'Daddy's special place.'

Even in the half-dark she can see Sylvia's eyes are puffy and bloodshot. 'Special place?'

'I asked him where he kept my school photos, they were on the press for a while, then disappeared. He said they were safe, in a special place.'

Sylvia nods, whispers, 'Safe. I've kept you safe.'

Roisin's throat is scratchy. She navigates the hallway by

touch. The kitchen is lit by the glow of the modern LED lighting from the service area behind. She picks up a beaker from the draining board. As she empties the dregs into the sink, the unmistakeable whiff of brandy hits her nostrils. It's the same smell that follows Anne Marie about, with her hands clasped around a coffee cup, thinking nobody will notice. Roisin rinses it out, pours herself some tap water and drinks, wrinkling her nose at the tang of alcohol. She opens a cupboard and lifts out three half-drunk bottles that she knew were hidden behind the baking ingredients. Sylvia could definitely outdrink Anne Marie. She takes one of the bottles, and a fresh glass, into Sylvia's bedroom.

'Drink?'

Without taking the bottle, Sylvia runs her hand along it, almost like a caress, and shakes her head. 'Not anymore. I don't need it.' She pushes it away.

Roisin drops cross-legged to the carpet, resting her back against the door. 'Right then. All these photographs. The newspapers. What's the story? Let's start with you and Nanny, and Conor. How do you know them?'

'Don't you know the story? I thought your nanny would have told you? It was years ago. I was on holiday, walking past the farm–'

'Come on, now. Don't be giving me that crap about fecking coincidences. Even if it was true, and we both know it isn't, at some point you found out I was Rosie, the kidnapped child, and you decided to keep it secret. Why?'

Sylvia's lips tremble then twist. Her eyes dart from the door, to the window, across the photographs. Twin red spots on her cheeks are visible even in this half-light. She scrambles to her feet, walks to the window, and her hands drop to her sides. Exhaling deeply, she seems to relax, as she says, 'I found you. It's true. I looked for you, and I found you.'

'Oo-kaay... and how come you found me, and the police didn't? Cos by all accounts' – she sweeps a hand towards the newspapers – 'everybody was looking for me, for a very long time.'

'There were things – the police weren't interested. They bungled it, I suppose. I tried to tell them, but they wouldn't believe me.'

'You told the police you'd found me?'

'No... no, once I found you, and you were so happy, and your daddy and nanny, and everything was so, well, so perfect, that I agreed with your daddy that I wouldn't tell the police.'

Roisin jumps to her feet while Sylvia is speaking and paces up and down the room. She puts her hands over her ears and her voice rises. 'I cannot believe you did that. You knew my real mammy and daddy, and my big brother, Jake...'

Sylvia holds out her palms to Roisin. 'Please, please, you must understand. He– Conor – he'd have gone to prison, for life. Your nanny's life, too, would have been destroyed. Oh, I know Conor had done wrong, but he'd more than made up. I thought about it, long and hard. In the end, I reckoned you were so happy there, you were looked after, and they, Conor and your nanny, they loved the bones of you. I couldn't imagine how it would be any better, if you came back here. Your mother was in hospital by then, she'd been sectioned, and your father was starting up with one young girl after another, all of them half his age, and–'

Roisin paces past Sylvia, and slaps her hand against the wardrobe door. She speaks very quietly. 'You made a fecking decision for me, about my life, just like that. Who the feck do you think you are?'

Sylvia covers her eyes with her palms and curls into a foetal position against the bed. 'I'm sorry, I'm sorry, but–'

'But what? Are you fecking mad, you stupid cow?'

'I think I was, yes, I think I was a bit mad, well, probably a lot mad. My boy, Dylan–'

'Who's Dylan?'

She's wide awake in bed, in Dylan's room, thinking about Jake, thinking she can smell him on the sheets even though she saw Sylvia changing all the bedding. She remembers everything. There are no pictures, no colour, just the raw burn of the feelings. The shock of being picked up by a stranger, the rage when she is thrown into the back of a car. Trying to get away, hardly able to breathe, the heat from a hand pressing on her, for a long, long time. Then the cold, the smell of the sea... but how would she know that at four, nearly five years old? She feels terror, then hears a noise, like no noise ever before, then loud ringing fills her ears, so she can't hear herself breathing. She doesn't dare to speak, in case that noise comes again.

At the crematorium, Rosie sits in the memorial garden. Her hood is up and a scarf is wrapped around her face, which works as a disguise but also because the wind is biting. The tinted car is parked over by the main gate. The hearse pulls in, followed by a black car. The man she now thinks of as her birth father, and the women she saw at the hospital, follow the coffin into the building. She could go up to them. Make herself known. What would happen? Would it be like one of those dum-dum moments in *EastEnders*? Except it wouldn't end there. She thinks again, about the Gardaí. Not for Sylvia. She doesn't really care what happens to Sylvia. But what Sylvia said about ruining Nanny's life if it was found out... Does she care about what happens to Nanny? The more she turns it over in her mind, the more convinced she becomes, that Nanny had known exactly what was going on.

The phone has a good signal here, and she thinks Conor would have made a joke about the Archangel Gabriel needing to get through. Nanny picks up straight away, listens to Roisin telling her all about what she'd discovered.

'Well now, isn't that the biggest of–?'

'Do not say it, Nanny. Do not say that word.'

She waits, listening to Nanny at the other end, also waiting, breathing noisily through her nose. Maybe one day, she'll admit it, but Roisin doesn't think so. She got her son home, whatever the deal, and that was all she ever wanted.

'Nanny? The boy, the one in the photograph?'

Nanny's breathing quickens, but she says nothing.

'He's going to come home with me.'

There is a long exhale, then, 'Well now, that'll be grand. Will it be tomorrow because I'll be doing some baking in the morning?'

As she cuts the call, she becomes aware of faint sounds of music; it's a pop song but it isn't one she knows. The familiar tinted car is still by the main gate, so that every vehicle will have to pass it on the way out.

When everyone has left, Roisin walks along the row of bouquets, with their *'Peace at Last'*, and *'Loved Forever'* messages. The tinted car has gone.

Sylvia walks towards her and Roisin thinks she is about to sit down, but she kneels in front of a stone. At first, Roisin thinks she's praying, but no, she's pulling up the weeds around the base of the stone, then polishing a little glass teddy bear with a tissue. Roisin stands behind her and reads the inscription.

'This is Dylan, then?'

'Our son. He died of meningitis when he was four, nearly

five. The same age as you, when you went missing.' She looks at Roisin. 'Like I said, I was mad for a while. No wonder Gerrard left me. Finding you, that's what saved me, in the end.'

'Gerrard? I thought his name was familiar, on the bus. He seemed a nice guy.'

'The best. I pushed him away.'

'Maybe there's a chance for the two of you?'

Sylvia smiled. 'Perhaps. It might be too late now.' She stands, knocks the soil from her trouser knees. 'I've had a word with Dylan. He wants us to get him a passport.'

'A pass – oh, I see. Yes, that's, well, it's a brilliant idea. Thanks, Sylvia.'

On the ferry, Jake walks up and down, up and down, then stops beside her. 'I feel as though I've been in a prison cell. Can't get enough of this air.'

She pulls up her collar, links arms with him and joins him on a circuit of the deck. She hasn't told him about Sylvia's role in all of this, not yet, possibly not ever. He's been through enough. Compared to Jake, she's had it easy. They stop, lean on the railing, watch the waves.

'It's not like you think, you know, Kilabran. It's quiet, like really quiet? Except for Clodagh, she's not quiet, and you'll like her. But you'll have to learn the farming, and all about the animals.' His eyes reflect the sparkle of the sun on the waves. 'Nanny's looking forward to meeting you.'

SYLVIA

2019

1

Roisin's voice is barely a whisper down the phone line. 'Anne Marie's here. She's going on at Nanny something awful, can you hear her?'

Sylvia recognises the high-pitched voice in the background but can't make out the words. There's a shout followed by the crash of pottery.

'Jesus, did you hear that?'

'What's happening, Roisin?'

'Ah, Sylvia, I don't know how she got wind of it. She was here the other day and they were having a massive row about the farm, and... well then, yesterday, I couldn't find my file with the newspaper cuttings...'

Sylvia slides down the wall until she is squatting, the telephone gripped between both hands.

'I think she must have it. She says she's going to contest the will, take Nanny to court if she has to, to make sure me and Jake don't get the farm. She's ordered one of those paternity testing kits and it'll be here in a couple of days. She wants to take my DNA sample. Sylvia, what am I to do?'

Sylvia's stomach clenches, and she swallows the vomit rising in her throat. 'Tell her... tell her you don't know anything, but – no, I tell you what, agree with her. Say you've been trying to find out about your real mother and that's why you went to England, and say – say Sylvia knows the story, she'll go for that. Tell her I'm coming over, and I'll explain it all to her.'

'Better be quick, she's threatening to go to Father McDonnell and to the Gardaí.'

'Tomorrow. I'll be there tomorrow. Ask her will she meet me from the airport and then we can have a chat, and I'll give her the whole story.'

'But, Sylvia, will you tell her–'

'Don't worry, leave it with me. Just keep her busy so she doesn't have time to do anything about it today, and make sure she meets me from the airport.'

'You're going to fly, Sylvia? But–'

The telephone starts to slip out of Sylvia's hand. She grips it tightly. 'And, Roisin–'

'Yes?'

'Nobody else. Just Anne Marie. It's important that I see her on her own. Understand?'

As she gets off the bus, Sajid says, 'Do you need a hand with that, it looks heavy?'

'No, but you could do something for me. Give this letter to Gerrard.'

'Pleasure. He's on a day off today. Is it urgent?'

She picks up the box, wraps her arms around it. 'Tomorrow would be perfect.'

He calls after her, 'You're looking well, Sylvia, good to see–' as the door closes.

She unpacks the shredder and plugs it in. With her back against the wall, she arranges the piles of newspapers and three shoe boxes from the wardrobe shelf into a semi-circle around her. She takes out each item: the pictures Rosie drew at primary school, her school photographs, all the letters from Nanny, twelve sets of Christmas cards and birthday cards, the short notes from Conor, and she shreds them one by one.

In the kitchen, the contents of the fridge go in the bin, then she cleans it out and turns it off, hanging a tea towel over the door to stop it closing and going mouldy. She carries the bin bag, the box of shredded paper, and all the newspapers, bundle by bundle, down to the recycling bin in the service area. When the washing machine has finished its cycle, she takes the last of her laundry out and pegs it on the line over the bath.

Checking that her passport and all her cash are stowed in her handbag, with her coat and hat on, she walks through each room once more, before leaving the flat.

Anne Marie is waiting in the pick-up zone outside Arrivals, tapping her fingers against the steering wheel, smoking through the open window. Sylvia slides onto the passenger seat.

'You don't have a suitcase?'

Sylvia doesn't reply. Anne Marie throws her fag end into the road. A yellow-jacketed man on the opposite pavement shouts and Anne Marie flicks him a V-sign.

As they pull onto the airport ring road, she glances at Sylvia.

'So, what's the big secret?'

'I told you I'll explain, and I will, but let's get on the road.'

'Well I hope so.' Anne Marie taps the mileage display.

'Nearly three hundred kilometres. I'm not an airport taxi and I'm not here for the good of my health.'

'I'll pay you the petrol money, don't worry. I thought it would be an opportunity, you know, to have a private conversation.'

Anne Marie glances at her. 'That's okay then. I presume you're going to tell me that this Roisin is really the child who was taken during that robbery all those years ago?'

Sylvia doesn't answer. They reach the junction with the M50 and Anne Marie accelerates down the ramp onto the motorway, squeezing the car in between two lorries and moving into the middle lane.

'Will you look at the traffic? I need to be in Kilkenny in time to pick up Niall since I have the car. And isn't it typical that after days and days of fecking rain, the sun would decide to shine today of all days, right in my face, so I can barely see?'

Sylvia drops her sun visor to study the traffic through the vanity mirror.

'And I've always wondered where you popped up from, Sylvia, all those years ago. You're in my mother's back pocket. Every time I want to know anything about that girl, it comes back to you. What's your hold over our family?'

Horns blare. Airbrakes scream. Lorry headlights flash blindingly through the back window.

Anne Marie smacks Sylvia's arm away and swings the steering wheel, swerving the car back into the inner lane. 'Jesus-maryandjoseph. Get your hands off the fecking wheel, Sylvia, you'll have us – what are you doing?'

Sylvia has released her seat belt and is twisting round and up, to kneel on her seat. She throws her upper body onto Anne Marie's lap, presses down hard on Anne Marie's right knee, and as the car accelerates, grabs the wheel with her left hand and twists it as far and as fast as she can.

THE END

ACKNOWLEDGEMENTS

I hope you enjoyed reading this book as much as I enjoyed writing it. The landscapes of Sheffield, Lincolnshire and Ireland feature large in this story; all are very familiar to me, and I have enjoyed placing my characters within them. Readers who know these places may be wise to not try to pin down the exact locations – I have been fairly free in mixing fact and fiction in the geography.

My main source of encouragement and support throughout the development of this novel has been the network of writers and poets at the Monday Morning Writers Café. Thanks to you all for reading, listening, commenting and suggesting. Special thanks go to Christopher Sanderson and Kate Harrison of Louth Creative Writing, for hosting that group, and particularly for keeping us going on Zoom during the lockdown.

Thanks as always to Hazel Mitchell, my home-grown forensic scientist, for her expert advice on bodies left lying around in various locations (I am responsible for whether I followed the advice). Dave Start accompanied me on two tours of Ireland, during which he peered at archaeology as I plotted how to weave that lovely landscape into the story, while peppering him with thoughts and ideas.

The Good Housekeeping Novel Competition 2018, by putting this story in its shortlist of five novels, gave me the inspiration to keep going.

I am grateful to Betsy and the hard-working and efficient team at Bloodhound Books for believing in this book and giving me such a good experience of the publication process; and particularly to Ian Skewis for his attention to detail and helpful suggestions in the edit.